Hollo

by **D**evon **M**ichael

SNOWFAIR BOOKS

Copyright © 2015 by Devon Michael
www.devonmichael.com

Published in 2016 by Snowfair Books
www.snowfairbooks.com

Editorial: Em Morrison
Cover Illustration: Sol Metcalfe
Book Design: Jordan Michael

ISBN-13: 978-1944635022
ISBN-10: 1944635025

Table of Contents

Chapter One
A Prologue and a Birthday

The house didn't look like anything, didn't look inhabited, nor tidy, nor dirty; quite unnoticeable really, due to the careful work carried out to make it unnoticeable. The man who lived inside, was, like the home he lived in, easy to overlook, and he'd cultivated that to live in secret. Though keeping brilliance behind closed doors is a lonely way to live, thankfully this man was never completely alone, not in this house.

He had been working in the attic lately because the size of the space was right. The room appeared empty except for the delicate thing he had been building there. It was made of thin wires hung in a precise web. Dangerous, as you couldn't see them, and if you didn't know where the wires were strung, and didn't know where to step, you would run into them. They were so fine and indestructible that if you missed a step they might run right through you. Fortunately, that was not what they were meant for. If his plan worked, and he was almost certain it would, then his house would no longer be lonely when he was away.

There were, let's guess and say…a thousand of them. Every thread was vital and thoughtfully placed around the room, threaded from hooks, around pillars and over rafters before meeting at the center of this invisible web, where each fit into its own piece of wooden machinery.

The man himself had placed them, and though it was finished, he sat before it questioning his next action. He had calculated so carefully, done it all perfectly, everything was as it should be and yet he hesitated. There was a choice he had to make now, and it was not an easy one to make. There was a storm of indecision raging in the man's head.

The sun had set on him while he sat there, and enough time had passed that now the moon began to shine through the little window and cast its light into the otherwise dark therein. The enormous tension in the attic suddenly split as the man moved, his hands flying off his lap, one hand cracking a snap between two fingers causing all the wires to shiver with anticipation, while the other hand lowered down to his feet where all these thousand threads met one another and waited.

Between his thumb and forefinger, he drew the wound thousand off the ground, careful not to tug. Should he tug them they could slide right through the wood beams holding them up and destroy not only all the work he had prepared, but also his attic as well. He was careful, so very careful in pulling the wires as he pressed them against his forehead.

"Hollo," he said in a whisper, and the wires heard this name and came to sudden, bursting life. Light grew in them, a thick molten gold that saturated the threads he held. This liquid light began to trickle down from his hand into the rest, and all at once the golden light burst outward, illuminating the web and tracing the invisible pathways of the threads until finally meeting one another in the center, where the light found its home in the finely shaped wooden parts assembled together at the center of it all.

"Hollo," came a voice, much smaller than that of the man. The light faded, though not entirely; there remained the heat of it in the wires, a dull, smoldering gold. The man rose immediately and in his body shone the same molten warmth as in the wires. He took several steps through the web, and as he stepped through them the threads melted and fell weightlessly to the floor, undone by the brush of his stride. His hand swept over the wooden form in the center of the room as if waving ashes, and those that ran into it turned to dust and fell away. He knelt over the wooden body, but his hands remained an inch above, nervous to touch.

Burning hot golden eyes opened to look into the man's face as he hung there. "I'm Hollo," the puppet said.

And a curious thing happened then. The man, a sophisticated, well spoken man, could think of nothing better to say in reply, other than, "I'm Fredric."

The two of them held gaze for a long moment.

"What am I doing here?" asked the puppet.

Fredric opened his mouth, and although a tear fell from his cheek, he said nothing.

"You cry for me?" asked Hollo.

"No, no…for me, I suppose," Fredric answered, wiping his face and gathering himself enough to continue. "I'll tell you why you're here. I am going to teach you," he said to the child, who lay, all engendered there before him.

In a drawer at the edge of the room, was folded a tiny frock-like dress. Fredric picked it out and presented it to Hollo.

"Am I a girl?" Hollo asked him.

"I…" he began, startled by the question, and changed his words. "It's all I have that will fit. Does it suit you?"

Hollo nodded. There were tiny flowers on it, and tiny flowers suited Hollo immediately.

The moon had just reached the point in the sky where it shone directly on her face through the window. The silver of Moon's light filled the light of her golden eyes, which opened wider in contact with the moon.

"I know this place," Hollo whispered. "Where is this, where did I come from?"

Fredric opened his mouth to answer, but again was astonished by the question. As much as he knew about the world, he found that he didn't have an answer to this either.

"This is the earth, this is your life," Fredric said slowly, and then added, "does it suit you?"

Yes, Hollo decided, it suited her immediately.

Chapter Two
Another Birthday

Early in the morning the Casters set to their work. Artisans owned most of the lots in this part of the city, and the property adjacent to Hollo's was home to the bronze workers, who cast their commissions within their workshop to then set their wares in a private, overgrown garden against the back of Hollo's garden beneath her attic bedroom.

In the north wall of her room just below the ceiling there was a round window with a flat ledge large enough for a tiny body to sleep in. This space, in summertime, was where the sun shone at first light to warm and brighten an otherwise dim attic room. This was where Hollo woke in the summers to watch the Casters set out their new works of bronze in the morning sun in their secret garden below her. She was already awake, lying as she had been sleeping, though with her eyes open and on the craftsmen. They pried with their metal tools, the three of them cutting into the ceramic casing of their latest project. The moment of all their work coming to fruition captured her imagination so much that she lay motionless on these mornings, interrupted from sleep by their shouting, though willingly and excitedly waking for the enjoyment of their labors.

The statue was the size of a man, though lumpy, bulky within the ceramic, and hidden. Her imagination was alight with expectation of what may be inside, what new artistry was to hatch into life in the garden beneath her bedroom window. The mold came away at the highest point, revealing the helmet, gleaming in the morning light; then more revealing the face of a man, a soldier. A bronze casting of bronze armor, a bronze moustache, and the face of a hardened leader of men shone for the first time in the sun. In all the ferocious gaunt solidarity of the figure's face, he was to Hollo but a newborn thing, seeing the world for the first time, how she herself had come into the world suddenly, so that the world was made to learn of her as she was, not of what she was to become.

Throwing open her window, she leaned out and laughed with delight. The men below heard nothing of her excitement, nor saw her. She knew she could not be seen by those looking in, this house was to them an empty place, an uninhabited and unwanted relic of some past place of business. She knew this, knew she was invisible to the world, but not to all the world. The birds saw her, as she had learned by the encounters they had with one another in this attic which she defended as her own. They would have tried to roost in her window if not for her extending offerings of friendship; friendship not declined but elegantly accepted by the feathered miscreants. Their flapping and bother was as unnoticed by the men below as she herself was.

From her window, she reached out to the rope that was hung from the peak of her house down three stories to the ground below. Swinging out into the air, she was careful to shut her window, else the feathered pirates in the neighborhood would claim her belongings as their own. The wind blew her this way and that in the air, crisp and cutting, but aroused her senses and sharpened her from her morning drowsiness, and with her new alertness, descended down the rope to the garden below, passing by her father's room on her descent carefully, not wishing to wake him just yet.

In her own garden she crept across the stones, choosing a silent footing she knew well from her numerous secret ventures into the neighboring yard. She knew how to get past her father's barrier through a secret hole in the fence where her own magic allowed her to step through from her hidden world into the world she watched from her bedroom window. There was, however, an obstacle she was faced with. There hung a tiny, decorative mirror from the branch of the lemon tree at the edge of the yard, but Hollo had learned a way to outsmart it.

She slept fully dressed, high socks and knee-pants under her short flowered dress. The clothing, she had found, was useful beyond keeping warm, and served well for many types of sneaking around. The socks, which kept her wooden footsteps soft against the rocks, also could be used to capture the little mirror. She rolled the knee sock off her leg, and then crept up behind the little glass, slipping it up under it gently so as not to rouse it and alert her father of the activity in the garden. Satisfied by her wiles, she hurried to her hole in the fence, reaching her fingers into her front dress pocket, and pulling from it her long circular thread. This game, her string cradle, was her secret from the world and from her father. Weaving it between her fingers, she began her rhyme while twisting, tugging, pulling and shaping her thread into a design that mimicked the one she saw her father use in his own manipulation of doorways. The rhyming, however, was hers, and rhyming was how she had discovered her magic.

"Under fences, here and back, open little door. Let me through and I promise I'll come home again once more." The silver thread glowed briefly and then faded, and nothing further happened, as she knew it wouldn't. In fact, she didn't know if the chant had any real affect or not, but since it worked for her father, she assumed it worked for her as well. Tucking the string safely back into her pocket, she was through the fence, into the wildly under-tended, thorny brush of the bronze garden.

The three Casters were gone, working furiously amongst themselves in the shop. This she knew by the smoky smell of their molten copper, which meant they were occupied indoors, and beside the smell, she heard them cursing at each other, such words that Hollo didn't know and would ask them if only she could, though approaching the men was out of the question. Beside the fact that she was strange, being wooden, she imagined they would not appreciate her messing about as she did in their garden, and tampering with their hard work. Not to say that she was disrespectful of the statues, contrarily, she loved them. She found them beautiful and perfect, and delighted in the feel of their familiar, solid bodies. The bronze was smooth and still cool despite the sun, and her hands scratched softly as they ran over the delicate folds of the Knight's bronze cape. She marveled up at the face of the frowning military man, his eyes piercing and forward. She giggled at the thought that such a newborn thing could be so grumpy looking. Hollo had come to understand that it was not unusual for statues to look as if they were in the midst of some terrible conundrum, or had recently become aware of some foul smell. She preferred to imagine the latter.

Just once more, she thought, reaching into her pocket for her thread, and checking over her shoulder to make sure the three Casters remained elsewhere, just this once she would ask the statue this very question. She grinned to herself, knowing herself to have told herself 'just once more' on many occasions, but it just couldn't be helped. Metal fascinated her, she was drawn to it, and it seemed beyond her ability to not be drawn into conversation with it. But before any conversation could take place, she first had to wake the newborn statue up from his furious slumber, and there was a very special kind of cradle she had invented herself for just this purpose. It was only the tiniest, faintest bit of magic that was nearly unnoticeable by anyone looking for it. Being careful with magic was essential, since she knew the consequences of magic being noticed. She only dared so much beyond the safety of her home where magic could not be seen, for her father's magic was of the largest variety, and the magic keeping it hidden was even larger.

Weaving the loop of thread between two hands at first, she then worked it into one hand, creating a circular web between her five fingers. Once finished, she checked on the Casters again, and then once sure she was alone, made her rhyme.

"Little baby of copper and tin today is the day your life begins," she sung softly beneath her breath. "But only just to talk to me, cause if you're found they'll capture me," she finished, feeling a shiver of excitement run through her as her five-finger web came to golden, glowing life. She placed it against the bronze, feeling the same shiver as in her body then in the bronze statue, who in an instant, relaxed from his stiff bold posture and turned his wild, fearsome features down at the child who had bothered him.

She beamed up at him expectantly, putting a finger over her lips, miming quiet to him. He nodded slowly, confused for a moment, and then gathered his dignity and resumed his pose.

He sniffed loudly, causing Hollo to glance fearfully back towards the shop for a moment, though knew all the ruckus of their work would drown any noise the two of them could possibly make.

"Ugh," the bronze man grimaced. "What's that putrid odor?"

Hollo's eyes widened. "I knew it!" she muttered to herself.

"Oh dear," the man said with his pompous air. "Is that my smell? Is that smell of burning coming from me…" he looked down at himself, seemingly aghast. "Ah blast! I'm covered with the stuff, what terribly, terrible rot!"

"You're made of it," Hollo said up to him. "You're made of metal."

He frowned at her, as though she had been insensitive. "And you're made of wood," he grumbled at her, returning the insult.

"Yep," she nodded.

"Hmm," the Knight said, inspecting her. "Doesn't seem to bother you much, certainly, wood might be a little more comfortable than metal. What ever do you want, anyway, little wooden girl?"

"I wanted to say hello. I watched them make you."

He snorted pompously at her.

"And wish you a happy birthday," she smiled.

"Indeed," the Knight raised an eyebrow. "Why yes, indeed, I suppose it is, isn't it? Well that's charming, my birthday, indeed!" His moustache curled into a knightly smile.

"I had to come see you," Hollo continued. "You and I share a birthday, that makes us something, I suppose," she said.

"Is it really?" the Knight looked so very amused now, transformed from his former irritation, which Hollo had come to expect from newly awoken statues, because, as she imagined, it was a hard life to be made of metal.

"Well, indeed that makes us comrades-in-arms of birthdays, or some such something..." he pondered. "Well, my little wooden lady, a very happy birthday to you."

He returned to the height of his initial rigid posture as Hollo's weave began to grow faint, and his animation faded away. "What wonderful...luck..." he trailed off.

"Happy birthday to me," she whispered.

A clatter of anger arose from the workshop, and Hollo quickly hid herself out of view as a voice announced the irritation of the largest and oldest of the three Casters.

"Magical taxes!" the big man she knew as the leader barked. "Again they're robbing us!"

"Chester, now you know they've ears and all round the world," the skinny apprentice said.

"I've told 'em before and I'll say it again I've no use for magic in m'work!" the leader, Chester, bellowed.

"But they's sure it's you making the witchcraft and not the Engravers across the way?" asked the apprentice.

"That's wot I said to the damn Magickers! They're sure that there's magic in m'bronze, and I said 'no, sirs, no certainly!' And do you know what they said?" he asked the skinny one. "Nothing!" Chester spat. "Not a thing, help me, besides that there was magic in m'bronze!"

The third Caster arrived, a younger man, though older than the apprentice. His name was Kit-Falermeyer, Hollo knew, and had heard the name bellowed by Chester from her room even with the window closed. Sometime he was called Dammit-

Falermeyer, when something went wrong, and other times, he was simply called Kit.

"Dammit-Falermeyer!" Chester shouted, as was appropriate in the circumstances. "I tell you to find me copper what's not been tampered by the Hermetics and you bring me this!"

Hollo saw the young man shrug. "Well you can't have it all in life, Boss. You've only what you've got and nothin' more."

"What the blasting-wax does that mean!?" Chester yelled. "What I've got in life is now the less in the amount of..." he trailed off to inspect the letter further. "*Fifty-seven marks of steel or the equivalent in copper,*" he quoted. "They're charging that for what I've not even done, all cause you can't find me honest raw metal! What's next might be m'firstborn son if ever I do anything against the law!"

Kit nodded sagely. "You're a lucky man then."

"How's that?" Chester grumbled.

"You've no sons, Boss." Kit replied cheerily. "Only Timtree and he's just a statue."

Chester set off on a wild bout of oaths and curses and stormed back into his shop. The apprentice wrung his hands with a fearful expression, looking imploringly at Kit.

"You think we'll be run bankrupted?" the youngest asked.

Kit laughed. "Not a chance, we've that much spare copper lying in the waste around the shop. Isn't a bother to ship it to the Practitioners. You don't fret, and leave the arithmetic to me and we'll be fine."

The younger looked worried still. "You've not really had dealings with Hermetic Magickers, right Kit?"

Kit patted him on the head. "Silly question, 'dealing wit Hermetics', like I'd know how to find one!" he laughed. "That's what makes them Hermits, their not wanting to be found. If the Practitioners have so much trouble tracking the rogues down, how's you suppose that I, myself, can find one?"

Kit started wandering through the garden at that point, trolling his way in Hollo's direction, with the young apprentice following closely after him. "Besides, metal changes a lot of hands before it comes to us here to be melted and cast. Suppose at some point someone uses some magic to shave a little profit off the top for themselves. Just the way the world is nowadays, us common folk payin' for the ill dealings of those with the power to abuse. Can't be helped, really. I'd do the same if I could," he added reasonably, a grin spreading on his face. His wandering had taken him to the statue of their mornings work. "See there?" He pointed up at the helmeted, mustached face. The apprentice went pale. "Sure enough there's magic left in the metal here, our gaunt brigadier-general got a smile on his face just now!"

Hollo heard this as she slipped back into her world, through the fence into her own yard. She felt a sudden clumsy guilt, having left the statue not as she found it. She knew better than that, she chided herself, and continued to listen, wondering if there was to be trouble.

Kit burst out in laughter. "That's marvelous! Think what 'ol Chester'll say when he sees this! Shh, don't say a thing to him. It'll be funnier if he finds it himself. The Practitioners'll be having words with him about this pretty soon, I'll bet."

Hollo let out a sigh of relief, glad to have the boys be so easy in believing that her tinkering was the result of some far away, other mischief. Once the boys could be heard indoors, and the copper smoke fumed again, Hollo slid the sock ever so carefully off the mirror, and back onto her foot, and then peered into it. Deep in the dark of the glass she could make out her father, asleep in his bed, his mouth open in what she could guess was a snore. She raised her wooden finger and tapped on the glass. He gave a start, vaguely acknowledged her, and then rolled away to fall asleep again. She grinned, drew her golden thread around the mirror in several loops, and spoke into it.

"Dad!" she squeaked. "Guess what today is?"

He rolled back towards his bedside mirror, regarding her with one eye open. He took hold of the mirror, and then from nowhere drew a golden tread from it and held the other end in his mouth. "Well," he began speaking into the thread. "That is a good question. Whatever could today possibly be? I'll take some tea with that riddle if you don't mind."

Hollo smiled and left the mirror hanging from the tree, returning to her bedroom rope while humming rhymes to herself, and helping herself back up into her attic room. By the time she had made her way downstairs, her father was already at his desk at the kitchen window, writing, holding a golden thread in his mouth that ran to the ceiling, and through the rafters in a web that spread through the rest of the house. Pointing at a boiling pot of water, he yawned at her, and she hurried to make a cup of tea, presenting it to him.

"Now," he said, sipping. "You'd put forth a peculiar question as you woke me, for whatever reason, from the garden, where you've been playing at the crack of dawn for no reason which I, in my boundless worldly wisdom, can puzzle out."

She bounced on the balls of her feet, her excited hands weaving her silver thread into a quick series of shapes. "S'my birthday!"

"No, no no," he waved a hand at her, with a sleepy half-heartedness. "Not 'till the twentieth, silly. You'll have a birthday tomorrow."

"But it *is* today," she grumbled.

"Nope, certainly not today, it is most certainly tomorrow," he sung at her. "Tomorrow is your birthday."

"Dad!" she whined. "It is the twentieth! Today it is, you're wrong!"

He quickly appeared affronted, and turned in his chair to face her. He cleared his throat pointedly as she glared at him. "As you'll find," he said airily. "I am never wrong, I'm your dad and dads are never wrong."

She rolled her eyes. "And then they get old and forgetful, and then they're even wrong about being right."

He gasped, apparently slighted. "I'm not old, I'm yet thirty!"

"You're at least a hundred and forty," she corrected.

"Nonsense, that's not even a real number!"

She nodded airily. "You are."

"We'll see about that," he returned the silver thread to the corner of his mouth and a pulse of golden light beaded through the wire and away into the ceiling.

He gasped. "This treacherous home of ours seems to agree with you."

Hollo jutted her jaw out, triumphant.

"You two are always ganging up on me," he grumbled, and then gasped. "But then, if that's true…and I'm a hundred and forty, which is just silly, then *you*…"

He seized a fresh piece of parchment paper, and with an elaborate show of difficult calculation and arithmetic came to a gasping conclusion.

"Why Hollo," he began slowly. "You must be twelve years old!"

"Yes, yes!" she pleaded. "I am, I am twelve."

"You silly girl," he shook his head. "You've almost missed your birthday."

"It's today, today's my birthday," she bounced, tugging at his waist jacket.

"Not according to that face of yours," he shook his head. "You don't look a day older than a teenager, and surely not near as young as the single digits."

"Yes yes! It's 'cus I'm twelve!"

"Well how wonderful!" he said, and then turned thoughtful. "You know it's a good thing I happened upon a present for you, else the house would've locked me out of the bathroom again."

"What is it?" she hushed to a whisper. "My present?"

He smiled, and opened his mouth, then paused, feigning confusion. "You know, I just can't seem to…"

She squealed, and bolted away as her hard wooden feet, though muffled by her socks, went pattering like rapid gunfire away and up the stairs.

Fredric smiled to himself, returning to his writing, and returning the silver thread to his mouth. "And *you* don't give it away."

The house settled and shifted in the morning warmth.

.   .   .

In the attic not a trace of present could be found. Not a glimmer of gift made itself known from the piles of things she knew so well. The house was very cleverly packed full of things, very useful and rare things which Fredric used for his work. Hollo knew nothing of their uses, though knew everything of their residence. You'd think finding the new, secret thing would be easy amidst the familiarity of this house.

"*Perhaps the thing you want to find hides somewhere else frozen in time,*" Fredric whispered cryptically from the attic mirror.

Instantly she was off, to the broken clock in his bedroom on the floor below, and when she arrived, flung the glass door open.

"*No, no silly me sorry,*" spoke the hand mirror on his dresser. "*Not there, maybe...perhaps you seek to find instead, a package in the house of bread.*"

"House of bread," she whispered to herself. The eighth, Virgo," she recited from her books. "The virgin...the painting!" she cried, assuming the young woman in the oil painting was indeed a virgin.

"*Erm, no, the pantry.*" He mumbled.

"Aha!" she sped downstairs.

The pantry would forever smell of dried fish, and the thought occurred to her that if this was indeed the final resting place of her present, it would be a present which forever would smell of fish. It was true that even if this house fell down and was taken apart, that pantry, even without walls, would smell of dried fish.

Zooming past Fredric through the kitchen she shouted at him. "Is it here? Is this it!?"

"Well now," he mumbled to himself. "From what we know, I'd say it's unlikely."

In her excitement she had forgotten to turn the handle and it very nearly came off in her hands. She took a calming breath, lowered her expectations, and then half-heartedly drew open the pantry door. Dried fish grinned at her from the racks, and on the floor in the middle of the little walk-in there lay a bundle of brown packing paper. Eyes wide, she sat down, then had to scoot herself closer to it. The parcel was not square, not a box, nor any particular shape. It was lumpy, and bound by warm golden string she recognized as her father's. Only her father could cut them. She approached him and poked him in the lower back, then lifted the parcel up to him as he turned around.

"Oh, wow," he said. "For me?"

She smiled.

"No, no. I can't," he said modestly. "It won't fit me, surely."

"Is it a dress!?" she brightened at the thought. "A new dress?"

Fredric touched the tip of his ring finger to where the two molten threads crossed at the center of the bundle, causing them to fall weightlessly away from the paper. She placed it gingerly on the ground and opened it.

There was cloth inside and a small breath escaped her, drawn from the delicacy of the fabric. Such cool, smooth wonder this thing had, Hollo had never felt such softness at her fingertips. Unfolding it, she pulled it up and around her body, finding the cloak to be much thicker than she first assumed. From her shoulders it reached perfectly down to the floor, and the heavily weighted hem scratched softly against the wooden boards as she turned this way and that, inspecting herself.

"It's a cloak," she whispered.

"Nope," he corrected. "It's a mantle, for a grownup, but for you it's a cloak."

"Is it old?" she asked, her eyes tracing the silver threaded outlines of the floral pattern on her shoulders.

"Very old," he nodded.

"Who's was is?" she asked.

"A very tall woman," he chuckled. "Much bigger than you. It hung to her waist, was very stylish once upon a time." His hand fell on her shoulder, and as he did so, the delicate silver threads glowed. The three large iron buttons at Hollo's chest fastened themselves, and the hood, enormous and heavy, came up over her head. She peeked out at herself, completely taken by the extraordinary vestment she hid beneath. It was so beautiful.

"You're stunning, my darling," Fredric smiled, his cheek propped on his fist, leaning on the arm of his chair. "Absolutely marvelous. You'll make people jealous, surely."

She turned her eyes at him, wide and wondering why he would tease her like that, if only…

"What good luck," he said. "Since I was going on an errand today, and you look too splendid to leave home alone."

Nervous anticipation seized her as she saw him smile. "You mean, out the front?"

He nodded. "I have a letter to deliver, and it happens to be near the marketplace."

Her jaw fell open.

"Maybe we could stop there on our way back?"

"Yes!" she cried. "Yes I want to, can we?"

"Unless there's something else you want to do with your birthday."

"No no! Nothing, I want to go out to the market! I…" she trailed off, choking back tears. "I want to see the market, yes. More than anything I want to!"

"But we have chores to do," he said somberly. "Beds to be made, dishes to wash, and locks to undo."

"But," she whimpered. "But we'll miss the market!"

"Ah yes," he said, turning frightened. "And you want more than anything to go, don't you?"

She nodded desperately.

"You're gonna tire me out before the day even starts, Hollo, but maybe just this once!" he said with a showy flourish of his arm. He rose to stand while holding several threads in each hand as he did so, letting his golden light out into the house.

With a glimmer of wonder in her golden eyes, Hollo sat on the floor, curled into her cloak, watching her father work his craft as she had only seen a few times before. The house responded to his threads, opening windows, curtains, letting light spill into the kitchen as an earthquake of activity sounded on the floors above them, where Hollo knew in her mind's eye that beds hurried to fold themselves and clothes set themselves to wash. Hollo hurried after her father, just in time for her favorite moment; the opening of the door. He placed both hands on the face of the wood as Hollo hid behind him. Silver threads crept out from the sleeves of his white-cuffed shirt. As snakes weaving side to side and licking the air, the threads coiled around into many shapes and spirals, weaving among themselves a large series of concentric circles. For a brief moment, the silver shone gold, and then fell away as molten smoke to the floor. The door was freed, and in such slow measure it let loose from frame and swung out into the yard and the world beyond, as it always had, as she had seen before, though this time was different. This time the door was opening for her, into the world that lay all undiscovered before her.

Chapter Three
Mr. Packerd Bae-Binn

It was one thing to know the world by taking tiny, daring steps into neighboring yards, staying hidden, within a few strides of home and safety. This new venture was another matter entirely. In Hollo's dreaming and wanting, she hadn't quite taken into account the largeness of the city streets. She had guessed, but nothing could have prepared her for the sensation of stepping out into the revealing sunlight, the bustle of errand-goers, and the volume of a world at work.

"Are you frightened?" Fredric whispered to her.

Hollo squeezed his hand tight, holding her hood for fear of the wind.

"Yeah...me, too," he said. "Sure hope we make it home."

"We'll be fine, dad," she said, unsure of herself. This outside world was one she knew well from her books and from her tiny round window in the attic. She had seen so much of it from her hidden room, but now, confronted so close, she felt she knew nothing of the people passing by, nor understood the mechanics of their toys, their clothes, or their vehicles. Sure she knew how they worked, but you can easily know how fire works and still have not the faintest idea how to remain calm in the midst of it.

In a snarling frenzy of stamping and clapping of hooves, Hollo suddenly lost any small illusion of her safety and seized onto her father's arm, shrieking, forgetting herself, and forgetting her fear of being noticed. She trembled at the monsters that had just rounded the corner in front of them. The enormity of them shocked the feeling from her limbs as she was instantly scooped up in her father's arms as he picked her off the ground, and together, they dove behind a pile of barrels. Hollo dared to peek her eyes out to watch an enormous horse-drawn carriage, headed by a pair who stood fifteen hands, many feet higher than Hollo, trundle past. They snorted and grumbled, very close to where she and her father hid.

"What on earth!?" he hissed at her. "We're done for!"

"Horses," she said in wonderment. "Huge horses!"

"Horses?" he repeated, following her gaze after the beasts. "Oh my, yes, you're right."

He stood, brushing himself off, casting his gaze sideways at her. "Are they dangerous?" he asked, taking her hand and walking her out into the street again.

"No," she said sheepishly, averting her eyes from the several bystanders who had stopped to stare at them and their bizarre behavior.

"You sure?" he frowned at her. "They're not poisonous are they? Your books wouldn't leave that out, right?"

She shook her head, trying not to smile.

"Well, tell me next time," he grumbled at her. "Now everyone thinks I'm silly, diving away from horses like that," he glanced around ashamedly. "Looking at me like I'm a scaredy-cat."

She laughed at him as he hurried her away from the reproachful eye of the barman who was inspecting his barrels for evidence of tampering.

"C'mon," he tugged her onward with a grin. "I think they're onto us," and they set out at a run. "Enough of these sour faces, hmm? We'll deliver my letter to Mr. Packerd before the market."

"I like their sour faces," Hollo muttered curiously, likening them to the statues in her garden beyond.

Her father chuckled. "Then you'll love Mr. Packerd."

They skirted the market, giving Hollo only a moment to gaze with longing at the cobble square in the center of town. The morning trade fair was an elaborate showcasing of the city wealth, and the artistry that rose organically in such a large and wealthy center of commerce as the city Hollo lived in. She had read this in trade articles, though knew artistry only through the workshop lying directly beside her house. She had little imagination for the crafting of wood, which made up the vast majority of what she could see from this vantage point at the edge of the square.

Just before they had entirely passed out of view, she caught sight of something marvelous. "What's that?" she tugged her father to a halt, then remembering her wooden fingers, quickly hid her hand.

"The white statues?" he asked. "That's marble."

Hollo gasped, allowing him to draw her onward. "They make people from stone, too?"

"Of course," he said. "You can make people out of just about anything."

Hollo was fascinated that each of the marble men and women had the same precise detail and life-like size as her beloved, bronze friends. There was, however, a key difference. The marble faces had a look of such peace and serenity about them, as if proud of their gleaming, pale beauty. They appeared almost vain, these pale, stone people who sat naked in the daylight, drawing any wandering eyes over their perfect sculpted bodies. So it was that bronze people looked fearsome, and so it was that marble people looked so effortlessly content.

"Why are metal people made to look hard, and marble people made to look soft?" she asked Fredric.

"For the same reason that wooden people are made to be so clever and wise," he answered easily.

She frowned at him, confused by the answer. He sounded like he was complimenting her but hadn't answered her question.

He continued, "People don't like to guess. It's easier to know something by how it immediately appears. Dark, hard metal is known as it appears, and so dark, hard people are built from it. Marble is smooth and pale and bright like the faces chipped into it. But that's something about life, what you think you know about a thing is always the first obstacle you face when trying to get to know it better. If they could speak, do you think they'd all be the same?"

Hollo knew exactly how she felt about that; the statues she befriended in secret had no such predictability. She kept silent though, choosing not to give away her meddling in the neighbors' yard. She wanted to keep that secret from her father a little longer.

Now he asked her, "Who would you be if you were made of something else?" This was a question that had not occurred to her. She frowned again, struggling with the idea. She couldn't imagine a body different from her own.

"I'd still be Hollo," she said as if it were obvious.

"Yes I think so, too," he nodded thoughtfully. "So we'll have to let people think they know everything about statues, but we'll know that it's not what you're made of that makes you. Does that sound right?"

"That sounds right," Hollo agreed.

Besides making vain statues, Hollo now saw that marble had another use. The building where they came to deliver Fredric's letter was made of the stuff. Great, pale, swirling columns stood on both sides of the door, though the upper floors seemed to be made of wood. It appeared as if they had begun the construction and then run out of stone midway through. Etched in large bold letters across the front of it read "Packerd's Historical Halfway and Pawn Broker". Both of those things meant nothing to Hollo, and her curiosity piqued as she followed her father inside.

A man sat with his back to them, his enormous backside hiding whatever chair held him there. His gigantic, squishy-fat torso hunched over the appraisal of some bits of metal that he searched closely with a monocle. Hollo gaped at the great lump of human, having never seen someone of such unnecessary size in her life. This was another great wonder of the outdoors that she placed on her list of things to ask her father about when they got home. Fredric saw her awe, and a devious smile crept into his mouth. He bent down to whisper in her ear. As she listened, her eyes widened and she shook her head. He pushed her forward, and with some nervousness, she came to stand beside the imposing Mr. Packerd, who didn't pay her the least of his attention even as she stood so close. Not knowing how to react, Hollo stilled, her nervous fingers alone noted the passing of time. The room had muffled itself in stillness also, so when he finally spoke, Hollo startled.

"What?" the giant mumbled without turning.

"Umm…" Hollo whispered, glancing back at Fredric, who nodded encouragingly.

"Spit it out, what do you want?" Mr. Packerd said irritably, again without looking up from his trinket.

She felt stupid, and didn't want to, but her father seemed so pleased with himself as he stood silently cheering her on. She took a breath, and lowered her hood back with shaking fingers. "Boo," she whispered half-heartedly.

"Boo?" He grumbled as the monocle fell to the table and his great big sausage fingers rubbed his eyes. "What on earth do you mean, 'boo'?" he straightened, turned and squinted at her face.

All in a moment, gelatinous face trembling and eyes widening, he shrieked with all the high pitch and volume of a terrified child as his undersized stool shot out from beneath him and he fell to the floor.

Fredric doubled over and bellowed with laughter, but Hollo, with shock and concern, watched the fellow flail under his own weight, screaming and lashing terror.

"Damn you, Hor-Gauer!" Mr. Packerd said, catching sight of Hollo's father and holding his chest.

Hollo mouthed the name at her father, who put a finger to his lips with a smile. She didn't know this name, nor why Mr. Packerd knew her father by it, but that would just be another item on her list of questions for now. Mr. Packerd heaved and panted, his face red, sweat beading from his receding hairline. "You're trying to kill me again, Hor-Gauer?" he bellowed, returning his attention to Hollo. "My god, man. What on earth are you playing at?"

Fredric latched the door behind him, drawing a curtain across the window so that their meeting could be held now in private. He was still laughing, and Hollo's fear of the giant had melted away and she shared in her father's joke. Mr. Packerd, however, did not, and instead leveraged himself up onto his feet before falling back into a sofa-chair in the corner. Still panting, he dabbed his sweaty brow with a handkerchief.

"Enough," he pleaded. "Enough, both of you...erm, rather...Hor-Gauer. What is this toy, this silly thing?" he pointed at Hollo, who glared at the insult.

"I'm Hollo," she said. "Are you Mr. Packerd?"

He went from red and flustered to stark pale as she spoke. "You speak," he whispered, looking between her and her father. "She speaks? This is new, not even Bander-Clou ever managed to seal a person's soul and have them remain as much themselves to speak about it. How extraordinary."

Hollo understood none of this, clearly the man was confused about her, as much as her father warned her others would be. Brushing it off as tactlessness, she smiled at the large man, attempting to make a good impression. She smiled, and offered her wisdom, "What you think you know about someone always gets in the way of knowing them better."

Mr. Packerd simply goggled at her, shamelessly appraising her as if she was a piece of merchandise.

"You," he pointed at Hollo. "Do you know spirits? Could you tell the difference from my other bottles and fetch my brandy? How old are you, do you know what brandy is?"

"I'm twelve," Hollo answered.

"It's her birthday," Fredric added.

"Hmm," Mr. Packerd frowned. "Then it'll be the round bottle with the donkey on it. Make sure it's the donkey, not the horse, if it's the horse bottle I'll be blind on top of scared to death. I'd ask you to do it," he glared at Fredric. "But I don't trust you with my things."

Her father grinned with an almost evil display of pearl white teeth at Mr. Packerd, whose rancorous glower amused Hollo and reminded her of her statues. She left the two of them like that, and once in the pantry she took a moment to be struck with wonder at the volume of food she found therein, which answered Hollo's question of how a man could become so round. It seemed that whatever Mr. Packerd did for a living with his trinkets and furniture, he afforded quite a lot of food and drink. Locating a round, donkey bottle was not so easy a task amidst such a trove, and she scoured, climbed and searched for some time.

"I hear your clambering in my larder!" came Mr. Packerd's voice from the other room. "The bottles by the cutting board m'dear, do hurry or my death will be on your hands as well!"

She located them. Lifting herself onto the countertop, she riffled through the numerous dusty bottles. Some, she noticed had not been touched in some time. These, she assumed, were the bottles Mr. Packerd did not care for. There were also larger bottles without dust, whose contents were nearly depleted. These were certainly the ones she was looking for. The problem that now faced her, was the fact that she was unsure what a donkey looked like. From what the man had said, it was mistakable as a horse, which seemed easy to her in theory, but the drawings on each bottle were poorly done, and four legged animals seemed to be the stamp of choice in labeling liquor. She drew a number of them out from their fellows, examining the pictures of what she could only imagine were the images of a horse, a cow, one of a bull, and three or four more which she couldn't puzzle out.

"The middle one," her father said from the ornamental mirror on the pot of a houseplant beside her. She seized it and hurried back to them, hearing Mr. Packerd chastising her father with ardor as she returned.

"Don't do that in my store!" he pointed his sausage finger accusingly at Fredric. "They've already got me paying through the teeth for some of the stuff I've had come through here, last I need is a taxing on glass. Those are steep penalties you inconsiderate bandit."

Fredric stepped away from the standing mirror in the corner, throwing his hands up pleading innocence as Hollo handed the bottle off to the flushed, squishy fingers of the upset Mr. Packerd.

"Now," he choked a little, licking the traces of it from his lips. "It's your birthday, girly?" he rounded on Hollo, shifting his weight sideways to crane towards her over the arm of his chair.

She nodded, wrinkling her nose as the silky fumes on his breath hit her unprepared.

"S'cuse me," he apologized, taking another draft of liquor, his neck jiggling as it helped the putrid liquid down. "Well, this is a terrible way to spend a birthday!" he shouted at Fredric. "Pretty, little lady with a fine cloak like that should be out at the fair, letting a boy buy you things! Certainly, I wouldn't dream of keeping you indoors like your father has. Why don't you have a run on round the corner and get yourself something nice in a comb, or..." he fumbled, eyeing her hair as if unsure whether or not the golden threads on her head even required brushing. "Or maybe, I don't know, whatever you like in a picture book. Hmm?"

Hollo didn't know what to make of the man. Fredric's expression had changed, and seemed guarded about letting Hollo off alone, as well he should, and Hollo expected Fredric to rebuff the fellow, telling him it was out of the question. She waited patiently for him to say this. A venture alone was an absurd thing on only her first time out of doors. She waited to hear these words from him. And yet no words came. She looked at her father.

"Well," he said reasonably. "It is your birthday."

She dizzied for an instant, struck speechless.

"Here," Mr. Packerd barked, pointing at a drawer by his desk. "There's a pair of little lady-gloves what used to belong to my dear, departed wife."

Hollo found them, smooth leather of high quality.

"You can have those," Mr. Packerd said with a wobbly smile. "I've no use for them anymore. Your father'll pay for them, anyway. She was a teeny, little woman, my poor wife. Those gloves should almost fit you."

"She died?" Hollo asked, holding the gloves to her chest.

Mr. Packerd smiled sadly. "Ah yes, well, things happen, dear."

"How?" she asked curiously.

"He sat on her," Fredric whispered with a sad nod at Mr. Packerd.

"How dare you!" Mr. Packerd scowled contemptuously at Fredric. "Mocking my dear, departed Elba like that, you scoundrel. We'd be having an entirely different conversation now if what you said wasn't…entirely untrue." Mr. Packerd stared deeply into his glass bottle for a long moment before remembering his company, and his hand dove into his breast pocket, found two large silver coins therein, and presented them to Hollo with a giant, kind, winking smile.

Fredric opened the door for her, raising her hood up over her head and then helped her into her gloves. "Now, it's your birthday," he said to her. "So find something you like, and I don't have to tell you to stay safe. You're a smart girl, you know how to stay safe, right?" She nodded eagerly, casting a nervous eye into the street outside.

"Then take this," he handed her a tiny little brooch from Mr. Packerd's jewelry case. In the center of the ornament was fixed a small circular piece of reflective glass. "You can always find me with this. Now run on, have fun while I finish the boring stuff with Mr. Packerd."

With a new lightness in her heart, Hollo's feet reached the stone street of a city that now opened its arms wide in endless opportunity, for her pleasure, and for her birthday. It seemed that the sun had risen that morning for no reason other than that of celebrating her life and her twelfth year.

. . .

"You've a terrible debt to pay the world, Hor-Gauer," Mr. Packerd proclaimed solemnly as the door shut behind the girl. "To put such a heavy burden on so young a spirit as she."

Fredric grunted distractedly, peeking out through the curtain to watch Hollo make her way back towards the square, and to her romance of the city trade center. Heaviness sat in his stomach, an ancient kind of anxiousness that lives deep in the hearts of those who love deeply. With a sigh, he reminded himself of her cleverness, and leaned against the wall as she disappeared from view. "A debt, you say?" he mumbled, more to himself. "That's what magic has come to these days, surely."

"And how I make a profit," Mr. Packerd said. "We're all sinners, Hor-Gauer. You not least of all, not surely the worst, either. What are you playing towards bringing her here?"

"You wouldn't believe me without seeing her," Fredric replied.

"That," Mr. Packerd said with a cutting bite. "Isn't true, as I still don't. She's a human girl, isn't she? Who was she?" he pointed an accusatory finger at Fredric. "You've started playing with Souls again, I knew you would. You've sealed a poor girl in a Stone, that's dark, sir, very dark."

Fredric shook his head. "Never human, not her."

"Then," Mr. Packerd lowered to a whisper. "Then she...the girl is just a puppet?"

"Just?" Fredric raised an eyebrow. "Certainly not."

"Then, how?" Mr. Packerd asked.

"You don't want to know, do you?" Fredric smiled.

"I carry more of your secrets than I can count," Mr. Packerd grumbled. "Just knowing what you look like would bring me a world of torment if they found out. What's one more?"

"I have your secrets too, Packerd. Don't forget to trust me in hiding you. Or rather who you used to be, back in your more active days."

"You're a scoundrel," Mr. Packerd grumbled. "A criminal of infinite variety, and I'll not soon forget you blackmailing me. When they count your indiscretions at the gates of the afterlife you'll surely hold the line up for a full day!"

Fredric shrugged, reached into his jacket, and pulled out a letter. He flicked it out from two fingers like a disk and it spun through the air and into Mr. Packerd's chest, who fumbled the bottle from hand to hand in a failed effort to catch it.

"One more secret in good faith, then. It's there, in my letter. You'll surely read it, so no use for me explaining."

Mr. Packerd's eyes widened as he unfolded the paper, scanning what had been said was a letter, but finding instead pictures and numbers, equations and calculations. With a pair of dwarfed glasses held at arms length, the giant examined them carefully. "Useless," Mr. Packerd said, pleadingly at Fredric. "What's all this, are you sending a recipe?"

"Something like that," Fredric nodded. "Hopefully the Practitioners pass it on to Him. They wouldn't understand it otherwise, I'd bet."

"Who…Bander-Clou?" Mr. Packerd whispered. "You mean for *this*…to find its way to Bander-Clou?"

Fredric nodded. "I would wager that in giving this to Bander-Clou, if he's still alive, and I'm fairly certain he is, we could save his next victims. If he makes the Stones in this way, as I have done, no one else needs to die."

"But people *will* die," Mr. Packerd pleaded. "Imagine Bander-Clou at the head of an army! If he's alive he needs to be stopped, not helped!"

"Well," Fredric said reasonably, "as soon as you stop him, I'll stop meddling. In the meantime maybe I can spare someone."

"I didn't mean *me*," Mr. Packerd grumbled.

"Then who?"

Mr. Packerd drank with frustration, then muttered "The younger ones," before continuing. "The only reason Bander-Clou's rampage stopped was because he ran out of the necessary kinds of Souls when the Practitioners finally found him out. Countless more may die if Bander-Clou does what you say he will."

Fredric shook his head. "He'll find more Souls if he keeps going as he has in the past. He already has many who he's turned into wooden soldiers; mindless, caged Souls who forget who they are. They are completely under his power."

"But he always needed bodies before," Mr. Packerd said. "That was all that slowed him down in making an army. Now you're sending a recipe to make soldiers without needing a human to rip the Soul from. There's no limit to what he could do if he figured out how you made the girl! If he figures out how the girl works he'll have as many soldiers as he wants!"

"Yes, but imagine if those same soldiers could *think* and *feel*, and be moved by morality."

"Oh," Mr. Packerd said, disappointment slowing down his voice. "So that's your plan? You think they'll turn on him?"

Fredric thought carefully. "I think that he is not the kind of man who can inspire faith or loyalty, much less, love, in real people. He's too greedy not to try it, you see, and that's why I have to send this letter, because he's much too eager to understand the *risk*. He'd just think he was making another puppet. He isn't clever enough to really understand what he would be drawing out of the dark."

"But you," Mr. Packerd pointed at Fredric with a dark, sarcastic grin. "You've done it, have you? With nothing but your arithmetic and cleverness, cracked all the secrets, hmm? You can just make people 'poof' into the world. How'd you do it? Did you dangle one of those little metal balls out before the void and say '*oh please wherever you Pneuma may be, won't you come live in my Zygotic Stone? It's ever so nice a place*'…"

Fredric met the man's eyes and they regarded one another without amusement. Trust had been hard for them over the years, and this year was no different.

"You were very kind," Fredric said. "Giving her Elba's gloves. You saw her smile, didn't you?"

Mr. Packerd's cheeks flushed a little.

Fredric continued. "Tell me, then, if I've 'cracked the secret', as you say. You met my daughter, you tell me if she's only wood and magic and my will made manifest, or if there's something else in those eyes. Something, maybe, that caught you enough to give away your wife's gloves."

Mr. Packerd frowned. "There are children who believe, for all the world, that their toy animals are real. Doesn't make it true."

Fredric sighed, looking out into the street again. "So you think I'm playing?"

Mr. Packerd nodded fervently. "A very dangerous game, yes. I know how good you are, Hor-Gauer. I know the things you can do, cause I've seen it. You've a solid head for solving problems, you're a clever man, and a good man, too, despite your pretending. But that's where I see you losing sight of things. You're a good man, Hor-Gauer, and good men lose sight of the truth sometimes, they prefer their hopes."

"Yes that's true," Fredric said, softly. "And that will never change."

Mr. Packerd grumbled. "Well you've heard me, at least."

They were silent for a while, save the frequent sound of the bottle swishing up and down, back and forth to Mr. Packerd's mouth.

"You can get my letter to the Practitioners, right?" Fredric asked without turning away from the window.

"O'course I can," Mr. Packerd replied bitterly. "Whether I can get it to them without them tracing it back to my hands, that's another question. My reach in town isn't quite what it used to be."

"Should I find someone else?"

Mr. Packerd responded with a growl of some odd word that didn't quite translate into any language Fredric knew.

"Just asking," Fredric said with a private grin.

"You should let her out more often, shouldn't you?" Mr. Packerd said, suddenly. "I mean, keeping her cooped up in there like a caged chicken all day has to be bad for a body."

"Even a wooden one?" Fredric asked sarcastically.

Mr. Packerd shot him a tested look.

"You believe me then?" Fredric continued.

"I believe what I feel like, and a'sides," he waved his hand through the air. "I've raised children before, and whether or not she knows it, she gotta get out into the world now and again, for her own good."

"I'll make a note of it," Fredric said. "Hmm," he squinted his eyes out the window. "That was fast."

The door came bursting open, and Hollo flew inside, a great red feathery lump in her arms.

"Well now!" Mr. Packerd bellowed as she came to a halt in the room. "What on earth you buy a chicken for?"

Hollo beamed and set the bird on the floor. "His name's Flynn! I traded for him, those two shiny coins for him."

"Two silver?" Mr. Packerd said, looking struck in the face. "A hen isn't worth two silver, much less a cockerel."

"Not normally," Fredric said, smiling. "But that magnificent fellow is surely worth at least two, if not three. Good choice."

"It's funny," Mr. Packerd barked, glaring at Fredric. "We were just talking about caged chickens. How come you picked the cock, hmm?"

Hollo sat, hugging the giant monster of a bird to her chest. "He was hung up in the air by his legs, the woman was 'bout to cut his head off," she sniffed, flicking curiously at the lobes of red on Flynn's throat. "So I told her to stop, and gave her the coins, and she stopped, and gave him to me."

"A chickens not worth two silvers!" the man yelled from his chair. "My god, girly, you've been done tragedy by your father, that much I knew, but to be without schooling in business…so great a crime is unjustifiable!"

Hollo glowered at him, the obtuse man who insulted her chicken, and her judgment. "I think he's marvelous."

Fredric smiled. "Very well put. And it's about time we be on our way."

Hollo gathered her prize rooster up in her arms again as Mr. Packerd put his hand up in the air.

"Look," he said flatly. "Why not, er…what I mean is…it's no good for a young mind to be wasted indoors. If you'd like, you can come here some days."

Fredric raised a bemused eyebrow at Mr. Packerd, who glared back at him. "Rather," he turned his attention back to Hollo. "You can have a job round my store if you care for it. I'm not so mobile anymore, and a strong young lady would be a happy help. I'll pay you a decent starting salary, and then you can rescue as many chickens as you like. But only after you learn the value of things."

Hollo looked all round the shop, taking in the wonder of Mr. Packerd's wares. What a bounty of knowledge this complex, unlikeable Mr. Packerd must have. What she might learn from him here…daring the trip across the square would certainly be an obstacle to overcome, but worth it? Mr. Packerd's face had set into the jiggling disapproval that defined him, and how it reminded her of the bronze garden caused her a smile. "You know," she told him. "If I didn't know better, I'd say you were made of metal."

She scurried out of the door, into the street where she released Flynn to follow her like a happy dog on his way to receive a cookie.

"Wait," Mr. Packerd called Fredric back as he was about to follow. The man poked his head back in.

"Why the letter?" Mr. Packerd asked him. "Why bait him like this? You're only making trouble for yourself and for her. Why send a piece of a puzzle if it will only frustrate him?"

"So long as Bander-Clou is hunting me, he's not hunting anyone else."

"Noble," Mr. Packerd said. "But doesn't that put the little one in danger?"

"Well," Fredric began, a complex series of emotions shadowing his face for only a moment. "One day, most likely, she'll be found out for what she is. And the world needs to know about her before it can accept her. This is the best I can do to give her a chance. The letter, besides being a trap for Bander-Clou, is a hint that she exists, and a hint about what to expect if they try and do to her what they did to her mother before her."

Mr. Packerd sat up a little straighter, a sudden thought pinching his face and he began to speak very slowly. "Hor-Gauer, you've been in that house too long. You're not sending them a recipe…not a recipe at all and not a warning either," he took a vicious swig again and frowned a deep, knowing, and all too familiar frown. "You're trying to pick a fight - like a boy in school whose been teased too long."

Fredric made no sign of having heard him, and instead hurried away after his daughter. Now Mr. Packerd sat alone, the footsteps of his visitors long since blended away into the noise outside. He took another long draft, quelling his secrets, quieting away his forbidden knowledge, and held out the letter to review it again.

"You think you can keep her safe?" Mr. Packerd said to an imaginary Fredric. "You're a good man to hope, Hor-Gauer. A foolish good man."

Chapter Four
The Hunter

Summer began, and the long days had Hollo wishing for the outdoors, but instead, she came to be inside, in a dusty, grumpy, fat man's live-in store front. The first thing she learned about Mr. Packerd was that he had sold his home across town just after his wife died, and in the years since then had lived here in his shop. Hollo thus began her education in the field of housework, becoming reluctantly fluent in the disposal of garbage and the upkeep of lanterns, doorknobs, piping, and a variety of other things Mr. Packerd had become too large to attend to. Her work, she had hoped, would've allowed her to learn more of Mr. Packerd's odd wares and their uses, but instead she became not unlike his maid, but of course one who peeked over his shoulder, listened to his conversations with customers, and scoured the house in search of the warmth she knew in her own home, which she could not seem to find here.

Not to say she was bored, Mr. Packerd's home fantastical in the most mediocre of ways. Her interest piqued by the upstairs tenant he claimed she must not bother, but who she never seemed to be able to cross paths with. She started to wonder if there was actually someone living up there, or if Mr. Packerd simply told her this in an effort to keep her out of his business; an effort he repeatedly wasted. Hollo was twelve, and Mr. Packerd was continually reminded of that fact. Not that she was irresponsible, but more that responsibility is a quality that grows with the diminishing of imagination, and Hollo seemed to be at constant odds with Mr. Packerd's responsibility/imagination ratio. Although he could not fault her for the work she accomplished, she always found more time to let her curiosity lead her than he agreed with.

They were at odds, though there is an advantage in youthfulness and over a short period of time he was worn down in his resolve and instead allowed her the occasional duty of minding the storefront while he took naps, strolls, and more often than not was occupied by heated arguments with himself or occasionally his old friends. One such man happened by on a particularly warm, summer afternoon, late in the day, but still light and not yet cooling into evening. It was this afternoon that Hollo had been placed in charge of the store while Mr. Packerd popped out for an errand in the garden behind his home. Hollo heard the front door from the kitchen, and stealthily maneuvered her way to peek out and see who had come. Walk-in customers were rare, and the even rarer sale that she made to them when Mr. Packerd was away always resulted in a fight between her and her disagreeable employer, since the two of them had very different ideas about the worth of things. She wondered if today would be the same.

A white-haired man, old but not frail and with impeccable posture, held himself straight and proud in the middle of the store. His hands were folded against the small of his back, and his eyes drifted with disinterest over the things for sale. Hollo made certain her hood covered her face before peeking around the corner at him.

"Mr. Packerd will be back soon," she said, drawing an instant sharp turn from this formal man. His eyes were wild, military and ferocious for an instant, bright blue and electric, and they grabbed onto her with a physical grip, steeling her legs while caught in their pale glittering intensity.

"Perhaps you can help me," the man said, changing in the same instant, the power of his presence lifting off her, relaxing into that of a kind man, one who perhaps had children of his own who had taught him softness in light of his warrior's countenance. His smile was kind. "I haven't had refreshment in some time on the way here. I'm so very parched of thirst and Mr. Packerd kindly allows me a cup of tea when I visit. Perhaps you could help an old man?"

Hollo smiled and nodded, scampering off to the kitchen to fetch his drink, something Hollo knew very well how to do perfectly. She tore her gloves off to handle the hardware better, and filled the kettle. The water was cold, but her interest in the man had caused her impatience, and so her eagerness to speak more with him had her immediately reaching into her pocket for her string. Heating water was simple, unnoticeable magic. No harm could come of it, she reasoned, whispering to her thread, bidding it into heat and touching her fingertips to the kettle.

"Save me trouble, time and toil, fire in water, heat and boil," she chanted under her breath, knowing the man couldn't hear her anyway, but safety was always worth the extra caution. Rinsing the cup with sugar syrup from Mr. Packerd's kitchen bar, she made her tea as she always did, with the faint lick of sweetness how her father always liked it. She hurried it to the man, setting it on Mr. Packerd's desk.

Her gloves were still in her pocket, she realized suddenly, jerking the little cup as she withdrew her fingers back beneath the hem of her cloak. She glanced quickly at the white haired man, who stared at her. Her breath held, she waited in fear for some shock or question, but none came. His eyes flicked only once, back to their stark staring intensity for a single blink. Instantly he was transformed, and then just as quickly shook it off, smiled at her, and returned to his soft kindness. If he had indeed noticed, he obviously dismissed it as a trick of the light. She breathed easily again, retreating back to the doorway as the straight-backed man bowed curtly and picked the cup off the table. He made a gracious show for her of savoring the aroma with closed eyes, giving her a small wink as he took a sip.

"Exquisite," he said with a smile. "You're very kind, might I ask who you are?"

"I'm…" Hollo began, unsure whether or not to lie. There wasn't any harm he could do her by her name, certainly. "Umm," she faltered.

"How rude of me," the man said, straightening more formally and placing a hand below his chest. "Myself first, of course. I am Amit Torrenet-Bluf, an old friend."

"Hollo," she said.

"Might I say," he chuckled. "You've a lovely pair of eyes, child."

She lowered her head a little, to hide herself, yet warmed at the compliment all the same. "Are you here to buy something?" she asked the man.

"Not today, merely visiting. He called on me, you see. Perhaps I can do him a favor in return for your fine cup of tea."

She smiled, returning to the kitchen then, struck by the thought that the man might care for a pastry with his tea. She knew the piggly Mr. Packerd was a man who kept a generous stock of delicacies at hand for just such an occasion.

"What are you doing, robbing me of sweets?" Mr. Packerd laughed as he returned through the kitchen door to find Hollo digging a scone from out of his pantry.

"It's for mister Amit," she explained, finding a pretty saucer. "He's having tea."

Mr. Packerd smiled broadly, calling into the front of the house. "Is that you, Amit!"

"Certainly!" the man returned.

Mr. Packerd laughed heartily, turning to Hollo. "I'll be talking with him for some time, Amit is a good friend of mine. Why don't you nip off home, I'll be closing up now."

She was disappointed not to stay and talk more with the old man with the wild eyes, but she knew Mr. Packerd must want privacy with his friend and so accepted the coin for her work and resigned to walk back home and enjoy Flynn's company instead.

"Nice to meet you," she called to the man out of sight.

"Goodbye, child, thank you again," Amit called back, and as Mr. Packerd waddled himself away, Hollo helped herself to another scone, stuffing it in her cloak pocket. Today she would go home early, give Flynn his pastry and tell him of the curiously complicated eyes of the man she had just had the odd pleasure of meeting.

Mr. Packerd shook his hand, enthusiastically exchanging a greeting as old friends do, though with a dignity befitting the lordly, military stature of the elder Amit. Mr. Packerd locked his front door and drew the curtains closed so they could visit one another undisturbed. He then settled himself into the chair at his desk, offering his guest the comfort of his best armchair, and offering Hollo's scone to him, which he accepted happily. Amit tasted it with relish, while gesturing with his cup of tea. "A fine young apprentice, a very kind girl. It seems I've promised you a favor for such a charming lady's doting hospitality."

"Convenient," Mr. Packerd chortled. "As I do have something for you." He handed over Fredric's letter. "If you could have that to the Practitioners in anonymity I would be indebted to you."

Amit took it with a chuckle, brushing away the debt with a sweep of his hand. "An easy thing, never mind your debt," he said, finishing his biscuit while unfolding the paper. "May I?" he asked, flourishing the letter. Mr. Packerd gave a permissive tip of his head.

"Oh my," Amit grumbled after scanning the paper. "Trade in secrets much, Mr. Packerd?"

"I've no idea what it's about, so don't ask," he winked at the older man. "Not that I'd breach contract and tell you if I did."

"Oh of course not," Amit replied. "I wouldn't ask, but from what I can tell on light inspection, this smells of some calculation in devilry."

"I'd say so," Mr. Packerd agreed. "Much as magic tends to, I've been smelling quite the trails of it around my sources and less respectable customers lately. Great for business when there's tension building in the world. Quite a commotion I hear coming from the lawmakers these days. What news?" Mr. Packerd asked eagerly of his politically informed friend. "You're better than a trade journal for the happenings behind the curtains."

"Ah yes, well, there are those who come to me, yes," Amit sniffed. "They won't leave me alone these days, with so much venom on all sides, everyone wanting security counsel, it's become something of a business for me, might start charging for my time, certainly there are those who can afford it."

Mr. Packerd guffawed heartily, leaning in closer. "Go on, tell me what the fancy people are up to now."

Amit shrugged and sighed, seemingly exhausted by the information he was burdened down with in his age. "Well certainly, there's upset around the secrecy of the Practitioners, and the hunting of those who keep their craft hidden away. Since the late King Haddard passed many of us question the right of the Practitioners to exist at all. The Mad King appointed them and we must wonder if he did so in madness. Especially now the Hermetics are hunted so viciously, despite all laws protecting human rights, but then, most of us would rather not know and just let magic and devilry destroy itself. And then there are the poorhouses, struggling to keep their doors open. Money, I'm afraid, is at the root of many of these problems. An irritating thing, economics, a subject I have little authority in."

"Does the government dare challenge the Practitioners?" Mr. Packerd asked in a whisper, enthralled with the gossip. "They've been looking for a chance for years."

"They would lose much in challenging those who deal in devilry," Amit said wisely. "I fear for them if they do."

"That's their business though, isn't it?" Mr. Packerd asked. "They've allowed the Practitioners to gain so much strength in politics, won't they ever declare their work unlawful? I heard they're hunting the Hermetics again, and that's quite riled everyone, you know. I hear the Hermetics growing more frightened. I hear whispers of resistance. Laws and rights be damned if they do, there'll be witch-hunts again if they're not careful. The higher-ups must know this, and yearn to take action?"

"No one wishes to confront the Practitioners, those in political standing are afraid of losing their station. The Practitioners still retain the blessing the king who organized them, mad or not, their power over the city is not without substance. You know as well as I do the stories of what it was like before the Practitioners. We need someone to be responsible for these people, without the Practitioners there may well be mayhem."

"But the Practitioners are crooks," Mr. Packerd said.

Amit nodded, his tone turning dark and deliberate. "More alarming is that they appear to be behaving with a sense of some urgency. They are becoming rash, making hasty decisions, and that is very dangerous. What's more is that they've grown lax in their morality." He raised an eyebrow at Mr. Packerd and hushed to a whisper. "You know, there is a rumor that the Practitioners intend to have a huntsman once more."

"I heard," Mr. Packerd said darkly.

Amit stared pointedly at him. "Perhaps you heard who they say will be re-elected for the position? They say it is to again be the fabled dark puppet master, Bander-Clou."

"No!" Mr. Packerd exclaimed.

Amit shrugged. "That's what they say. The Practitioners whisper, so I hear, that despite being thrown out of their order years ago, they want him back now that Hermetic mages are coming out of the woodwork and parading their power around in daylight. The Practitioners are taking action, reinstating Bander-Clou to do the very thing that got him thrown out in the first place."

Mr. Packerd rubbed his forehead in distress. "The Hermetics will be hunted again, murdered even. That is grave, very disappointing. But how do they know that there even are still Hermetics?"

"They are younger people," Amit said with an odd bite of frustration. "The ones who learned their craft from beyond the grip of the Practitioners. The next generation of Hermetic magic now has a lust for attention. You know there are Hermetics on the high seas now, beyond law. Even in our own Artisan District there are upstarts vying for attention, like the Black Rider, who they say hunts the Practitioners themselves. Everywhere there are stories of danger, magic, and devilry. The young mages will surely have the attention they wish for unless they keep their heads down. There will be blood, always blood, and I only hope it won't be the blood of children."

"Yes," Mr. Packerd muttered gloomily. "We shall see. Here," he offered as Amit raised his cup to his lips. "Let me freshen your tea, it's gone cool by now."

"Contrarily," Amit said, his eyes twinkling with an odd intensity, intensified further by how slowly and pointedly he now spoke. "It is very much as hot as it was."

"Ha!" Mr. Packerd shook his head. "Imagine that."

"Indeed," Amit smiled, and then changed the subject. "Do you know much about Bander-Clou?"

Mr. Packerd frowned. "Can't say that I do. I know of his legend, the stories of what he did to the Hermetics he hunted down. Heard that he rips his enemies out of their bodies and seals them away into puppets. What about you?" he leaned in again, eager for more gossip.

"Hmm," Amit tapped the cup of steaming tea before him. "I hear he's always been hard to find. He moves easily in the world, from circle to circle, certainly it could be that he's been nearby many people without them knowing who he is. I don't know that anyone really knows his identity."

"Odd thing," Mr. Packerd said taken aback. "Why would you assume that?"

Amit stared into space for a long moment, then his fingers crept slowly to the folded piece of paper on the table beside him. He opened it casually, eyes darting all around it, then widening slowly. "Odd indeed," he muttered distractedly. "Who did you say this was from?" he asked.

Mr. Packerd's neck jiggled as he shrugged. "I do various things for people so long as they pay, and not knowing who they are is one service I am valuable for."

"Clever," Amit mumbled. "Very clever, yes, you are, aren't you…"

"Well," Mr. Packerd frowned again, put off slightly by his guest's changing mood. "Not so clever, just a scoundrel for the right price."

"Aren't we all," Amit said quietly. Folding the paper together again, his eyes fixed on Mr. Packerd. "Well if you know little of Bander-Clou, perhaps you also know nothing of the other puppet-master, Hor-Gauer?"

Mr. Packerd shifted in his seat, struck with agitation by Amit's wild stare. "I'd say you're right about that," he answered. "What's all this now, Amit? What's riled you?"

Amit tapped again on his teacup, sniffing his sharp nose into the steaming tendrils.

Mr. Packerd frowned at him, eyeing the tea, seeing the steam wafting up in front of Torrenet-Bluf's face, clouding his already cloudy-blue, wild eyes. It was an odd intensity, one Mr. Packerd did not recognize in this man who he considered a friend. There was something definitely amiss in the room, and Mr. Packerd had now begun to put the pieces together as to what.

Amit continued to tap on the teacup. "Your assistant has an uncanny skill with making tea. How rare it is to find good help, especially for a man of your…financial overhead," he eyed Mr. Packerd's overlarge midsection.

"My assistant," Mr. Packerd tried to chuckle amusedly, but it came out very much uncomfortable sounding. He began fumbling clumsily with some of the odd ornaments on his desk; casually fogging a hand-mirror with his breath and wiping it clean with a sleeve. "Ah, yes. She's burned my mouth out many times. Has a charming knack for making tea much too hot."

"Indeed," Amit replied coldly, drawing the letter from the table beside him, and examining it once more. "So now...pretense aside," he said conversationally, causing Mr. Packerd's blood to run cold. "Hor-Gauer lives, does he?"

Mr. Packerd gulped slowly, determined not to show his agitation. "I don't-"

"Pretense aside!" Amit hissed at him. "There will be no more lies out of you, now, tell me," he raised his eyes to Mr. Packerd's, the kindness gone from them. "Wherever did that little girl run off to?"

Chapter Five
Black Rider

Fredric sat perfectly still at his kitchen desk, listening to the two men speaking. He knew both, he knew Mr. Packerd, and he knew the devil across from him. The white haired man's pale eyes glittered in the mirror on Fredric's desk. Mr. Packerd had done right by using the mirror to alert Fredric of the impending danger, and he listened carefully for the information that he hoped with all his being that Mr. Packerd would give him. It was essential for Fredric to know where Hollo was at this moment, and it was also very important that he be told whether or not the elder man knew Hollo's secret.

"The girl?" Mr. Packerd was failing at feigning comfort, his voice was shaking and strained, despite his calm words. "Why, she must be off home, it's past time for her to be off. Why...erm...why do you ask?"

"Off home to Hor-Gauer?" the white haired man said. "Well why don't you call her back, I'd certainly like to meet her properly." Fredric saw him holding his letter. "I'd certainly like to see what she knows of the *taste* of the tea she makes."

Fredric knew clearly what needed to be done. Years of preparation came to relevance now that the secret of his life with his daughter had been revealed. Golden threads met his hands as he reached for the ceiling, and one of the threads met his lips.

"Quickly now," he spoke into the room. The mirror on his desk went dark, and then illuminated into a distant wooden room, where the hanging chandelier swayed ever so softly in the air.

"Eferee," he said loudly.

A young girl raised a fist as she turned towards the wall he spoke from. A moment of wild ferocity dulled only a little as she saw who called on her.

"You," she said with distaste. "What do you think-"

"I have few seconds to spare, so listen carefully," he said, and she fell silent, regarding him in a way that made her face appear ugly. She clenched her jaw and dried what appeared to be moisture off of her clenched fist with an already damp kerchief.

"Fine," she mumbled.

"I've been found," he said.

"By who?"

"Bander-Clou."

She spat on the ground, appearing ferocious again. "Well, that was stupid. I always pegged you for-"

"Just listen," he cut her off. "You know what I need from you, and you know what you owe me. I can't ask anyone else, will you help?"

She rolled her eyes. "It's out of my way."

"Eferee…"

"But I owe you, don't I?" she spat. "Your so-called 'guidance'. How would I have survived without you whispering at me from your damned mirrors? You're not my dad, Hor-Gauer."

"Are you nearby?"

She raised an eyebrow.

"Tell me," he pleaded.

"Where do you think I am!" she yelled furiously. "I'm on my damned ship!"

"What dock?"

"The Artisan Harbor."

"I hoped so. Can I count on you?"

"We'll see," she grumbled.

"Eferee," he pleaded again.

"I said we'll see!" she shouted back through the mirror, and then pulled open her desk drawer and found a silver locket. Giving a sarcastic show of bowing and putting the locket around her neck, she then glared at him one last time before storming out of the cabin.

Fredric let the mirror fade away, concentrating harder than before to bring the next person into the glass. He saw only darkness, but he could hear a white noise of stormy weather behind the thudding pulse of a heartbeat. He bit down on the thread between his teeth, and shouted as loud as he could. "Open the locket!"

A moment later, the mirror came to life with a face, and a blinding flash of lightning that knocked Fredric back in his seat.

"The Mirror Man," came a thunderous voice from the other end, though the face remained hardly discernable.

"I'm in trouble," Fredric said hurriedly.

"What do you want?"

"I have to leave my city, I need a guide and I need protection. Do you know where this house is?"

"I know the house, yes," he said forcefully.

"Then I'll see you here," Fredric said desperately. "I have to go. I'll look for your coming."

"Watch the sky," the voice boomed back. "I'm days away, but I will come."

"Thank you," Fredric shouted back over his shoulder, leaving his mirror, leaving his house, and even leaving the front door open behind him, and with that, ran with all his might along the road to Mr. Packerd's shop.

. . .

Amit drew out from his jacket pocket two identical objects, both made of metal, elaborate in their ornamentation, and held them out for Mr. Packerd to see.

"You say Bander-Clou seals enemies away in puppets?" Amit said. "That is true, just as he seals away friends. Perhaps there is room for you in his collection? Tell me, have you ever seen a Zygotic Stone before?"

Mr. Packerd tensed his body, gripping the edge of his desk with white fingers. Amit's own fingers had grown hot against the metal orbs in his hands, and as he released them they did not fall far, but instead floated, hung by soft blue threads of light that led from his fingertips. In a great scrape and bending of solid material, the wares of Mr. Packerd's shop came to life and began to be dismantled by invisible hands. Great clocks and mirrors, gadgets and toys lent their pieces into the construction of two bodies that rose around the metal orbs, rose, and stood mismatched, though strikingly human in appearance. The humanoid beings remained silent, staring dully at their feet but with only dark vacant spaces for eyes. Amit released his magical hold on them and strode lazily around the shop, rifling through Mr. Packerd's items of clothing and picking out a pair of thick cloaks. Mr. Packerd feared to move, though his fingers reached again to fiddle with the mirror on his desk. This small motion was cut short by the cracking snap it drew from the closest wooden man, whose head jerked up to him, halting Mr. Packerd's movement immediately.

Amit dressed his creations, and was met with no objection, covering both their hairless crowns with the dense fabric of the heavy hoods. "This could be your fate if you wish," Amit told him. "Perhaps I could save you from the weak, gluttonous heart that troubles you?"

Mr. Packerd's hand went to his chest, which indeed tightened under the stress of such impending danger. "What are you going to do now, Amit…" he trailed off.

Amit, whether or not his name held the same deceit as his eyes, didn't bother to reply. The answer came with the other of his wooden men raising his head. Amit leveled his eyes at Mr.

Packerd as the puppet's body then jerked to life and strode forward, leaving by way of the kitchen door after Hollo. Amit didn't speak, only held gaze with the fat man, telling him without words that the question was not what he was going to do, but rather, what did Mr. Packerd dare do to stop him.

Packerd's fingers pressed harder into his chest as beds of sweat ran down his forehead and nose as his body slumped forward in his seat.

"Well?" Amit asked coldly. "Not long for you now, wouldn't you rather a more resilient shell than your aging one?"

Mr. Packerd heaved and fell to the floor while Amit let out a sigh and turned away from him. As Amit muttered to himself, Mr. Packerd's hand dove into his lowest desk drawer, drawing out a short-barreled single-fire musket.

Amit turned slowly as the pistol clicked, a dark, dangerous expression then shadowing his face. "I thought you were strictly a man of sabers, Packerd? Perhaps it's true what they say about you, that you've lost your magic. Certainly, there are limits to how much magic can do, and you have become rather overgrown since your days of glory."

Mr. Packerd pulled his trigger, loosing the shot and a screen of gun-smoke into the room, hiding the two men for a moment. The smoke dispersed, revealing the shattered wooden arm and damaged torso of the wooden man who had shielded Amit from the blast.

Amit brushed splinters from his sleeve, standing straight again. "Really now, Packerd. You surely…" he fell short, realizing he was now alone in the room, and a smile then crept onto his face. "Ah…I see, Mr. Packerd. Then I was right in guessing who you used to be. A fine clockwork man you'll soon become."

.   .   .

Having been sent out the back door had changed Hollo's plans on the way home. Since she came out on The Etcher Road instead of Casting Street, she made it her plan to find the store front which belonged to her favorite Bronze workers, and perhaps slip secretly through to their garden. Since she had a little of the afternoon to herself for once, she intended not to waste it. She wondered what it would be like to strike up a conversation with the foul-mouthed, head bronzer, Chester, or maybe even the charming and attractive Kit-Falermeyer. The thought had her giddy and excited to meet them, finally, after years of spying.

The warmth of the summer day had lingered into late afternoon, though somehow the heat in the air didn't warm her. It was this odd feeling in the wind that first caught her attention. She shivered a little with what might have been excitement, but as she came closer towards the bronze smith's workshop, she found there to be commotion and confrontation commanding what should have been a lazy summer afternoon. Men in uniform were gathered in the area. She noticed them walking in twos and threes with larger huddles talking amongst themselves. She curled herself out of sight in the side of an alley so as to overhear what the trouble was. She waited for some time before a younger pair of soldiers came to stand near her, mumbling and arguing with each other.

"Sixth time I've seen him, I swear. Haven't had a good look, but he's easy to spot at a distance," said the smaller soldier. He appeared the younger and definitely the shorter of the two, and his youthful face was wrinkled by the constant, squinting shut of his left eye. Hollo listened closer, careful not to move and give herself away. At least they were looking for someone else, she thought, and not for her. She had felt a grip of fear with so many men near her home. She was relieved that it wasn't a little wooden devil they spoke of, but instead a criminal on the loose in the neighborhood.

"So what are we supposed to do about it?" the tall soldier muttered. "Gunfire does nothing, they say. He's toe to head in old-fashioned armor."

"Gimme a rifle with a good eye-piece on it and this mess would be sorted," the other answered him. "Just takes a shot in the right place."

"Oh ho!" the other laughed. "You could hit him off a horse, could you, one-eye? Well aren't you the boss marksman! This is the first I'm hearing of it."

The smaller one whose left eye was apparently missing behind the squinting shut quickly riled. "I am, if only the Captain would requisition one of the fine long arms from the armory for me. I keep telling him, but I'll be damned if he listens."

The taller one shook his head with a condescending smirk. "Not a chance. We haven't even got an order to kill him yet, I don't think. They want him stopped is all. Practitioners want him, dunno why they've got us out tailing the brute."

The one-eyed youth swore. "I dunno even if he's done anything, asides his illegal magic. He's not yet attacked anyone, so why all the bother, I wonder?"

"Captain's calling," the tall one said, suddenly. The pair hurried off to join their party, and Hollo rose to watch. It seemed someone had broken the law with magic. Hollo knew there were penalties for magic, but hadn't known it was so serious an offense that it merited twenty armed men. She knew she must be careful never to give anyone a reason to come hunting after her, aside from the fact that she existed at all. Her thoughts turned to the image their description of the perpetrator left in her mind. A man in armor, riding a horse. Her imagination filled in the form of her recently acquainted bronze Knight, and an awful thought occurred to her. What if she had done wrong in waking him? What if she had somehow let too much of her magic into him that he had got loose and found a horse? She shuddered at the thought that this all may have something to do with her. She began to construct a plan to sneak past the soldiers, or around them somehow to get into the garden to check on the bronze Knight, to assure herself he still stood there. She realized she was being silly, that she could simply go home and see from her window. Certainly it was the less amusing option, but very much more responsible. Mr. Packerd would be proud of her thinking responsibly.

Sudden calamity broke out amongst the assembled soldiers and a voice boomed out over them; a Captain shouting orders at them to form ranks and to fire. Hollo ducked herself back, watching them from safety as the yelling was interrupted by noise so deafening her hands flew up to her ears. A horse, equally as large as the ones she had encountered on her first day out of doors, and carrying a man on its back, broke right through the ranks of gunmen, scattering them. The rider came down the street in Hollo's direction, the hard clattering of metal hooves making so much more noise than any horse Hollo had ever heard. The beast wore armor, dark, almost black-looking plates that covered its whole body, and the rider wore the same. As he passed her, she heard the man laughing loudly, calling obscenities over his shoulder, words Hollo had heard before, from Chester. Halting a few yards from Hollo's alley, the man reared his animal onto its hind legs. Waving at the gunmen like a madman, the black rider screamed challenges punctuated with rude gestures.

The soldiers were verbalized back into ranks by the leader. The Captain, remaining calmer than his units, raised his voice to hail the outlaw. "Stand to be judged, Rider! Else we shall fire and have back your stolen items from your corpse!"

The rider cackled and his steed's hooves shattered chips of stone from the cobble street as they stamped back down from the air. His voice returned, even louder than the Captain, as if his mask magnified his voice. "I've stolen nothing, and you shall have nothing from me. But know that I will ride, until this city comes crashing down around the feet of my horse, and the Practitioners are routed from their dens, I will ride, and your stone and guns and fire will break against my armor, and fade around me!"

The Captain hesitated for a solid moment, before shouting his command. Though his soldiers were rattled and unsure of themselves, they fired well, even at the length of street that separated the rider from his foes. Hollo couldn't help but whimper as shots landed, ricocheting from the plates that covered the rider. A second volley had the same effect, emitting no sparks from his shields, but rather tiny puffs of smoke. The third and final volley came a second later, a shot hitting the rider between the eyes and knocking his head back a few degrees. Hollo clapped her hands over her mouth as she saw this, fearing the shot had found his eye, but the rider drew himself back quickly, unharmed, to speak at them again. "You men, you soldiers are not who I want. Send out a better fighter. Send me Bander-Clou. Send me the puppet master."

"I don't know who that is!" the Captain shouted back, and Hollo now saw that a military saber was in his hand, and that his men had fastened knives at the end of their muskets, turning them to spears.

"He fights for the Practitioners. He is a huntsman and a murderer. Send your soldiers to them, and make them fight their own battles!"

The rider turned away and charged on, away from the soldiers, and away from Hollo. The soldiers gave chase for all the good it would do them, and Hollo hid in the shadows as they passed by her. She shook and trembled now, now that the fighting had moved away from her. She couldn't wait to speak to her father about this, and how many questions it had raised for her, how it was that magic had such a place in the world, to be feared, to be used for war and making threats. She held herself, calmly breathing, noticing now that people had come out of their houses to talk amongst themselves and stare down the road after the rider and the soldiers. She thought to go and listen to them, to hear what the common people had to say about such things, but she thought again, and decided it was time to be home, and be safe. She knew the alley she was in, knew she could take it all the way to Casting Street, and be home shortly after. These alleys ran between houses, expanding on the grid-like structure of the city streets. Assuming this alley was like all the other alleys, it would come out nearby the square where the market was held. In fact, as she thought about it, she figured the alley may come out where the barrels were stored beside the bar near her home, where she had hidden from horses not too many weeks ago. She smiled, noticing how brave she had become after being so afraid of normal horses, and how she had learned to be brave of horses, and now how she was learning to be brave of giant magical black horses carrying outlaw Hermetic mages. Her father would be proud, and she brimmed with self-satisfaction.

The alley was not perfectly straight, and turned several times, not so much that she became lost, but enough that she started to wonder if she had been right to decide to take this route home. She could ask, she knew, but there were no people she could find. She imagined that this was because it was around time for dinner, and most must be indoors with their families. She began to hurry herself, walking quickly, eager to get home before night set in.

Turning another corner, she found someone walking slowly, and she ran to catch up.

"Excuse me, sir!" she called, then realized that she didn't know if it was at all a 'sir' or not. The person wore a heavy cloak that covered their body, though they did indeed stop walking when she called.

"Sorry," she said, unsure why she was apologizing. "But I might not know where I'm going." She then wondered why such a heavy cloak would be worn in the heat of summer, unless, she rationalized, perhaps this person planned to be out late into the night. Still, she became suddenly a little nervous. Standing several paces behind the cloaked person, and not wanting to go closer, she now wished desperately that the stranger would say something, anything, to put her at ease. No words came, but rather, as the cloaked figure turned, there came the sounds of mechanics, of metal and clockwork, and the hard step of a wooden foot against stone.

Chapter Six
Puppet Masters

Before she had a chance to see a face, or wooden face, the cloaked figure turned away again and walked on, away from her, his feet clacking dully against the stone. "Wait!" Hollo heard herself say. She knew she must distance herself from him and go home, but a wooden man was something she had never known existed. She herself was unique, as her father had told her. She was the only one who had ever been born into a body like this, but now she had found another, a wooden person who walked as she did. He didn't seem to intend her any harm. She was unsure if the man could even speak…she had heard Mr. Packerd say something to that effect when he'd met her. Something about how other people in wooden bodies couldn't talk, besides her. She searched her memory for the rest of the conversation, and as she did so, realized that she had begun to follow after the wooden man as he slowly strolled away from where she was going, back in the direction of Mr. Packerd's shop.

Her curiosity had absolutely gotten the better of her now, and she surrendered to it, following at a little distance from the man, intent on at very least seeing where he was going. She decided that since the man paid her no attention, he obviously didn't care if she tagged along, though still, she hid her pursuit from him, always keeping at a distance. When he turned a corner, she would hide there and watch him walk until he turned another, and then run to catch up and watch again. All the while she replayed what Mr. Packerd had said to her father about her, how puppets didn't speak, how they were people once, human people. And a name surfaced out of that memory. Mr. Packerd had spoken of a puppet master, Bander-Clou, the same man the black rider had called out to fight him, and whose dark tinkering had hushed Mr. Packerd's voice to a terrified whisper as he spoke of him.

What was a moment ago simply a curiosity now transformed into something greater than that; the idea that she had stumbled into something dangerous. Hollo felt a fear set in that she couldn't explain, as if someone had turned off the light, and the world that had been familiar a moment before had been instantly turned into one where things moved about in the shadows intending to harm her. They were very near Mr. Packerd's shop now, but in the maze of alleys behind it. Where exactly, she didn't know. The buildings here were tall and without gardens on the sides of them. She wanted to go home, wanted to be rid of her situation, but felt that there was no turning around, no escape from the maze and puzzle laid out for her by the cloaked wooden stranger, who still had not turned to her, not noticed her, not made any sudden movements other than to lead her onward.

He disappeared around a corner, and Hollo's well-practiced system of following brought her running after him, to then peek delicately around to watch him walk on, but this time the alley was empty. She had lost him, or he had gone through a door perhaps. A moment of relief swept over her, in a way glad to be done with the chase, glad at least that the wooden man was gone. For all her curiosity, he also frightened her.

The calm she felt left her body as she realized that she was lost again. Wherever the man had led her, it would be a long walk to try and get home, and she didn't plan to ask for help from anyone else. Hiding herself within a pile of boxes beside a door, she sat quietly listening to this afternoon darkness. There was little human noise, a baby crying in the upper story of a house, a small sound of work in a kitchen, and a far away drunken argument. The argument caught her attention, the grunting of what might be fighting drifted towards her from the far end of the alley, where the clockwork man might have escaped to if he had suddenly run very quickly. The noise grew louder, the sounds of fighting escalated, and Hollo, despite her fear and knowing better, decided to pursue it.

At the end of the stone corridor she peeked very carefully around to see, and found the culprit of her fear. Her senses and tingling intuition had been correct in making her afraid, and as she peered around, found a struggling battle between two bodies. The rotund backside of Mr. Packerd was towards her, and the wooden man she had followed here wrestled with his hands. For all his size and subsequent strength, Mr. Packerd was grappling with all his might just to remain on his feet, such was the strength of the wooden man who wrestled him. Gaining the upper hand, he threw his enemy to the ground, then brought one enormous heel crashing down into the wooden pelvis, repeatedly, attempting to cripple the flailing construct. Hollo held both her hands over her mouth, assuring no noise escaped her and alerted them of her presence.

At the far end of the alley came another hooded figure that ran towards him. Mr. Packerd growled with his fists clenched, when at that moment his body began to glow with a trace of pale yellow light. It was as if the structure of his bones had illuminated within his body, changing the ruddiness of his complexion into a soft yellow. He bellowed, taking a few slow strides, and then reached a sprint very quickly as he raced forward to meet the charge of his new foe. They met halfway down the alley, Mr. Packerd slamming the entirety of his considerable weight against the cloaked wooden body, sending the puppet through the air at an angle and into the wall, where it bounced off and crumbled amidst the garbage and lay silent.

Mr. Packerd heaved with deep exhaustion, holding a hand over his heart, sweat beading at his hairline. He doubled over panting, dripping moisture from his head to the ground. Hollo wanted to run to him, but her fear held her out of sight. She dared not go to him, she dared not step over the body of the unmoving wooden man between them whose legs were broken. She wanted to call out to him, to let him know she could help, because if more wooden men came, Mr. Packerd would certainly be outmatched, even with his magic, or at least the faint lingering traces of what might once have been great power. She saw a strain in Mr. Packerd as he wheezed and grabbed his heart, and she wondered how much toll this use of his dying power had on his body. She wanted to help him, but what strength did she have to lend? Then she realized there was something. She could lend her own magic; for what good it would do, it was still better than nothing. She ran out of the shadows and rushed to him, drawing a terrified gasp from him as she did so.

"Hollo! Get out of here, run home, girly, it's you they're after!"

"I can help!" she said.

He rounded on her, red and furious, yelling for her to flee, but then paused as a clicking wooden clamber sounded behind him. The broken puppet had revived, at least enough to stagger upright. Mr. Packerd went pale, raising a fist in the air, perhaps to try and break it against the wooden man. Before he had a chance, the puppet leapt, its fingers finding a solid hold on Mr. Packerd's vest. Hollo screamed, instinctively running the threads through her fingers, but no words came to her mouth, no clever rhyme to aid in the situation. She had been paralyzed by fear as she watched Mr. Packerd struggle with the grappling, wooden man, whose one, intact hand refused to release him. The other hand, Hollo saw, had been splintered, broken into a jagged pointed spear.

A spatter of blood hit her in the face, though drew no flinch from her; she remained rooted to the stones by the sound that followed. Fat, clumsy Mr. Packerd had landed on his meaty knees with both hands at his throat, his enormous mouth unhinged in a silent yell, his eyes bulging. The sound didn't come from him, rather, from the wooden noise of the cloaked assailant, whose damaged body rattled in what sounded to Hollo to be some kind of sick, mechanical laughter.

Hollo gulped, the gold of her gleaming eyes then catching the attention of the hooded, broken man, who, with creaks and whines of strained wood, turned to her. She saw the blood on the broken stump of his arm, and simply stood transfixed as a wooden finger rose up and pointed at her. It took a step, and with an explosive snap of some internal mechanism the wooden man had broken. The rest of his body then gave way, from his feet up through his legs parts of him fell with hollow noise to the ground until all at once his torso gave in, releasing the head to roll to a stop at Hollo's feet.

A whimper escaped her, quickly followed by her hand again covering her mouth for fear of being discovered. She realized what would become of her if she were seen here, what it would mean for her, and for her father. A broken puppet at the scene of a murder, and her, a living puppet, standing over it all.

"You might be blamed for this," a spoken voice nearby seemed to read her thoughts. She shrunk into a corner of wall as she met the wild, cloudy blue eyes of the man, Amit. He was stock still in his grand posture, a mild frown hung beneath the commanding clutch of his stare as he probed the remains of his puppet with his boot. "They don't last long, some longer than others," Amit said conversationally, looking down on his broken puppet, and then his eyes flicked up onto Hollo, something like lust in them. "Not like you…"

She shriveled within her cloak, staring up into the face of her betrayer.

"Your maker," Amit continued. "Where is he?"

Hollo shook her head dumbly.

"He'll come for you," Amit said confidently. "He will most certainly come for you. I warn you though, he may die when he does. Does that worry you?"

Hollo choked, her eyes darting to Mr. Packerd's unmoving body nearby. Amit followed her gaze, looking at the body with distaste.

"Not like that, no," Amit said casually. "No, Hor-Gauer will go to the Practitioners first, as they want his help. They need his mirrors, they think they can force his cooperation so that they don't need me anymore. They want to find the rest of us," Amit then spat on the ground. "But the fool will refuse, I know. I know him very well, actually. You'd be my god-child if you like, once he is incarcerated."

"Why?" she pleaded at him.

"Why what?" he barked.

"Who are you?"

His mouth curled. "I am Bander-Clou, and like your father I make doors and cages. Unlike him, I do so with pride, whereas he hides things away. Like you."

"What do you want with me?" she whimpered.

"To know how you came to be, and to see if you can be controlled," he replied with a scientific air. "Do you know what you are? You are a Zygotic Pneuma, do you know what that is?"

Hollo shook her head weakly, chewing over the odd words in her mind and spelling out Zy-goh-tick-New-ma with some difficulty.

"A soul," he simplified. "One like mine, one which is very unique and very powerful, but you're different," Amit elaborated crisply. "Because you have a body that does not age, and so your magic may, or may not, be inexhaustible. A body that does not tire, does not drain of life. Power," he said loudly. "Without consequence. Can you imagine what that would mean in the world? I've worked so hard to build what Hor-Gauer managed to make in you. They call us devils, you know, Hor-Gauer and myself. They say we are thieves of souls, and your father hides in shame because of it. Don't you want to help him? Wouldn't you like to see your father live in the high regard he deserves?"

If it meant her father would be like this man, she wanted nothing more than for Fredric to stay hidden in shame for the rest of his life. Hollo believed deep in her heart that this kind of cruelty and deceit was something her father entirely incapable of ever possessing.

"You obviously don't think so," Amit said, reading her face. "Which is irrelevant."

Tiny threads, like her father's threads, snaked out of his sleeve and down to the ground towards her.

"You may be unique, but you are still a wooden puppet, no matter what else. I wonder if you'll obey a marionettist the same as these broken men?"

She shied away from the probing strings as they teasing her, lashed towards her, threatened to grab hold of her and take command of her body with the same pale blue, glowing anger that filled the man's eyes.

"What are you doing? Get away!" she cried, swatting her hands at the threads.

"I'd like to explore you," he answered simply. "I'm very curious to see how you work."

One of the blue threads evaded her hands and hit her in the forehead. It felt like a needle, white hot and electric. She immediately went numb, her arms falling limp at her sides, and her knees giving out so that she fell to the ground and lay without the ability to move. There was a horrible noise and vibration from the thread, the electric feeling changed to a deafening roar of white sound as he probed her mind. She was helplessly examined, however he was doing it, she then felt her body lift into the air, and a dozen more threads connect to her legs and arms and torso, each one white hot and harder to bear than the last. Her sight remained her own, though was clouded. She could only watch as her body was forced into an upright position. He was making her move around, playing with her, dancing her about like a puppet on strings, controlling her with his commanding blue threads. She obeyed helplessly, turning slowly in a pirouette as he squinted his hateful eyes at her.

The wooden men on the ground, broken and motionless now seemed to have a new kind of life as she watched them through her semi-controlled eyesight. There was a torch within their bodies that she could now see clearly, a flame that burned around a metal orb in their center. This orb, she saw, was a cage. It housed a person, trapped inside. She felt them, the humans trapped by Amit's will. She felt them, and now heard them whispering over the white static in her mind. They seethed with fury, blind anger and murderous intent, and not just at their captor, but at her as well, and at each other. These were not souls at rest, but rather the souls of people whose fury had overpowered all else after being sealed away in the trinkets of this dark man with his blue wires and tiny prisons.

She burst out in a yell, not knowing if she had made the noise in the real world or only in her delirious state of helplessness, but as it happened, she fell to the ground and the invading mind of Amit released her from his control.

She scrambled, using this moment to try and escape from the man, but was halted by a new voice. Amit was no longer alone. Someone had arrived, and before she could wonder, she found herself enveloped by the hugging arms of her father. She didn't say anything, or cry, or breathe; only held herself completely still in his embrace. He was speaking to her but she didn't hear him, only shivered and held on tight. In her relief, she still knew there was danger. Her father was very powerful, but she did not know what kind of man he was when faced with battle and fighting. She couldn't imagine him brawling and breaking things as Mr. Packerd had done.

After a moment she wondered why Amit hadn't yet attacked them, hurting her father as he assured her he would. Removing herself from him, she peeked over his shoulder and found the reason for Amit's delay. There stood another person, heaving with exhaustion, a little way behind her father. The figure, a girl, straightened, and steadied her breathing as she ran a damp cloth through her hands. Her hair seemed so aged, while she herself was very young. "Hor-Gauer of the Mirrors, and the Puppet-Master Bander-Clou," she began, radiating dislike with her words. "A fine night for it, gentlemen."

Fredric stood, keeping a hand on Hollo's shoulder to steady and reassure her. She squeezed against him, hugging against his leg as he replied.

"You came quickly, thank you," Fredric said. "Sorry for pitting you against Bander-Clou like this.

She scoffed. "As if I'm afraid of the likes of him. Bander-Clou!" she shouted past Fredric. "You're advised to leave and hide."

Amit spread his arms at her. "You'd have to force me, and I think you'd be advised not to provoke either myself or..." he gestured at Fredric. "my esteemed colleague. Perhaps you'd like to dampen that attitude of yours."

She spat on the ground and unfastened the clasp that buckled her short, long-sleeved leather jacket across her chest and let it fall away. Her sleeveless vest beneath, Hollo noticed, was studded with metal. This woman must be a fighter, Hollo decided, and it was confirmed as the young woman widened her feet into preparation for an attack.

Amit went on. "You're a child. You've been hiding, by the looks of it you've hidden on the seas for some time. It is a mistake, what you're doing, you don't know who I am."

"I know who you are," the young woman said with a smile. "It's been a long time since I've seen you, Puppet-Master. The sad thing, Bander-Clou, is you don't know who I work for. He's in the market for bodies of men like you."

"So you're a bounty hunter?" Amit laughed. "Just like me, but perhaps it didn't occur to you that two bodies are worth more than one. You'll find a good price on Hor-Gauer's head, not to mention the little one."

Eferee's eyes flicked from Fredric to Hollo several times before frowning back at Amit.

"Come now," Amit said. "Perhaps you've heard the stories about Hor-Gauer."

Eferee blinked at Hollo, obviously surprised she was there, but then shrugged and smiled.

"Eferee," Fredric said forcefully. "Don't get ahead of yourself."

She seemed resistant to answer.

"Listen to me," Fredric continued. "Don't get greedy, you need my help, you can't stop him alone."

"You don't know," she bristled. "You don't know what I can do. I know you though, both of you."

"Then you know what we're guilty of?" Amit asked her. "Whatever price is on my head goes the same for my partner here."

Fredric's shoulder sank a little at these words, his body growing tired as it was only just reminded of the weight his shoulders bore.

"Nothing to say about that?" Amit jeered at him.

"Listen, Eferee," Fredric pleaded. "It's not what you think. Remember who I am, what I've done for you."

"What, blackmailing me?" she asked viciously. "Who cares what you know, you wouldn't be able to tell anyone about me anyway! You know what?" she smiled. "Maybe he's right. He thinks that he can get the better of me by dividing us, but he's wrong. I could do without you haunting me, Hor-Gauer. I'm tired of you trying to tell me what to do!"

"Eferee listen to me!" Fredric yelled, but there was only enough time to be astonished before Hollo registered Eferee sprinting forward, and a moment longer to see the watery green glow of her hands as she darted towards Hollo and her father. Water dripped from her fingers, leaving a trail of puddles behind her that glowed with the blue-green briny taint of the ocean. Raising her palms forward, Eferee lunged, kicking one foot out in a long, leaping stride and hitting them full on with the cold weight of her aqua aura. The pushback was mild, though as Hollo tried to regain her balance, she found herself off the ground, hung in the air, and buoyant. It was not quite wet, though not dry either, somewhere in between, as if the air had turned liquid within this undulating globe. The aqua-green light swam softly around her. Beside her, her father was trapped in the same bubble. It was like swimming, how weightless they were, though without the silence of submersion. Hollo's hands were free to move, though very slowly, and she reached for her string, but Fredric's hand closed around her wrist, stopping her.

Slowly, she turned her body to follow his eyes behind them and heard the confrontation Eferee now had with the man Amit.

"I cannot be caged!" he bellowed with laughter as his blue threads whipped around his body, splitting the bubbles of the girl Eferee as she assaulted him with unrelenting ferocity. Her strategy seemed to rely on fury, and indeed all the rage of the seas seemed to live in the palms of her hands. As Hollo watched, wondering who would prevail, she then felt a tug at her wrist where her father held her. She found him smiling at her, calm and disarming. His other hand came to his lips, gesturing silence, indicating he was about to tell her some secret.

"I'm scared," she mouthed at him, hearing her own voice but being unsure whether or not the sound had come out or not. He nodded but did not speak, instead whispered in a way that she heard him in her mind without his mouth opening. He said: "I'm sending you away from this."

She shook her head knowing she needed to stay and help.

"I know, sweetheart. But we can't stay here, I have to send you away for a little while. I'm sending you to family, they'll take care of you."

"Family?" She mouthed. Whose family?

"You're wonderfully clever," he continued. "But there's things you have to learn about the world that I can't teach you. I wish I had time, but I've only time for one more trick tonight."

"Won't you fight them? Aren't you strong?"

"I won't," he smiled. "I can't, but there's a better way, now…" he put his fingers back to his lips again, and Hollo steeled herself for whatever magic her father had planned.

While Eferee and Amit were distracted, Fredric's golden, glowing threads struck outward and freed them from their prison. The bubble burst, and Hollo fell to the ground as the next part of Fredric's magic took effect. The world went white with bright light. She was momentarily blinded by it, but through the white-hot glow she saw thin lines around her feet snaking out shapes against the stones. A series of her father's threads were at work creating a large, circular, magic seal beneath her.

A sudden, dull pounding caused her to look up. Beyond the glow she could see Eferee, at the edge of the light, fighting with the air, beating her blue-green fists against an invisible barrier while water sprayed from her fists with each impact. Then Hollo saw what danger the girl was in. Glowing blue threads arched up from behind, and before it even occurred to Hollo to shout a warning the blue threads pounced, striking the girl in the back. Eferee crumbled, and her body was then slowly dragged away into the darkness as Hollo feared to move, forced to watch helplessly. Dread twisted her stomach as the last of the other girl's fingers slipped away into the shadows, and in her mind Hollo was almost sure she could hear cold laughter from away in the darkness.

Her father was at the edge of the light, smiling at her, but the smile no longer felt reassuring to her. She just remembered that he had made it sound like he was planning to send her somewhere without him, and now that he was smiling at her from outside the barrier she had to begin struggling with the idea that her father might mean to abandon her.

She clenched her fists in desperation but found them numb, and, looking down, caught her breath. Holding her fingers out in front of her in disbelief, she found that she could see through them, and that her hands had lost color and boundary and become only a faint white-hot shadow like that of the etched drawing on the ground around her. Through her fingers, across the glow of the magical furnace she lay in, she saw her father again, but this time a scream escaped her. His face had changed. The warmth of his blood had left him, the softness of his face hardened, and the hair on his head seemed to die and fade from brown. He hardened, not his expression, but rather that his face became solid and wooden, and small lines began to reveal themselves where the moving parts met against one another. His fingers on the ground broke apart at the joints, separating into the hands of a wooden man, though losing none of the power that held the barrier around them. She scrambled towards him, clawing out at his face but finding that her hands passed through him, that she was no longer solid at all, that she had become ethereal and without affect.

He was but a wooden man, staring at her with all the same love and warmth that he always did, though no longer with his own body, but a body of inorganic construct. He spoke again, in that way that made himself heard in her mind. She saw now how he did this, how one of his threads had attached itself into her forehead, exactly how Amit had done, but this thread, her father's thread, did not hurt or change her.

"Hollo," he whispered in her mind. "You'll be safe, I promise. Don't lose faith in people, never be afraid to ask for help when you're lost. You're so clever for your age, perhaps more of me is in you than if you had been born human. Don't ever regret your gift, and don't ever be afraid of people, don't judge them by what you've seen tonight."

The thought was then drowned by Amit's loud, cold laughter. Eferee was nowhere to be seen but Hollo saw Amit now standing at the edge of the circle, his eyes locked on the transformation of Fredric's body as the light from him grew brighter and brighter.

It was too hard to see anything clearly but she squinted through the light and noticed her father's hands moving, and in one of them he held something small and round. He placed the object on the ground and let go of it. She caught one last glimpse of her father's wooden face before the heat of the contained field blazed into an inferno. Hollo screamed out with the instant of pain it caused her as the glow became blinding before, an instant later, it all vanished, leaving her on cool ground in the nighttime, where wind blew and trees swayed above her, all indifferent to her sudden arrival out of the dark.

Chapter Seven
Alikee, or 'Ali'

"Daddy!" she screamed out, unconcerned by who might be near. She huddled, blind in the night, her eyes not adjusted to the lightlessness of this abyss where she had landed. Gasping and shaking, she curled into a ball underneath her cloak, letting it cover her completely, letting herself whine and cower and be loud enough to be found, to be rescued or killed, and at the moment it didn't matter to her which it was. For a long time after she stopped shaking she then lay still, her eyes closed, herself vulnerable and at the mercy of whatever fate lay waiting in the shadows beyond her field of vision. She knew she had to get up, and she whispered this to herself, but her thoughts continued tumbling around, jeering at her as she cowered. She knew it was important to move, to find out where she was, how far she had traveled, and whether or not the family Fredric spoke of was here to help her. Family, he had said, but whose family? Fredric didn't have any relatives she knew of, he'd never spoken of anyone like that before, but then, he hadn't spoken of many things; the nature of magic, the people who had attacked them, and the wooden puppets like her; people who lived encased in foreign bodies. How like her were they in the end? She didn't know what she was, to have found kindred spirits in the trapped killers and criminals like they who were owned by the puppet-master Amit. These things reeled in her mind: evil magic, violent people, spirits trapped in tiny cages driven mad, and she couldn't shake them, nor the nauseating image of her father turned into a clockwork man like those who had attacked Mr. Packerd. She remembered Mr. Packerd lying silent on the ground, and she recalled the blood. She had never seen death before. She wondered if she had seen it tonight.

Reaching to her face, she searched for the thread that had connected her father to her a moment before, but found it was gone. Trembling fingers pushed the hood off her face. She tried to stop her hands shaking but there was a dizziness lingering in her from the transportation she had undergone. Despite the uncontrollable sway of her body she came to sit upright, facing the space she had landed in. There was rubble around her, pieces of stone that must have been brought with her through the white doorway of her father's creation. Certainly it must have left a crater in the alley she had been sent from, and how far away from there she was she had no idea. She remembered the object her father sent through with her, but even in the shadow of night it was apparent than no small, round thing lay amidst the jagged pieces of stone. The ball had been his tool, she concluded, not a thing to help her as she had hoped for a foolish moment. The ball might have been not unlike a bomb; certainly the doorway had felt more like an explosion than a window. She knew nothing of her father's doorways or barriers, not how they worked, what tools he used, or how far the magic reached. He could have sent her anywhere. She may not even be in the same city anymore. Perhaps luck was on her side and maybe she had arrived in a city far away, where there was no magic, and no clockwork men or coiling blue wires to give chase. Her eyes adjusted to the darkness now, finding other stones here in a plot of grass and dirt that was illuminated at a distance by homes bordering the field. There were countless large stones stuck in the earth; some polished and others made of muted granite. This was a graveyard, she discovered as a tingling crept up within her. She had arrived amidst tombstones.

Hollo's eyes glowed a little in the dark. It had always been that way, and she had never thought about it before, but now the warmth that came from the ever-present golden power inside her body was casting a beacon into the darkness just when she wanted to remain invisible. The light made her vulnerable to danger. The thought of dogs crossed her mind, hungry animals that would see her and lick their overlarge and underfed mouths in preparation for a meal. These sounds crept towards her in her mind; the excited breathing and salivating of hunters. What would they do, she wondered, when they found no flesh on her? Would they leave her, or would they keep searching, tearing her body apart in search of meat, or perhaps tear her apart out of anger for fooling them?

A noise, a falling sound like that of something breaking sent a shockwave through her and she shrunk smaller, hunching into herself like a rabbit. How like a rabbit, she thought, as her only weapon in the darkness was to become still like a rock and hope the monsters in the darkness were outsmarted. The trembling of her shoulders made the cloak shiver, a frightened rock was no great illusion to the night, and her last layer cover was blown. Now at the mercy of her fears, it occurred to Hollo to wonder what it must be like to be a human girl. This was the first time she could remember ever wondering such a thing. There was safety in wood that was not found in flesh. Not that she was so indestructible, and not that she did not feel pain. She did feel pain, as Fredric had explained, she felt things in all the same ways that he did, he who was her father. As she felt all the same things he felt, so too she saw the same way he did, and heard and smelled the same way he did. A girl in a wooden body had some advantages, she told herself. She might not have a smell for predators to follow, and that was something. It might even be true that she had a greater kinship to the wooden trees that to people or rabbits, as far as monsters were concerned, and trees themselves had no fear of nighttime. If nothing else at least she had her father's bravery, and she said this to herself, and the thought made her stronger.

"At least I have my powerful soul," she thought, recalling what Bander-Clou had said, and though she did not fully understand what the man had meant it still comforted her. "Like Dad. Dad is not afraid of the dark, and neither am I."

Closing her eyes hard, she then reopened them with a different countenance and met the graveyard anew, introducing herself in a different way, now that she had decided that the noise must have been an acorn falling, and that the only dogs nearby were certainly scrawny, domestic, and subservient. In fact, a dog would be welcome, so she could hold it and be warmed by the animal's body. Looking around again, she searched this time for people, and she listened for human sounds but found none, no response to the initial cry that now left her feeling childish and stupid for letting escape her. She was smarter than that, she knew better. A sudden, odd relief swept through her, belying her shivers. The only people here were those beyond this world, deep in sleep under the earth and beyond it; people who didn't mind in the slightest her wooden parts or loud arrival. The graveyard seemed altogether uninterested in her, and she breathed easy now that she was invisible again.

She rummaged her hands around her pockets until locating the tiny, mirror-adorned brooch her father had given her from Mr. Packerd's shop. With her thread wound around it, she shook it, rubbed at the dark glass, and tried everything she could to make it connect to her father, who had assured her she would always be able to find him through the glass. The mirror reflected only the cold darkness of the night, remaining as lifeless as the bodies in the ground beneath her. Whatever had happened to him, the part of him that lived in the mirror's reflection had left the world, and Hollo was now isolated in a way she hadn't ever been. There was no one looking over her shoulder, no one keeping a cautious eye on her, nor anyone within reach who was available for conversation. This was a new world, one much colder than before. Though, after her experiences of this night, perhaps she preferred the company of corpses.

Standing slowly to her feet, she brushed the leaves and dirt from her cloak and searched around for an idea of where to go to find out where she was now. Fredric had said very specifically that he was sending her to family, someone's family. Perhaps he had relatives that he had never told her about, a thought that seemed preposterous at first, but then, her image of her father had changed. What she thought she knew about him hung in question, and even the face she knew and loved and trusted had become tainted by the image of his body turned to wood. Regardless of this, there was no one here, no one to keep her safe, nor anyone to explain her situation to her. There were only trees and graves, and at some distance from her, the lights of other people's homes. If he had thought to send her to people that could help her, he had certainly missed his mark, perhaps simply made a mistake. Whatever the reason for her arrival here, she was alone, and certainly in no state to ask for help from anyone. She pictured herself knocking on doors, 'are you my family?' she saw herself ask a stranger interrupted from their supper. She saw the horror on their faces as she, a strange magical puppet, begged them for help. No, she decided, she didn't trust strangers. There were homes in three directions with lights on and undoubtedly people inside. To the east however, there were no lights, she saw clearly silhouetted against the moonlight the black darkness of a city wall. She had come to the very edge of the city, hopefully her own. Certainly, as she peered into the darkness of the wall she could make out a figure at a distance that stood atop a buttress in the military fashion that was unique to the Artisan District. His rifle was visible on his right shoulder, and a long spear was held at arms length at a perfect 45-degree angle away from his left side. The stoic man guarding the wall top assured her that she hadn't left her city, that she was still home, though her true home might be still a very long way off. This was the east wall, though for all she knew, it could be the north or west. She had no knowledge of stars, and so couldn't place herself. The idea of walking home now was out of the question, and the question became what would she do until morning when the sun would rise in the east and tell her.

As she wondered this and pitied herself, her attention turned to the wooden home closest to her, where a scuffle drew her notice. A shouting man could be heard, venting his anger on someone whose voice was drowned by his fury. Not knowing what she hoped to learn from this shouting, Hollo made her way through the under-tended graves, through trees and brush until she could see through the front of this home, where a man had come out onto the porch. He was very tall, this man who now fell silent in his fury, choosing instead to put fire to his lips, and then pulled smoke into his breath and release it in a cloud before the lantern outside his house. Hollo watched him for some time, expecting that maybe he would speak, or go for a walk. A moment later, he did just that, yelling into his house and then leaving down the road. The girl he shouted at came to poke her head around the door, watching him leave. Hollo jumped at the sight of her, a girl her own age, or maybe a little older. At least, someone she might be able to trust to tell her where she was.

Once sure the man was away, the girl shut the door behind herself and began to walk in Hollo's direction. Staying quiet and out of sight, Hollo followed the girl from the shadows taking care not to scare her, since they were in a frightening place, but Hollo soon realized this girl had no fear of graveyards, as she had. The girl walked comfortably and purposefully, quickly and directly until she stopped still, and Hollo hid herself better to watch. The girl had come upon the stone rubble that Hollo's doorway had brought through. Slumping down, the girl began to move the stones away, picking them up and throwing them furiously into the bushes. Hollo flinched as a large bit struck her in the face and she let out a yelping gasp. The girl immediately wheeled about in fear, not speaking, but her eyes searching deep into the shadows where Hollo sat rubbing her face. Realizing her cover was blown, she moved forward out of the brush.

The girl said nothing to her as she came close enough to see, merely stared and seemed to crouch in anticipation to run.

"Sorry," Hollo whispered to her. "About the stones."

The girl glared at her. "You put them here? What for!" she barked.

"It was an accident," Hollo mumbled. "I'm lost."

"Oh," the girl said curiously, bending back down to continue her work. "Well be more careful, this is a graveyard."

Hollo watched her work for a moment, until the girl glared over at her again. "You gonna help me then?"

Hollo jumped a little, realizing how rude she was, and walked slowly to her side where she knelt down and started throwing the bits of rock away from the tombstone. A moment passed while she cleared the space until she noticed the girl's eyes on her. Hollo paused, and then realized, foolishly, that her hands were out for the other girl to see plainly. This girl stared dumbly at Hollo's fingers as they wrapped around a stone before Hollo squeaked and withdrew herself into her cloak. She cowered a little, waiting for the other girl to say something, or scream out, or shout for help or something, but after a moment, the girl simply returned to work, not screaming, merely frowning.

"Are you running away?" she asked simply.

"I," Hollo began, unsure why that would make sense to the other girl. "I suppose so, I mean...I don't know."

"Wish I could run away," the girl mumbled sadly. "Where are you going?"

Hollo pondered this. "I want to go home. But there's not going to be anyone there for me if I go back."

The girl nodded. "I did that once," she then pointed at the nearest tombstone. "That's my mumma. I ran away when they put her in the ground...but I had to go back."

"Why?"

The girl shrugged. "I was hungry. It was the Pig'n'Bowl that did it. I got caught trying to steal one, they took it from me, and I ran, ran all the way back home. Couldn't help it, the smell made my mouth dripping."

Hollo fell silent, wondering what it must be like to have this girl's life, to be trapped. Suddenly Hollo thought that she might have an idea of what trapped felt like.

"Sorry for messing the grave," Hollo mumbled quietly.

"You can't stay with me," the girl said after a moment. "But we have chickens, you could sleep in there tonight. He never goes in there, he makes me tend the roosts." She didn't wait for Hollo's thanks, but simply grabbed onto her wooden hand and led her into the darkness.

It was sudden, how tears seemed to spring up in Hollo's eyes, and how her throat grew tight. Only her father had ever held her hand, and the warmth of this other girl, this girl who just met her, who had not fallen off a chair when she'd seen her hands, who'd not attacked her when her cloak was blown off her, who had met her, forgiven her, and taken her by the hand and held it in her own. Hollo was absolutely certain not to make a sound, she was embarrassed to be feeling so strongly, even after all that had happened tonight, her tears seemed to arise at the least likely moment.

"It's okay," the girl said without looking back at her. "You can cry. I'd cry if I was lost, too."

Hollo swallowed, stifling her tears and noticing how attuned this girl was to the things she was feeling, perhaps even more so than her father was. It was worth wondering if all people as young as she was were so aware of what if felt like to be sad and afraid, and lost and alone, or if it was only Hollo and this girl who had this in common.

They arrived at the house, where the girl checked to make sure the man had not returned before leading Hollo around the back, into a yard where there stood small shacks and fences for the animals they kept here behind this cottage at the edge of the city. The girl led her inside, and the hens roosting made only small sleeping noises at the intrusion. She pointed to the hay bale strung together in the far corner.

"S'not so uncomfortable, sleep there. You need to be gone tomorrow, or else he'll get really angry if he sees. So...I'll maybe see you, or maybe not, I guess."

Hollo nodded.

"I'll bring you bread in the morning," the girl then faltered and frowned. "Or...do you eat food?"

Hollo shook her head.

"Lucky," the girl sighed. "You could run away forever if you wanted." She smiled and closed the door.

.   .   .

The chickens woke up early, before the sun fully rose over the city wall. Since chickens awaken with noisy falderal, Hollo was made to rise with them. The rooster seemed irritated by her sleeping in his hay, and made this obvious by lingering behind after the hens had made their way out into the yard in search of young shoots of weeds. He, the rooster, stood in the doorway at the tips of his feet, making many flustered movements. She tried to go back to sleep, but couldn't and it appeared the hospitality had run its course. Brushing herself of dirt and hay, Hollo stood to her feet, causing a whole new level of irritation in this Lord of the Roost, who darted left and right, seemingly torn between the will to battle her to the death, and the instinct to flee. Hollo kicked a little scrap of wood in his direction to shoo him from the door. This caused him to freeze into livid stillness, a single of his round, yellow, and seemingly bloodshot eyeballs glaring wide at her for so clearly daring to throw challenge in his own territory.

"Get over yourself," she grumbled at him, steeling out the door and making for the nearby brush of the graveyard, where she could perhaps catch a few more minutes sleep in peace. The rooster followed halfway after her, grumbling his lipless insults at her until he was sure she had quite been routed by his incontestable might. She missed her Flynn, she thought dismally, curling into the barbed leaves beneath an oak. He wouldn't have kicked her out at dawn.

Remembering the scone in her pocket, she reached in to find a very crumbled and stale mess inside. Figuring it couldn't hurt their relationship, she flung the crumbling pieces towards the yard. The beaked Lord scurried to them, cackling his genius discovery to his hens and thereby drawing them waddling over to feast. He stood tall and proud, appearing to believe that his ladies must think him wonderfully divine for having drawn such gifts from the sky. Hollo rolled her eyes, now feeling even less appreciated than before. Perhaps one day she could fetch Flynn across town to show this smaller monster a lesson in gratitude. The thought of Flynn again caused her anguish, though she knew he was most certainly fine living in a whole yard of grass and bugs to keep him fed. Still, she saddened to think of him all alone, much as she was now.

At least Flynn appreciated her, and he probably even worried about her, and perhaps he was the only one who did. Her father had sent her into this by his own hands, and it seemed so easy for him to trust her cleverness to survive the city on her own. But there was little confidence she had left in her cleverness as she lay in a ball in a bed of thorns, lost, and without an ally to speak of, except Flynn for all the use he was, and then, perhaps, the little girl whose mother's grave Hollo had trod upon.

There was no going back to sleep now. Tired as she was, Hollo's mind was already spinning her problems into a colorful collage. Ordering her thoughts and sitting upright with purpose, she realized that staying in the bushes wouldn't get her anywhere, and so she made a plan to find her way home. She had seen a little of the city, and if only she could find some trace of the market, then she would be able to get to Casting Street.

Standing to her feet, she made her way down to the wall by the road, hoping that she might spot a caravan on way to the Square's daily Trade Fair, and if so, follow the wagon to market. Much as she had hoped, no one paid her much attention as she strolled along, keeping her ears and eyes out for clues, and finding herself unexpectedly caught by a powerful sense of adventure as she set out with her secrets on a mission like some great adventurer. Getting a little ahead of herself and feeling braver now that she was moving, she chose

an ambitious detour, taking a small sideway between a few of
the taller buildings as her nose detected a most peculiar scent. It
was similar to the smell of the chicken coop she'd slept in, and
her curiosity of farm animals compelled her to track it down,
perhaps to a farm or something, but as she came through the
tiny corridor, she found herself gravely mistaken. She had
happened upon the pig merchant alleyway, here at the edge of
the city. The smell hit her full on; a smell of death and blood, as
the pigs were brought to butcher fresh in this unwanted nook
near the city wall where the stench could be washed away, and
where the pigs could be brought from the outlying farmland
just near enough into the city that no one would be offended
by their odor. Here, Hollo was offended and in her animus,
there rose a pang of guilt as she likened the heftiest of the
whining beasts to Mr. Packerd. The thought of him tormented
like this caused her to break out at a run through the
assembling merchants. Used to the scurrying away of
frightened children, they paid her no mind. Pushing the cloak
up over her nose, she squinted her eyes to blur out the
grotesque sight. She ran on, where at the far end of the pig-
alley, she found a way out. It was a tiny slip between two tall
buildings, barely a foot wide. She squeezed herself through,
huffing the scent out of her nostrils with distaste as she came to
a small street that intersected her escape route. Turning left, she
sighted a bustle of tents and activity in the distance, beyond the
reach of death's scent.

The square, it turned out, had been closer than she had
figured. And better yet, she now knew her home was much
beyond that. Her father hadn't sent her to the edge of the
world after all. The city, she realized, wasn't so hard to navigate,
and not so scary at all. She quickly learned many landmarks and
felt confident that it was only a matter of time until the town
was as familiar as her own garden. She let out a giggle of
excitement as she neared the dawn assembly of merchants who
set their wares out for the coming wealthy patrons. She
wandered aimlessly for some time amidst the working men,
women, and children, spying on their trinkets and valuables,

clothes and foodstuffs. A wonderful aroma caught her attention, the smell of some kinds of curry spices or exotic herbs. The cart responsible for this already had a cooking fire going, and was serving a meaty breakfast to many of the merchants. It appeared to be a breakfast of a bowl filled with a paste that Hollo couldn't fathom. Stuck into the mound of aromatic mash was a great, fat sausage that apparently was the delicacy of the day. Some of the larger people had even purchased a pair of them, and held one in each hand, talking animatedly with their friends and relatives. All were gathered around this cart and the big sign that hung over it. Hollo read, 'Fagg-Netten's Famous Pig'n'Bowl'.

No wonder the girl stole one, Hollo thought, it seemed an irresistible meal even for these people here who probably ate it every day. She watched on for some time, watched the happy faces of the younger merchant's children as they dug into their bowls of paste. She couldn't stand it any longer. Hollo knew the right thing to do would be to get one of these valuable things to repay the girl for her kindness. She still had the coin in her pocket from yesterday's labor. Unsure the value of it, she approached the line cautiously. People jostled her a little, unintentionally, though she feared discovery all the same and so was very careful to keep herself hidden, and her head tilted downward. A tiny child, almost half Hollo's size stumbled into her, a half a sausage clutched in his chubby little hand. His eyes widened as he looked up into her hood, as he squealed with delight. Fortunately for Hollo, the words he screamed at his mother, pointing at Hollo, were muffled by his mouthful of sausage, "I wan see da funny puppa sho!" She shied away from the boy and quickly handed over her silver coin to the man at the cooking fire and took the bowl from him before he had even let go of it.

"Hey!" he shouted with a dash of laughter as Hollo turned away. She froze, a tingle of fear clutched her.

"I've got enough to change this in my wife's purse, hold up little fancy-cloak!" he said good-naturedly as his large burn covered hand fell on her shoulder. Hollo flinched and he immediately drew away with a curious expression on his face.

"Imma keep the bowl," she muttered quickly, and turned away again.

"Well," the cook called after her. "Thank you much little misses! You hear that, the rest of you? The bowls are on sale today, special price of three-quarter sterling! Now if the rest of you bought your bowls for the same price I'd retire a young man!"

A cheer of heartfelt laughter followed Hollo as she ducked away from the crowd and slipped away under tables and between caravans until locating an alternative road at the south end of the market instead of the returning path of the pig-merchant alleyway, which she had no desire to revisit. She had now but to return to the house and wait for the tall, angry man to leave again. Then she could give the girl the Pig'n'Bowl she so treasured. Hollo was pleased at her successful purchase of the food, she barely felt she had started walking before she came the whole long way around the pig-alley and back to the dusty street that led back to the girl's house.

By now, the bowl had lost some warmth, and she wondered how much longer she'd have to wait for a chance to give it to the girl before the man left. Maybe if she returned early enough she'd find the girl collecting eggs before he rose. Certainly it was still very early in the day, and perhaps the man drank like Mr. Packerd, who had been late to arise more than once for the same reason.

Hoping this was the case she came into view of the house, and as she did so, immediately took shelter behind the edge of the building beside her. The little girl, Hollo saw clearly from her vantage point, was on the porch, but held aloft, her wrists bound in the single, giant hand of the man. He was alarmingly huge, standing an inch taller than the door behind him. With his hand free, he was smacking her with the indifference of beating a doormat.

Hollo remained hidden and watched until the man finally dropped the girl. The pain prohibited her from balancing properly as she stumbled backwards off the porch into their dusty patch of a front yard. The man went back inside and slammed the door. The girl winced as she limped away from the house. Heading towards Hollo's hiding place, the little girl crawled into a deep pile of abandoned, old wood crates. Hollo watched the house and once sure the man wasn't coming back out, she approached.

It took her a moment to find the entrance into the maze. "Hello?" whispered Hollo. "Where are you?" she asked, trying to be more polite than the night before.

"No boys!" she called back from inside.

"I'm not a boy," Hollo answered. "Do I sound like a boy?" she asked, more to herself than her friend. The girl poked her head around the corner to Hollo's left.

"Oh, it's you," she said, craning towards Hollo and squinting to examine the face she couldn't quite see. Her face opened in surprise as she inspected her. "You've beautiful gold eyes, haven't you? I didn't notice before," she said quietly, then retreated out of sight, where Hollo followed her into a less cramped, hollowed-out middle room of the box fortress where they had space to sit upright.

Hollo remained curled in her cloak as she sat down. The girl eyed her curiously.

"It's rude to come in without asking," the girl said, sitting with her chin on her knees, staring openly at Hollo across the tiny distance that was allowed to them.

"I'm sorry, I didn't know. Here," she held the bowl out with both hands, and the girl stared and blinked. She wiped her cheeks, though there were no tears, and took the bowl. "Didn't think I'd see you again. Why'd you bring me this?"

Hollo shrugged. "Don't have any friends."

"I put you up for the night didn't I?" she choked out through a mouth of sausage. "Wot you mean we aren't friends?"

Hollo smiled, embarrassed, and then asked, "who are you?"

"Ali," she sniffed, scooping into the bowl with dirty fingers and shoveling it into her mouth. "Tor-Atora. Wot's about you?"

"Hollo."

"Just Hollo?"

"…umm, yes."

"Why is your name only one word?"

"How many do I need?"

Ali frowned. "Not about needing. The names you get from your mum and dad. My name is Alikee Tor-Atora. My mumma's name was Tor-Falerum. My dad's name is Atora-Kruk. So my name is Tor-Atora. Since you're a girl your mumma's name comes first."

"I don't have a mumma."

"Oh," Ali saddened. "Yeah, me neither. Where are you from?"

"…umm, Casting Street."

"I'm mean where before that?"

Hollo took a moment, she didn't understand the question. "I've always been from Casting Street."

"You've lived here your whole life and you don't even know about names?" Ali didn't sound accusing, only interested. "What's your dad's name? You'd just use that one."

"He's just Dad, he only called me Hollo. Why do people call you so many things?"

"I dunno, so you can tell apart from other people whose name is the same, I guess."

"Are there a lot of people named Alikee?

Ali laughed softly out her nose. "You're funny."

"I am?"

Ali nodded. "Thanks for making me smile."

Hollo tilted her head to the side. "I don't see your smiling…"

Ali's cheeks reddened a little as the corners of her mouth curled.

"Oh, there," Hollo said. "You're welcome then."

They were silent for a moment, staring at one another.

"Who is he?" Hollo asked.

Ali's smile fell away, and her eyes followed. "He's Dad."

"Dad…" Hollo frowned. "My dad never did that to me."

Ali said nothing.

"Do dads do that?" Hollo implored.

Ali shrugged. "Mine does."

"Better to not have one, than to have him," Hollo said, anger filling her.

Ali smiled at her. "Thanks," she said softly.

Hollo didn't see why Ali thanked her. Before she could ask, "Alikee!" The shout came from the house and it instantly wiped the smile from Ali's face and replaced it with wrinkles. She held herself, shrinking further into her corner. "Mmm," she grunted, eyes crinkling into a frightened squint. "Mmmm," she whined softly, beginning to cry her dry tears.

Hollo had quite enough. She took hold of Ali's hand and pulled her forcibly to her feet and out of the hiding place and out of view of the house. "Let's go. We can leave."

"No!" Ali whimpered. "No I can't! You wouldn't understand, it's hungry out there by yourself."

"We can go home, there's food there," Hollo answered, checking behind them to make sure Ali's father hadn't yet spotted them. Ali struggled half-heartedly with Hollo's grip, apparently unconvinced, and Hollo decided there was no time to argue and instead pulled Ali harder by the arm, down the same street Hollo had taken to get to the market.

"Get back here Alikee!" cried her father. Hollo didn't look back, she didn't need to. Ali yelped, and Hollo knew they were being pursued.

"C'mon!" Hollo said, noting that her voice was shaking. A moment before, the thought hadn't occurred to her what it would mean if they were caught. "Run faster!" she said forcefully, knowing they could no longer take the road home. If they were in the open they would be caught since the man was certainly faster than them. Their only way to escape was to be smaller that he was.

"Not this way!" Ali groaned, now sprinting beside Hollo, equally panicked. Hollo ignored her protesting as she turned them right at the corner towards the smells of barnyard fodder, and into the pig-merchants' alleyway. The fetid odor nearly stopped them, their frightened breathing taking in huge gulps of the rotten air. Ali retched a little and held a hand over her mouth.

"Don't throw up," Hollo said quickly. "We can't stop now!" Ali gritted her teeth and resolutely stomached her nausea. The ground ran with pig's blood, through the stones and into the metal grates to the sewer below. It took great caution to avoid the slippery puddles.

At first, no one paid much attention to them darting through the crowd, under tables and occasionally leaping over pieces of fleshy scraps, but with Ali's father making such a commotion behind them, throwing people down in the attempt to catch up, the merchants and patrons quickly noticed what was happening.

"Knock them down!" he bellowed at the onlookers.

The girls' faces, so etched with desperation, must have inspired sympathy in the people nearby, because as he said this, those ahead of them made a pathway, gasping and muttering amongst themselves and shooing the girls onward, out of harm's reach. This only made Ali's father more furious, and he began attacking the few brave men and women who stood to delay him.

Hollo saw their escape. It was the tiny wedge between two stone buildings that led to the side street Hollo had taken to the square. The sideway was too small for Ali's father to fit through, he'd have to go around, a long way around, and by then Hollo could have Ali home. As they came to it, Hollo shoved Ali through, but her foot had caught, and she fell with a shriek of pain as her ankle twisted.

He had caught them, and with a single crushing blow from the side sent Hollo down into the stone street. Where she lay, Hollo heard a yelp and knew the man must have pulled Ali back through. He was yelling and shrieking at her, threatening her.

With one arm, Hollo dug her fingers into the gap between the stones, pulling herself away from the man behind her. She chanced to look back, seeing that the man had Ali in the air by the front of her shirt, and was screaming in her face. He then saw Hollo crawling away, and dropped Ali onto her already damaged ankle. His expression changed as he looked Hollo in the eyes, from anger to a murderous contempt. She scrambled onto her back, kicking her legs out to push herself farther away from the man until she had no where else to go and her head hit the wall. She was trapped, and in her frenzied attempt to get away, the cloak had fallen off most of her body. Now her wooden legs were splayed for all to see just what she was made of. There was a commotion of chatter from the frightened audience, whispers of puppetry, of magic and forbidden sorcery.

Ali's father hesitated as he saw her inhuman body. He grimaced, stepping backwards. "What kind of monster are you?" he growled with contempt picking up a heavy pig hook from a nearby rack. He raised the hook up in both hands as Ali screamed at him.

Hollo shook with deep sobs, clumsily trying to gather the cloak around herself, for all the good it would do to protect her from him.

"Stop, Carr stop it!" a man braver than the other onlookers spoke out. He looked to have the solidity of an oak tree and stood boldly facing up to the giant. Ali's father wheeled about on him, stepping close to the man's face. Though the man had the build of a heavy lifter, Ali's father towered over him, snarling into his face, threatening not only the lifter, but his entire family. Hollo sprang forward to reach Ali. She lifted her off the ground and pushed her again through the wedge in the building. Ali squeezed her way through, only to land once again on her already damaged ankle.

Hollo put one foot into the sideway as a giant hand fell on her head, lifting her off the ground and throwing her away from her escape. She landed in blood, a sticky, sickly red pool of pig's blood. Her scrambling was ineffectual as her feet slipped in the muck.

She saw the lifter, who lay with his eyes closed, and a terrible gash on his face while a woman knelt over him, attempting to revive him. Red traces of the blow could be seen on the heavy hook in Ali's father's hand, which now rose high into the air above her.

Hollo's hand struggled into her cloak pocket for her string, forgetting the consequence, forgetting her father's warning. Before she could stop herself, she had wound it between her fingers and was chanting her rhyme up into the face whose teeth clenched at her with all the rage and violence of a murderer.

"Up from earth, to get us home," she pleaded at him, quietly. "Up from earth, to get us home," she chanted, weaving her shaking fingers through the thread as fast as she could. "Up from earth, to get us home."

Ali's father laughed at her mumbling, arching his feet up onto tiptoes with the hook as high in the air as he could, determined to hurt her as badly as he was able with the first blow.

"Up from earth, to get us home," she chanted faster, "Up from earth to get us home,". "Up from the earth to get us home, leave him forever here alone," she sobbed at him, drawing her wooden fingers hard, stretching the thread taught with the final motion of her weave. "Turn the madman into stone!"

A collective gasp of fear silenced the marketplace as her silver thread glowed with golden light, tracing through her body and into the stone ground beneath her, then beneath Ali's father, who immediately froze in the downward swing, the hook halfway to her face, the murderous grin left solidly, timelessly, mocking her. From the ground came the stone, creeping up his legs, to his chest and out to his fingertips until he was entirely captured, suppressed in the cold of his rock coffin.

Chapter Eight
The Pig Merchant's Alley

Hollo heaved with fright, taking gulping breaths of air. Her name was called and she scrambled to her feet, rushing to the gap in the walls where Ali lay beyond, crying out for her. Shoving herself through, Hollo felt hands behind her, and heard a voice, or perhaps many voices trying to stop her. Her fear of capture helped her to be faster through to Ali, who she hoisted up, and, with Ali's arm drawn over her shoulders, took her away from the pig market. Ali didn't speak but did whimper on every other step. Hollo herself was numb with shock and couldn't feel her own pain. They ran, or rather, hobbled slowly down the deserted alleyway, thankful that no one was around since the last thing Hollo wanted at this moment was the help of others. She thought of the poor lifter who had been struck down, possibly struck dead after trying to help them. He had, Hollo then realized, saved her life. He had caused Ali's father enough delay that they had got away. Hollo couldn't begin to fathom how she could ever return that sacrifice to his family. Her unplanned, sloppy attempt at a rescue had ended in blood, and now she could do nothing but repeat to herself that they had at very least escaped away for a moment.

As they neared the end of the alleyway they heard the commotion of the market. She didn't know how to escape notice from here on out. The only way home was through the crowded market, and they would surely draw attention, herself covered in pig blood and with an injured companion who looked very nearly out of blood herself. Hollo let herself slow to a stop, closing her eyes and panting, fighting tears, fighting regret and guilt for doing such a horrible thing to someone as what she had done to that horrible man. Had she killed him? She didn't know, nor did she know enough about magic to guess.

Ali was bent double, examining her ankle with little hissing sounds of stifled pain. Hollo wondered what she would say next, if Ali would fear her, or hate her for killing her father, or just hate her for making her run away. Ali sounded like she was crying now, tiny whimpers not unlike the sounds she made after being beaten by her father. Maybe Hollo was now another person on the list of people who hurt her and betrayed her trust. Her crying was a little louder, and Hollo couldn't help but let go of the girl and turn away, overcome with guilt for having caused her so much pain and trouble in such a small amount of time.

Ali forced herself upright and grabbed hold of Hollo's arm, tugging her viciously around to face her full on. Hollo instinctively turned her face away, closing her eyes and expecting to be shouted at, or even struck by the girl, but what came hit her much harder. Ali threw her whole body into Hollo and the girls staggered backwards into the wall, where Ali clung, hugging her with loving ferocity. As Hollo stood in shock, her arms pinned forcefully to her sides by Ali's arms, Ali herself relaxed her embrace a little, and her tears switched to nervous giggles and then grew into laughter. Ali cackled with teary eyes, releasing Hollo and holding her by the shoulders, her grinning face an inch from Hollo's.

"I thought we're dead for sure!" she laughed.

Hollo stood in shock, her mouth hanging dumbly agape as Ali's hand wrestled with Hollo's pocket, finding her long circular thread and inspecting it with amazement.

"Wow!" she exclaimed. "How'd you do that? Is it you or the thread?" She then strung it through her fingers with just as much dexterity as Hollo herself had.

"I didn't know cradles were so fun!" Ali said. "I used to play with the twins before they moved away, you can play with two people you know!"

She set an elaborate show of winding the tread around her fingers and then began to direct Hollo in taking hold of particular treads, and like that, the pair of them traded the web back and forth, each time making a new weave, each one its own picture or shape, and with each one Ali had a new story of what they meant or resembled. Hollo followed obediently, stunned into silence by Ali's exuberance, which was infectious, and before long both girls shared the same smile, and the same exhausted triumph over the world.

"I can't believe you didn't show me sooner," Ali said, releasing her hold on two strings, which immediately transformed the ladder into a heptagram between Hollo's shaking hands. "You're amazing Hollo! I wish I was wooden and magical!"

"Am I?" Hollo heard herself mumble weakly.

"Wooden?" Ali cocked her head at her friend. "Yup, you sure are, aren't you?"

"No, I know, I mean…"

Ali grinned broadly. "Amazing," she said confidently, then hobbled a few steps away to stare upwards at the sky. "What I wouldn't give for your magic. I'd love to be strong like you, and made of wood. You don't have to hurt when you're knocked around."

"Yes I do…" Hollo said softly.

Ali's smile fell, and her wild energy came back to earth a little. She looked Hollo up and down a few times before the questions began. "But you don't eat though, right?"

Hollo nodded.

"Hmm," Ali shuffled around, experimenting with her damaged ankle and wincing. "Well, maybe you don't break quite as easy," and her smile returned.

Hollo smiled a little as well, gesturing at Ali's ankle. "Fragile, aren't you?"

Ali bellowed with laughter, then cut herself off with a heavy rumble from her stomach.

"Hungry again? Already?" Hollo smirked.

Ali blushed.

"Should have brought you two bowls, shouldn't I? There's food at home. You can eat as much as you like."

Ali lit up for a moment with a fierce greed, as her eyes glazed over and she wiped her mouth with the back of her forearm. "Can I?" she whispered, nearly inaudibly.

"Yes," Hollo said half-heartedly. "But I don't know how to get there."

"Casting street?" Ali frowned. "That's just at the far end of the square."

Hollo pointed at herself. "Look at me, covered in pig bits. We can't go that far. People will see us."

"Silly," Ali said jeeringly, limping up to Hollo and undoing her three large metal buttons. Hollo's head darted side to side to assure herself no one would see her as Ali mercilessly yanked the cover off her body and with a mighty flourish then replaced it again over Hollo's shoulders.

"There," Ali said triumphantly. "Inside out, and no one will notice."

Hollo was speechless, how simple the solution was that she hadn't thought of it. Elation washed over her, remembering loneliness of just a day before; to have now found someone so clever so quickly, washed her with gratitude.

Ali took her hand again and led her, limping, towards the market.

"Do you think he's dead?" Ali asked her as they braved the crowd through the square.

Hollo's heart sank with guilt again. "I hope not," she answered.

"I don't," Ali said, her face wizened with wrinkles that split into the youthfulness of her brown skin, cutting it with worry not befitting her age.

"You wanted him dead?" Hollo asked.

Ali didn't respond, frowning, not confirming or denying it, but certainly considering whether her anger at her father really went so deep as to wish him death. "He would have killed you," Ali said after a while. That, it seemed, was her answer. Hollo thought about this for a long time, reasoning that it was true the man had come very close to doing just that, and that if he was indeed dead inside that rock casing, then whether by accident or not, Hollo had simply defended herself. The guilt still did not ease.

"Do a lot of people try and kill you?" Ali asked, ducking under the swinging arms of an over-excited man haggling for a brass mirror.

Hollo barked a sharp laugh, but then was overcome with distress when she realized the answer was, in fact, yes.

"Who?" Ali continued.

Hollo was quiet, wondering if anyone had actually meant to kill her. She then winced, remembering the murderous souls trapped by the man Amit. She wanted, needed to talk it over with Ali, but would wait until they were safe indoors. They neared the pub and the alley full of the barrels that had once shielded her from horses. Home was now only a block away. She was thinking of how to explain to Ali about the other wooden people, when the sight ahead turned her thoughts into abject fear. She whispered, "the clockwork men."

Ali stared at her face, examining the open fear on her friend. Hollo took hold of Ali and ducked behind her to shield herself from view.

"What the…" Ali mumbled, but Hollo was quick to explain, whispering into her ear over Ali's shoulder. "That man over there, the one in the dark green cloak."

"Yeah," Ali whispered back nervously.

"He's one of them, one of the clockwork men."

"How do you-" she started to say, but then a gasp escaped her as the figure turned, and a momentary flutter of wind revealed the lower half of an inhuman leg, with the metallic three-clawed foot of what might have once been a large table.

At the sight of it, Ali shoved Hollo away to their left, past the barrels, down into the alley at the side of the pub where they scrambled into a fearful run.

"That's horrible!" Ali said. "They're after you? Will you be safe in your house with them searching?"

"Yes!" Hollo said with confidence. "They'll never find me there, they can't."

"Can we go around this way? How far is it?"

Hollo didn't have a good answer for that, as this was the same maze of alleys she had gotten lost in and stumbled into the clockwork man the first time. She said this to Ali, who groaned, her eyes darting all around as they turned a corner. In this direction, Hollo hoped they would at very least come out again on the Etcher Road, and maybe if all else failed they could sneak through the bronze garden and into her backyard, preferably without anyone seeing them.

After turning several corners, they stopped for rest. Ali was very pale, from fear, or pain, or both. The pair of them breathed heavily, exhausted, listening all around for the sinister sounds of heavy footsteps. But the sound that came was not footsteps. Just as they began to breathe easier, they heard instead a distant thunder of galloping horse hooves, pounding the stone streets, growing louder with the passing seconds. Hollo remembered the fear of horses that had numbed her limbs on her first day in the outside world. In that moment she knew that these hooves were harder than those, sharper than organic, angrier than she remembered, and much faster; growing close so quickly that they had only enough time to turn before the beast was upon them. They glimpsed a great black mount, clad in so much black metal that no living animal was visible in the shell of armor, and whose master sat in the same metal, crouched over the massive steed and kicking it onward with shouts of mad, bellowing laughter. The black rider, the Hermetic outlaw Hollo had previously watched in safety bore down on them.

Ali and Hollo froze in the light of this monster that would run them down. Hollo remembered that this neighborhood was indeed where the magic rider roamed, but what could have given him cause to charge at them down this alley was beyond her imagination. There were only seconds allowed to the two girls before realizing there was no room to move out of the way. There were no doorways along this alley, only walls of stone too high to climb over, and so as one, they turned to flee, hoping the man would stop his mad charge by enough to let them out of the alley ahead of him. The sound of racing hooves suggested that wherever the rider was heading, he had no intention of being delayed by children in his way. Hollo and Ali dared a look backwards, and again in unison, grabbed onto each other and collapsed to the ground as the iron horse took a great leap into the air. Their eyes followed as the great plated underbelly flew over their heads, and landed beyond them.

Hollo heard men shouting from where the horse had come, and saw armed soldiers giving chase on horseback, all the while the black rider's cackling laughter taunted them onward.

The great, black horse had cleared the girls, but the smaller, military horses were not likely to be as capable, and now, Hollo and Ali realized that there was no stopping these men either. They turned to run once more, but found their way blocked. The black rider had halted his mount, and sat twisted in his saddle, the eyes behind his iron mask fixed on the children. His eyes locked deep into Hollo's, until their stare was broken by the sound of gunfire.

Ali shrieked as a bullet bounced off the stone wall near her face. The soldiers had opened fire, so intent on downing this man who escaped them that Hollo and Ali's lives had become forfeit in their fury. Seemingly uninterested in the gunfire, the black rider dismounted to examine the girls more closely.

Ali tackled Hollo down to the ground as more gunfire bounced around them, some of the shots finding their marks, hitting the metal rider only to bounce off with tiny puffs of smoke. The girls held themselves, waiting for a stray bullet to catch them. As if in response to this, a great cacophony of metal scraping came from the black horse. The armor, seemingly unbidden, came away in pieces to reveal there was no horse at all. Instead, being reassigned, the tons of metal flew past the girls, plating into a barrier that filled the alleyway side to side and twenty feet high. The gunfire did not cease immediately, at least not until the bellow of a soldier announced that the gunfire had ricocheted and hit one of their own. A moment later there was banging and prying as the soldiers tried to penetrate the solid metal shield, but to no avail. An officer ordered a retreat, and Hollo heard the protest of horses being turned about-face in the narrow corridor.

A hundred paces behind the rider, foot soldiers with guns appeared. Hollo watched them form into a firing squad, the first line dropping to their knees as they trained rifles on the black rider.

"Take aim!" a commander barked from a distance. The rider again made no motion, remained facing Hollo, but now the metal vestment on his person peeled away with the same sounds as the mount. Plate upon plate of the thick black shields came away, flying with purpose off his body and creating the same metallic barrier, as the bellowed command unleashed a volley of ammunition against the magical, immovable irons that had them now sealed in this hallway. The wall rose higher as the last remaining plates came from his chest, then shoulders, and lastly, from his face.

"Hiya," said the rosy, cheery voice of the assistant bronze-smith. "Guessing you're the one what's been messing up my statues in the garden."

Hollo gasped.

"He's beautiful," Ali whispered in wonderment to Hollo so that Kit couldn't hear.

"You?" Hollo hissed at him.

Falermeyer nodded. "Call me Kit. Or call me Thanks if you want, since I've saved your life now. Or just a good word to your dad would be fine," he winked. "How's ol' master Fred puttering on, anyways? Older than ever before, I assume?"

Chapter Nine
The Rider Returns

"Taken!" Falermeyer hissed, his lightheartedness fading into fear. "Bander-Clou cornered you?"

Hollo nodded, but was unsure of the full truth. There was no knowing what had befallen her father after he had turned into wood and clockwork and sent her away. He had lingered, and not taken the doorway as she had done, and so she assumed he, or at least his wooden remains, had been captured.

Kit-Falermeyer's mouth fell open a little. He reached into his shirt, and pulled a necklace out, opening the locket and looking inside with a frown. He shook it at his ear, then tapped the inside, grumbling as he inspected the ornament for damage. He frowned more deeply and reached into his pocket to pull out another piece of metal to examine, obviously puzzled. "This isn't yours, is it?" he asked, holding the round metallic object up towards her. She shook her head, confused.

"Then I wonder what on earth it is..." he muttered to himself. "And Mr. Bae-Binn, too?" he implored.

"Who?"

"Packerd," he pressed. "The man you worked for, Bae-Binn, he's...dead?"

Hollo shrugged dismally, then nodded, assuming the worst. The man had been lying very still, and as she recalled the broken, wooden arm dripping with his blood her chest flooded with an icy cold and she shivered.

"That's bad, very bad," Kit's handsome young face tightened with worry, stuffing the metal ball back into his pocket. "Didn't even have time to give me a heads up, did he…where the flustered-frog-spawn am I gonna get my copper now?"

He paced around their enclosed space for a minute, muttering to himself, cursing as he had done when taunting the soldiers. "And he left you alone?" he asked Hollo, who nodded. "My, the tragedy," he shook his head. "Terrible burden on me this is, as I'm responsible for you now."

"You?" Hollo asked incredulously, drawing a stricken look from Kit.

"I'm very responsible you know," he replied in a hurt voice. "I've a mother's sentiment and a maiden's softness, I swear."

At that moment, the head of a particularly agile soldier poked over the top of the twenty-foot barricade, his face splitting into a triumphant sneer as he sweat and struggled to get himself over. Kit barely paid him any notice, and without turning, hit his metal wall with an open palm, sending a violent reverberation throughout. The soldier, and the human ladder of men he had been perched atop, were sent flying into the air like a flimsy pyramid of playing cards, to then crash to the ground in a metallic heap.

"Fred trusts me," Kit continued, as if nothing had happened. "He's always said that I might look after you if he needed me to."

"You're so young," Hollo said.

"Older than you." He jutted out his jaw.

"Then how do we get out of here?" Ali grumbled, seating herself against the wall, and gingerly touching her black and swollen ankle.

"That," Kit said reasonably, "is a valid question."

Hollo started. "You don't know?" Then with a high squeak. "So we're trapped?"

Kit resumed his pacing. "Didn't think this through," he muttered, scratching the stubble on his chin. "You wouldn't happen to know how to do the stuff like Fred, do you? The doorway thing? He's famous for that, you know."

Hollo shook her head, recalling the enormous power of that white light, and knowing that she could never be called upon to muster so much magic as that.

"You don't suppose they'll just get bored and leave, do you?" Kit asked.

Hollo raised an eyebrow at him. "You're the expert on escaping soldiers, aren't you?"

"Yeah, you're right. They'll stick it out, won't they…they're so keen on catching me," His chest pride-inflated as if these periodic antics were actually heroics. Hollo held her face in her hands, sliding to the ground against the stone wall.

"Hey!" Ali shouted as a thought struck her, causing the other two to jump. "What's beyond this wall?" she pointed across from Hollo.

"Mmm, gardens," Kit answered with a schoolboy's eagerness.

"And beyond that?" she continued.

"Mmm…" Kit chewed on his tongue thoughtfully. "Prolly more gardens, then maybe another one, then the garden behind my shop against the back of your house," he pointed at Hollo.

Ali jumped up with excitement, nearly falling down again with a hiss of pain. "So blast the wall!" she looked expectantly between Kit and Hollo.

"You got any dynamite?" Kit asked eagerly, his eyes alight with excitement.

"Well, no," Ali mumbled, deflated. "But, you two do magic, don't you?"

"Not with stone I don't," Kit mumbled, turning to Hollo. "What about you?"

Hollo furrowed her brow, regarding the wall and thinking hard for a rhyme that would blow it up without blowing the three of them up at the same time. It was a lot to ask for, to move that much stone; the wall was high, and like the other town walls, they were at least a foot thick. The use of force was out of the question, she reasoned, deciding that maybe there was another way, an easier favor to ask of the stones, and, if asked correctly, perhaps the wall would be willing to simply accommodate a doorway for a moment until they passed through it. She was a little shy in front of Ali and Kit as they watched, wild expectation in their eyes. She pulled the string from her pocket, weaving it between her fingers as she approached the stones.

Kit looked pleased. "That's a yes then?"

Ali nodded. "She did it today, made the stone move. A wall should be easy."

Hollo didn't share her confidence. The magic in the pig market hadn't felt like magic, more like a desperate plea. She hadn't really forced the stones, rather, she had begged them for help. Perhaps a similar approach might work for her now, she thought, but struggled to get her tongue around her words as her palms and thread pressed into the stones. "I know it's strange, but rearrange and try not being a wall, try a door here at the floor and with those stones...grow...tall?" She finished with uncertainty, unsure what she meant by this, but nonetheless, the mortar between the stones cracked and crumbled and the stones separated, moving amongst themselves, and opening a great arching door before them.

"Wow!" Kit exclaimed. "You've certainly got Fred's gift with doorways, don't you!"

Hollo gazed dumbfounded at the high archway, realizing she'd very much overdone it. This looked like the entrance to a grand cathedral, only two feet wide, but apparently the wall had taken her instructions seriously, growing half its height again with her magic. It made sense, she reasoned, that a wall's deepest aspiration would be to be as high as possible. The stones had been only too happy to accommodate her. But then, when the magic began to fade, the stones were reluctant to rearrange back, slowly returning to normal. As Hollo gazed at the wall, its mood darkened further remembering what it felt like to have been, moments before, twenty feet high and so very grand. Hollo smiled back, mouthing 'sorry', but her weave could not have lasted forever.

Kit led them through the hedges beyond the archway and across several gardens where he waved cheerily at any odd neighbor upon whose garden they trespassed. "Taking a shortcut, hello!" Kit relayed a series of pleasantries as he navigated the backyards under fences and over low walls. "Hello Missus, pleasant day, indeed! ...just giving a tour to new neighbors...yes...oh my yes...pretty young ladies surely...of course sir! ...oh and a lovely afternoon to you as well Mrs. Pad-For!" He sated the curiosity of their neighbors with a doggish charm that appeared all too easy for him.

Ali was blushing. Kit calling her pretty had a powerful impact on her. Seeing this, Hollo raised an inquisitive eyebrow, but Ali turned away, a grin spread over her face.

In the distance behind them, Hollo heard a great scraping of metal, and then the stamping of hooves roar away amidst the shouts of soldiers.

"That blasted Magicker!" Kit shouted in the direction of the noise as it receded into the distance. "What's he up to now, eh?" he asked of a nearby carpenter, who nodded his approval at Kit's indignation.

"You're right there, Kit-Falermeyer," the man said. "Staying out of trouble aren't you?"

"Not one for trouble, me," he responded congenially. "Like the life of honest work best!"

"Good lad!" the carpenter nodded approvingly at him, tipping his hat at the two girls as they scurried past his workshop.

What a pair of friends Hollo had, she realized. The clever bronze-skinned girl that was tough as nails, and the bronze-smith with his quicksilver, lying tongue. Though she was stunned by his blatant dishonesty, she appreciated how well it allowed them to slip through all these people's homes and into the bronze garden. Here they avoided Chester and his apprentice, and the three of them slipped through the brush, through the fence and finally into Hollo's garden.

Flynn, who had been pecking curiously at an infuriated garden snake, went into a heat of clucking and fluster as he caught sight of Hollo. She grinned broadly, working out the excuse she would give him for why she had come home a day late and entirely pastry-less. She bent down and opened her arms to him. Flynn's tongue, quite unlike a rooster, hung a little out of his mouth as he hurriedly waddled over to greet her.

"Pretty chicken!" Kit beamed as he came through the fence last. This caused an immediate reaction in Flynn, who, a moment before, had been on course to jump up into Hollo's open arms. He revised trajectory and barreled into Kit's leg with an impassioned rage of barking squawks.

"Monster!" Kit bellowed, sprinting away from the onslaught that Flynn whose neck feathers flared out like an umbrella. Hollo and Ali sympathized at first; that is, until Kit brought magic into the fight. Disassembling an unused wheelbarrow, he drew it into protective casts around his legs. Seeing his attacker outsmarted, he taunted Flynn as the rooster's spurs rattled ineffectually off the metal.

"You're cheating," Hollo grinned at him as she scooped the enraged bird up into her arms.

"S'not cheating," he retorted. "What, should I just let him pulverize my legs until he's satisfied?"

Hollo shrugged and stroked her bird as Kit dodged a lunging peck at his face. Hollo turned and handed him off to Ali. His eye facing her closed contentedly, while the other bored accusingly into Kit, who reflexively took a step backward. Hollo meantime, opened up the back door of the house and beckoned to her friends.

"Pantry's inside. Flynn can come in, too."

Ali carried Flynn inside as Kit gave them a cautious berth. As Hollo entered, she breathed the sweet, welcoming air of her home. Just then, behind her, Kit let out a short grunt. Hollo turned in time to see him airborne, flying some twenty feet before landing in some standing water at the other side of the yard. Before she had any thought about whether or not he was injured, she cast several quick looks around to see if anyone saw the magic of her home at work. Remembering that they were safely within her father's barrier and knowing that there was nobody who could be watching them, she hurried to Kit's side.

"Why?" he whined, cradling his elbow.

"I got through fine," Ali said from the doorway. "Why didn't it bounce me like that?"

"I'm sorry," she mumbled quickly. "My house is protective, I guess the barrier was still up. Prolly cause you used magic to fight my chicken." She helped Kit up as best she could.

"S'cus I'm a guy maybe?" he glared at the doorway. "Hardly 'bounced' me, Ali. More like slapped me upside the head like Chester used to, except instead of a hand, this felt like a great big invisible frying pan, surely." He touched the back of his head where it hurt most and his hand came away bloody. "Maybe I'll say goodbye for now, not sure I wanna play anymore."

Hollo took him by the wrist, leading back to the door, though he struggled as they neared. "Come on Kit, you're bleeding, we've got to fix you up."

"No I'm not," he shook his head desperately, cowering before the doorway. "I'm fine, really, sleepy though, want to go home to bed right now."

"No," Hollo said sharply. She needed him to talk and explain himself, and no protective doorway would keep her from having her explanations. She stared frostily up at the house, wondering if she'd have to resort to trying some chant, but she was no match for her father's work, and she knew it would be in vain. She decided to try and reason with it instead.

"He's a friend," she whispered to the door. "And he's saved us both, me and my friend Ali." She thought about this and realized that Kit had only saved them from the soldiers that were after him in the first place, but she knew that would be unwise to mention. Should the house know that he'd been responsible for guns being fired at her, the next blast of the barrier might break the young man.

"Please, let him in," she whispered again, tugging forcefully on Kit's arm as his other hand flew up to shield his face as he winced, preparing for the magical impact.

He opened his eyes when Hollo let go and found himself not only inside her home, but unscathed. He cheered up, straightened his clothes and gave one of his best adorable grins. Hollo directed him into a chair and then set tea to boil. Meanwhile, Ali located a clean cloth to wash the wound on the back of his head.

"This is lovely," Kit said with a happy sigh, accepting the offered tea as Ali mended him. Looking askance at Flynn who nibbled at a cookie in the corner, he raised his cup towards the bird and said under his breath, "Who's the center of attention now, you red-feathered weasel?"

Flynn gave a single, short, and very loud cluck that certainly sounded like it translated into something rudely offensive. Kit grumbled into his teacup.

Sitting herself down opposite him, Hollo's arms clapped against the wooden chair as she settled herself. She locked eyes with him.

"Ahh," he said sheepishly. "Something on your mind?"

She nodded. Ali came and sat beside her; the two couldn't contain their curiosity. His eyes darted back and forth between them and then casting his eyes ceilingward, he asked out of nowhere, "Can either of you cook?" Ali's hand shot into the air eagerly. "Good, good…" he mumbled. "We'll be at this table for the rest of the day, I think. I suppose I'll be taking dinner here."

"I'll feed you," Hollo said dismissively. "But you need to explain yourself and what you were doing out there with your metal magic. First though, I want you to listen to my story 'cause I'm thinking you may be the one to help us get me my dad back."

He let out a pensive sigh through his nose, eyes darting around the room for a moment before nodding his gradual consent. He looked at Ali and frowned. "You better be a hell of a cook then."

Chapter Ten
The Lightning Man

Faint chords of a deep resonating warmth hummed through the house as it changed and settled in the dimming daylight, as dusk cooled the summer day into a mellow evening.

Inside, three young runaways sat in conference. Kit listened openly to the story, gasping silently at times and looking politely fearful when appropriate, but it was not until Amit was mentioned that a dark crease soured his face. Kit did not elaborate on his deep-running feeling towards the man. He did not interrupt and Hollo, who had noticed his reaction to Amit's mention, didn't ask. He was listening carefully now and even the house remained silent.

Ali set herself to work in the kitchen, her limping eased as she set herself to examining the contents of the pantry. She continued listening to Hollo though, keeping her rummaging to a whisper, and quieting her stove work with the soft setting of pots and pans upon it, careful not to disturb.

"So you met them?" Kit asked. "Those who Bander-Clou have trapped?"

Assuming what Hollo had thought was indeed true, and the souls inside the wooden constructs were indeed human souls, then yes, this was true. Though 'met' wasn't the word Hollo would use to describe her experience with them. Oddly enough, as she thought about it, the wooden men hadn't raised a hand against her. Perhaps that was because Amit wanted her unharmed, but somehow she didn't believe that the man preferred her intact. There was no reason the wooden man she had followed couldn't have simply taken hold of her and forced her into Amit's hands. Instead he, or whatever was left of that chaotic soul, hadn't attacked, only led her on, allowing her the opportunity to leave, the opportunity to walk away from that night.

As Hollo wandered through her memories, Kit spoke for the first time. "Ill take your silence to tell you that Bander-Clou is a cold man, a man who has many enemies looking for him. I'm one of them."

"Why?" Hollo asked.

"What do you mean 'why'?" Kit puzzled.

"I mean why are you one of them?"

"My reasons," he grunted, and the house momentarily darkened, disapproving of his tone. He cast an eye around the ceiling, frowning deeper. "What's it that does that?"

Hollo shrugged. "This house has always had more to it than just the place my father and I lived. I dunno, maybe dad's magic is stuck in the walls."

"Feels different than Fred," Kit observed. "The light is a bit different from his. Bit more out to get me than he was. Not to say he was exactly supportive, mind you, but this place kinda feels heavy on the shoulders, like an angry hand or something."

"Not really," Ali said softly. "Reminds me of mumma. Reminds me of when she was alive."

Kit's face fell as his attention went to the girl at the stove. "Yours too, huh?" he whispered. "Was she a Hermetic?"

Ali shook her head.

"Mine was," he said. "And my father. Having magic gets you killed a lot of the time. What happened to yours?"

Ali's hands fell away from what she was doing, though she didn't turn to them. A whisper seemed all she could manage. "One day she was gone."

There was silence for a long while, and Kit had the decency not to probe further, perhaps due to Hollo glaring at him, or perhaps because he knew why the girl did not want to elaborate. Hollo wondered what this young man was really feeling behind his polished lies and hidden anger.

Kit sighed, the darkness returning to his face as he spoke up again. "Look at us, orphans the three." He grumbled to himself for a moment, chewing furiously at his tongue as Ali watched him, cow eyed, carefully alert to his changing mood. Hollo saw this happen; saw Ali reading him, standing very still and alert. Although this wasn't the kind of anger she'd lived with, the silent kind that sent Kit off into his inner tantrums. Still, this was anger and Ali had learned to be aware of any angry man.

"Kit," Hollo said sharply, failing to reach him back from his furious rumination. "Kit!" she said a little louder, probing for his attention, though not gaining it. Whatever he was thinking about had deafened him. She could feel Ali's fear mounting. Casting around in her mind for a new strategy, she thought back on the head Bronze Smith's tactics for garnering the youth's attention. She took a breath and bellowed, "dammit-Falermeyer!"

The young man went white with surprise, snapping out of himself and looking at her incredulously. "What?" he asked irritably.

"What's wrong with your face!" Hollo yelled, more upset than she'd realized. Kit scowled.

"Orphans, aren't we?" he said as if it were obvious. "You and I by the same hands, if you have to know," he spat.

"My dad isn't dead," Hollo shivered. "He's too strong for that, and I'm gonna find him."

Kit rolled his eyes. "Yeah, well, my parents were strong too. Didn't stop him catching them, didn't stop them being burnt. Fred's a survivor, yeah, but he isn't a fighter, what chance you think he's got?"

Hollo's throat burned for a moment, but she held his eyes, willing herself to defy his word. She held a retort in her mouth, but couldn't utter it; her throat had clutched the words like a doll and clung to them. Any motion threatened to let her tears spill onto the table.

"How could you say that," the words she wanted to say came from Ali, who faced him, her knuckles white for gripping the hem of her shirt. "Why would you say that!"

Kit rolled his eyes again and folded his arms in front of his chest. "I don't have to make it sugary for you. You want my help killing Bander-Clou, and you've got it, but don't ask me to lie to you."

"Why not!" Ali barked. "You're so good at it!"

He scowled again, looking a little dangerous in the dimming light. "You two are gonna need to grow up if you're to sort yourselves out. Crying and wishing aren't gonna bring back Fred."

"Being mean to Hollo isn't going to help either!" Ali fumed. "Take it back!"

He spread his arms wide as his eyes widened in disbelief. "What? She's fine!" he gesticulated wildly at Hollo across the table. "She's a strong girl, she knows what's going on. I'm just saying that if we're gonna get revenge on Bander-Clou, she's gonna have to go full force, and with her magic. That's the only way to kill the-"

"I don't want to kill anybody!" Hollo bellowed, as tears ran down her cheeks. "I just want my dad back!"

Kit's face opened for a moment in honest shock. Regret registered on his handsome features for a moment before he turned away to harden against his private feelings.

Hollo hung her head letting her tears fall. As they landed on her folded hands, she watched the wood darken where they landed. She clutched her tear-stained hands into angry fists, preparing to yell at Kit some more, to tell him he was wrong, to say that he should be more sensitive, and above all, she wanted to tell him that magic wasn't meant to kill people. She would never, ever do something so horrible, and yet she recalled that this very day, she might have. Maybe the young man was right, and she was the one who was lying. Maybe what she ought to do was hunt after the man Amit and see if he would turn to stone like Ali's father. She released her fists as the fight went out of her.

"Grow up, both of you," Kit shoved his chair away from the table and rose. "I guess you're too little to do anything to help me, so I'll go after him alone, like always."

He walked to the door, and then turned back. "You two just hide here, and don't do anything stupid. I'll come and check on you when I can."

"Don't bother!" Ali shouted, as the front door opened, to then slam itself shut behind him, perhaps trying to close on him before he had fully left. The young man was prepared though and jumped out into the street. He stuffed his hands into his pockets and stalked away, glaring up at the three-story home.

"He's probably right," Hollo heard herself say. "Dads prolly dead."

A pause, and then tiny brown arms circled her from behind. Ali didn't say anything, only rested her chin on Hollo's head and held her. They were still for a long while, the pair of them looking dismal, and together they watched Flynn rise from his business and cluck his way around the kitchen. He cocked his head up at the stove, looking appraisingly at the handle of the cooking pot. He saw it as a potential roosting spot, and just as Hollo realized the impending danger, Flynn was airborne, springing up to perch on it. His weight catapulted the contents off the stove as he burst into a fury of terror-filled screeching, flying away and into the hallway where he could be heard in a panic, running in circles. The food, meanwhile, had sprayed across the room, across the floor, and over the girls. Their burns were mild, but the mess was profound. Her cloak was now ruined on both sides, and Ali's filthy garments were filthier.

"Bath would be good about now," Ali observed.

"I don't take baths, it'll rub off with a wet cloth."

Ali frowned at her. "Baths aren't just for cleaning, c'mon, we gotta wash Kit's unhelpfulness off. Baths are good for cleaning thoughts too."

Under protesting, Hollo showed her the washroom upstairs, where Ali promptly began to pump the water into the copper basin. She searched around for the wood required to heat the water but bound nothing.

"What, did your dad take cold baths?" Ali asked, disappointed.

"No," Hollo said dully, and without thinking. "Just ask the house."

Ali's eyes widened with wonder. "No," she whispered, then looked excitedly all round the little room. "Hot water please!" she grinned shyly.

Hollo nearly had time to tell her that she should rhyme it, but before she did, the bath's steaming tendrils rose around her. Hollo forgot her grey mood watching her elated friend, who in a swift, well practiced few motions had removed her filthy clothes and leapt into the water. Re-surfacing, she reached out her hands and began rummaging through the colored bottles on a stone shelf beside her. She smelled them experimentally, and beckoned to Hollo, who moved forward curiously.

"C'mon," Ali smiled reassuringly. "It's not deep, you won't sink. We can both fit."

Hollo wasn't sure what to expect from a bath, but she wasn't fully prepared for how wonderful and comforting it turned out to be.

Ali seemed to have quite moved past the argument with the young bronze-smith, and was beside herself, adding colorful elixirs turning the bath into a mountain range of bubbly peaks and valleys. The steam clouded the room, and as Hollo began to lose sight of Ali in the thickening haze, the window above the bath opened up by its own will. It was strange how this alarmed Hollo more than Ali, who squealed and yelled 'thank you' out into the space of the washroom.

Was it because of the girl's manners that the house welcomed her so readily? As Hollo pondered this, her expression caused Ali to stop playing with the bubbles.

Unnoticed, she crawled over to Hollo and gently touched noses with her. Hollo gave a startled blink and and Ali grinned.

"Hey sour-face," she teased.

Hollo smiled, but only half-heartedly, as the hard knot of anxiety within her begged attention and refused to let her, despite the bath's comfort, fully relax. Worry for her father, worry for Kit, burning guilt, all of it tightened inside her.

Both girls' heads flicked up to the window at the same moment, having both heard the same noise. The roll of thunder was faint, but here in the quiet of the washroom it had found a way through the tiny window.

"Not the time of year for rain," Hollo whispered.

"Sometimes the storms come anyway," Ali said. "Have you ever heard about the Lightning Man?"

"The what?"

"One of the stories my mumma told me at bedtime," Ali explained.

"No, I haven't."

"I'll tell you then, little sour face," she cleared her throat and settled herself into a sitting position. Biting her lip, Ali stared upwards searching her words. "So one day, a baby was born, who cried and cried and didn't stop crying. His mumma would say, 'O how you carry on like a storm' and she'd say 'oh how the rain comes falling down when you whine', and as the baby grew up a little, he still cried all the time. Even past the age for crying, and his mumma would say, 'now stop crying or the clouds will hear you and cry as well, and then we'll be flooded and the harvest ruined, and it'll be your fault. And the little boy didn't stop crying, and kept going, day after day, until his hair grew white, and his face blue and swollen like a thundercloud. And when he cried, the sky would swell up and the rain would come, and his mother shook her head, and said, 'baby, you'll starve us all up if you don't stop crying,' and still the baby kept crying. He cried and cried and then his cries turned to screams and then the thunder came. The village got really poor, the vegetables all stopped growing, and time passed, and the baby grew into a boy. And when he grew, he stopped crying, but he'd done so much already that it didn't ever stop, and it had stormed and thundered for seven years without stopping so far, but only in his town. The town just down the road had no rain, and the town up the road had no rain, but his village was always raining. The other villagers knew it was because of him that the rain fell, and it was him who made the thunder roll in the night. The village up the road had a drought, and they were thirsty, and one of the villagers said 'bring us the boy who makes it rain'. The boy, whose hair was all white, and his face the color of thunderclouds, well, he left his mother's house, and he went up the road, and sure enough the storm followed him there. And the people were all happy for the water, and they danced in the rain, and he lived there for a while and was happy to make people so happy. But then there was too much rain, and the lightning came, and houses were struck and some burnt down, and so they'd had enough of his rain and sent him home. But when he went home, he stopped on the road outside the town where his house was, and he saw how happy people were there, and how, since he was gone, the crops began to grow again, and little sprouts were popping out of the ground. He saw his own mumma, happy with his brothers and sisters building a new garden, and he grew sad. He knew he couldn't stay, and so he left, and he walked the road as far away as he could, and then kept walking after that, not staying very long in any place, because he knew he couldn't. Most places wouldn't put him up for very long, he was a stranger with the face of a storm and hair like lightning, and so he would leave towns quick, or even be chased out. He got older, and when he did, he also got more mad. And the sadder and madder he got, the worse was the rain, and the harder the lightning. They say he still walks the road, and you can always see him coming on the horizon, where great storm clouds follow him overhead; the man who's never seen the sun, the man who lives under the lightning. My mumma always told me that story when I was sad, when I was crying in my bed. She said I should feel better than the Lightning Man, because at least for me, I would get to see the sun in the morning, and I had a home and my family."

At that moment a distant clap of thunder found them again, rolling along the eastern plains and in through their window. The girls locked eyes, and it was a moment before Hollo realized her own mouth was agape just like Ali's. Ali leapt up, water splashing on Hollo's face as she reached up to the high bathroom window, and lifted herself to it while slipping around with soapy feet on the bath-side shelf. Hollo followed, and they looked out to the distant horizon, where they could see a fog of darkness between two mountains. It was a strange time of year for rain, Hollo thought, daring to wonder.

"That's a true story, you know," Ali whispered beside her. "Mumma said she knew him."

"Do you think it's him out there?" Hollo asked.

"Could be, maybe he'll come this way. We could search him out if he comes to town," Ali grinned ear to ear. "Maybe if the Lightning Man comes, then Kit won't go chasing that bad man. It must be hard to ride in metal when you're all wet."

Hollo smiled. "Maybe, if the Lightning Man comes, he'll lend me his lightning and help me make a door to get my dad back."

Ali gasped. "I bet he would! I bet that would work, too! Lightning is crazy full of magic I'll bet!"

Hollo brightened at the thought. She'd heard of lightning rods atop houses capturing the light from the skies. Maybe if she could muster enough of her own ingenuity, maybe she could use it for making a doorway.

"What are you thinking?" Ali asked as they slipped out the bath and into towels.

"Wondering if I could find some other magic, some big magic that could help me."

"Wish I could help," Ali muttered. "Wish I had magic to lend."

Hollo thought about this. This idea of lent magic, she wondered if this was possible. "Maybe," she said thoughtfully.

"Maybe I just need some more people. Maybe if I could find other people with magic, then we could all make one?"

"Probably," Ali said. "But where would you find them?"

Hollo pondered, standing there staring in the mirror at the reflected pair of them.

"C'mon," Ali said smiling. "You've got to dry off." She took the towel from Hollo's hands and began to rub her down. Drying wood was harder to dry than skin, and without realizing it, Ali's gently rubbing was getting rougher. Hollo almost lost her footing from being so jostled. She was about to object and pull the towel away, when Ali tossed the offending towel to the floor and obliviously proclaimed, "Done. Show me your room?" She marched out of the room triumphantly, leaving Hollo to grin and shake her head as her friend disappeared around the corner.

Hollo jogged past and lead her upstairs to the top floor and into her attic. Ali spotted Hollo's dresser and rifled through her clothes where she found a long, cotton shirt to wear. It was lucky they were about the same size. Hollo climbed up to sit in the nook of her round attic window. The stars were out now, the sky black and the tiny flashes of light on the distant horizon told her the storm had not changed place.

"You can sleep in my bed down there," Hollo said. "I'll sleep up here."

She looked down and found Ali snoring softly, sprawled out on the mattress. Hollo eyes smiled as she watched her friend sleeping peacefully. It wasn't until she felt her eyes grow heavy that she how tired she was. Settling down on the sill of her window, she pulled the blanket around her. When teetering on the edge of sleep, a thought seeped through. "I forgot to let Flynn out to bed," she muttered aloud from her half-dream.

"Go to sleep," whispered a voice in her ear. "I'll look after everything."

"Mmkay," Hollo trailed off, falling into an exhausted sleep.

Downstairs, the back door opened enough to let the rooster scurry out to the safety of his hay bale house, where the door of his cage opened, then closed behind him, and shut him inside, where he, too, dozed off.

The tub on the second floor drained of water, and the stove's flames burned out of wood. A broom scooped the mess of food up, and the floors were cleaned, quietly, so as not to wake the girls upstairs. On the desk in the kitchen, a book that had been locked away in a drawer now lay in the center of all the papers and mirrors on the desk's surface. It might have been wind that opened the heavy cover, and breeze that turned the pages. There the book waited while the breeze moved away.

Lastly, the lights in the house, the few candles that remained were blown out by these same ripples of wind. The only light left was the golden, humming glow deep within its walls where the last light lingered.

. . .

On a distant horizon, amidst mountains and under torrents of rain, there stood a man who saw the city. Visibility was poor and the evening was dark but still he saw lights, even at this great distance. His eyes were used to the darkness, and the twilight of thunderstorms. The glow of nighttime was his domain, and he saw clearly the walls and high buildings, as clearly as he had seen a hundred cities before now, from where he remained far away. Long years he had remained on the roads, having no human settlement to call home, and therefore the road was his home, and he lived off the woods, and the trades he made with those he met who were willing to do business with him.

Often met with fear, he did not make friends easily. The long, white hair and bluish color of his skin usually drew caution from travelers, who whispered as they passed him. For this reason, it was many years since he had set foot in a city as he planned now to do. An urgent invitation drew him to this place for a very important meeting. He sought a man who wrote stories; a man who, it was fabled, could see the world through a looking glass. A man named Fredric, who kept the secrets and identities of his kind recorded in a book of stories. He had even written the white-haired traveler's own story. He called him The Lightning Man.

Chapter Eleven
Reflections of the Mirror Man

"Your house is amazing!"

Hollo's eyes opened with a start, unused to being woken up in the morning. She was the first to rise, always, and if not, had only ever been called to rise by her father's voice from her mirror. Ali's head peeked up to her, over the edge of the window ledge where Hollo lay.

"I've been up since dawn, already let Flynn out. Made the bed, too," Ali pointed responsibly to the bedcovers that were laid respectfully in order as they never had been laid before. "I found a great book downstairs. It's really great, have you read it?"

"No," Hollo said, drowsily. "I dunno, what book?"

"On your dad's desk," she explained. "It's great, there's a whole bunch of stories. Come downstairs, I want to show you something, but you probably know already."

Hollo obeyed, wondering what Ali might have to show her that she hadn't noticed over the last twelve years of being confined to this residence. As it turned out, it wasn't 'something' so much as it was the lack thereof.

"No mess!" Ali said, pointing to the floor. "Your house cleans itself, how great is that?"

"No it doesn't," Hollo said with a frown, examining the spotless floorboards where Ali's stew had ended up, and should by all reason still be. "Not unless Dad uses magic."

"Well it was clean when I woke up, much tidier than we left it."

Hollo looked around, and was forced to agree. The house had always had a mind of its own, as was demonstrated by the disagreements it had with her father, though she had never thought to wonder if it was capable of doing things on its own.

"So are you haunted?" Ali asked, sounding thrilled by the idea.

"Am I what?" Hollo frowned.

"Haunted," Ali said slowly. "You know, haven't you ever heard stories like that before? Haunted houses, poltergeists and things, no? I'm sure there's some ghost stories in the book."

"What book?" Hollo persisted. She had read a great many of the books in this house, and no collection of stories had ever caught her notice.

"The one on the desk," Ali reiterated, surprised. "I figured you put it there, since it was turned to The Lightning Man, but maybe it was your ghosts…" she trailed off thoughtfully.

Hollo then saw what book she meant; the large tome that sat open on her father's desk. It was never left open on the desk, Hollo knew this from years of watching her father carefully remove and return the text from its dedicated drawer. Ali had speculated that it could be the work of the house's 'haunting', and Hollo now wondered something similar.

"The house hasn't ever moved things around like this," she said, hearing the concern in her own voice as she said this. "Something is different."

"Well, yeah," Ali said. "Your dad is not here, so what else is it gonna do? Seems helpful either way."

Hollo was emboldened by Ali's complete lack of perplexity. Since meeting the girl Hollo had realized that Ali was a person easily smitten with things; food and boys and haunted houses and such things. Perhaps it was that she was easy to assume best, but perhaps, given what Hollo knew of her life until now, perhaps Ali's sense of danger was simply more acute than her own, and should be trusted. Hollo had read stories of animals, and how they were attuned to things in a way different from people. They felt storms coming, and they had powerful and immediate senses of the character of strangers. Perhaps Ali, having been treated like an animal, had adopted this quality. The girl must be able to see deeper into things than Hollo did, like how she had responded to Kit. She had an intuition that wasn't to be ignored.

"I guess if you think so, maybe the house is trying to help us," Hollo said, taking a seat in her father's chair. "Suppose we should at least find out what it has to say. Have you eaten?" she asked.

"Mmm, not yet," Ali said carefully. "Was gonna ask…"

Hollo smiled. "I hope you eat it all before it spoils, I don't like cleaning the pantry."

Ali lit up with that familiar food-lust, and she bounded through the door to the treasure trove of edibles. Hollo turned back to the desk and focused her attention on the leather-bound book open in front of her. Staring up at her was the picture of a white-haired man. The title read, 'The Lightning Man'. Hollo began to read, finding the tale to be written very much the same as Ali had told her. It sounded like a children's story, a fable, and it certainly appeared as if her father had been the one to write it. She knew articulate handwriting very well. She had been enamored with it since she was very young, and had aspired to copy it as she had come to be taught to read and write. She had watched him work on this text for as many years as she could recall, and had never thought to wonder what he was doing, for surely it was some monotonous task, but no, he had been writing stories. Was he a storyteller, she wondered? Wouldn't she know if he had been?

Ali came back, munching at a rather over-sized apple. She draped an arm over Hollo's shoulders, the crunching amplified as her chewing came to be beside Hollo's ear.

"He has a whole bunch of them," Ali said as a little apple juice sprayed onto Hollo's cheek. "Stories about people like the

Lightning Man. I've heard a lot of them before, all over the place, at lessons with the twins, in plays in the market. Did he write them?"

Hollo shrugged. "Dunno if they're his, wouldn't he have read them to me? I love stories, I've read a lot."

"He hid it from you?"

"No," Hollo said, though was unsure. "But he never talked about it."

"Maybe he didn't write them, just liked collecting them?"

Possible, Hollo thought, but her father didn't seem like the kind of person prone to collections. She had always thought his writing was something important involving his work with magic. His commitment to the writing had taken so much of his time that Hollo found it hard to believe he was merely 'collecting'.

She closed the book, and then opened the heavy cover. She flipped through the first few pages, ignoring the body of introduction and paused on a page that caught her attention. It had a rhyme written on it; one that she knew. Her father had mumbled and hummed it, more to himself than to her, but she remembered the first short verse clearly. She hummed it now.

A-salt the walk, a-latch the lattice

Mad King Had come out to play

Latest hour, bedroom tower

Up till dawn, and dead by day

"I know that tune," Ali began to hum. "We used to play the game too, Mad Had."

"He must have written them," Hollo concluded. She wasn't sure why, but the odd, halting rhyme indeed sounded in her head identical to the way her father spoke when they had played. His clumsy way about words had a clear tone in her mind, and somehow, she knew without knowing that this was indeed his work.

"Let's read them," Ali said. "They're all about magic stuff."

The sound of a wall creaking on the floor above them caused Hollo to stiffen, and that tingle of nervousness came back to her. It was strange, how she was suddenly wary of the house she knew so well, the house whose characteristics she simply thought had been an elaborate and amusing game her father played for her. It seemed there was more magic in her home than she had known, and now that she had come to realize how little she understood about magic and its dangers, the more distrustful she became.

"I suppose," Hollo whispered, hoping not to be overheard by any 'helpful' entities that might be nearby, "Let's start by seeing if there's a story about houses that can make things move."

They decided the only way to read the whole book was to start from the beginning. In doing so, they naturally started with that the first story, and by coincidence, the exact story they were looking for. 'The Restlessness of King Haddard', it was called, and beneath it in smaller handwriting the alternate title read, 'Mad King Had', just as Ali had said. The schoolyard rhyme that began the tale was penned in tiny cursive, so that the girls had to lean in close to discern the words. They settled into the armchair near the back door, where their two small bodies fit side by side. They wrapped a blanket around themselves and began to read:

A-salt the walk, a-latch the lattice

Mad King Had come out to play

Latest hour, bedroom tower

Up till dawn, and dead by day

A'latch the lattice, a'lock the door
Mad King Had fell all the way
Poor King Had-oh, the witch's sha-dow
Darkens walls, and leads astray

A'lock the door, Afraid of shadows
Listen and you'll hear her say
At the latest hour, in your sleepless bower
Stay up till dawn and die to-day

The sleepless nights began in summer, and it was not until the late winter that the tragedy of King Had was immortalized in the rhymes of schoolchildren. In the spring before, the crimes of a woman had been brought to the attention of both royalty and common people by the gossip of scandal involving the husband of a young noble matriarch. It was normally beneath the business of a king to involve himself in such petty trials as the one of a young woman accused of nefarious magic. Such superstitions were not terribly common in such a cultured capital as King Haddard's city, but the particular case he involved himself with was not like any other. The young woman, they said, was an enchantress, and could captivate men in ways that bespoke of certain evil. The woman stood a head higher than even the formidable King himself; a quality that some believed proof enough of her use of magic, for how could such a very tall, and so very skinny woman capture the interest of otherwise healthily undersexed husbands?

While the King Haddard was not a young man, he was not old enough to be prone to such things as sleeplessness, like what the men who came into dementia suffered from in their twilight years. He was not old, even though his wife was long since passed away. He was not old, even though he had not taken a lover since her passing.

His maids spoke to each other about him, the man who demanded solitude when he rested. They whispered and he heard them whispering, he knew how they spoke of his failing virility. This bothered him, much as it would bother any man. Perhaps even more, having been born into a station that had shielded him up to now from any serious criticism in his adult life.

King Haddard had not won his throne by conquest in war or in politics, but quite unremarkably. He was born the only inheriting child of his family, the royal house before his own. He was born a king, and now approached his winter years as a tired, paranoid relic of his own father's glory; a man who had taken a hundred cities and a hundred virgins for his legacy. They spoke of this, the maids and footmen, they, who had once loved him for his gentleness now ridiculed him for it within earshot. They did not fear him; no one feared him, not until the winter.

The woman on trial was sentenced to imprisonment by the king, who attested to her use of magic himself. While she awaited trial, the King, in order to see what all the fuss was about, went to her cell and spoke with her. Their conversation was private, however when he came out of her holding cell, he proclaimed that she would be sealed in his castle's own, though long since unused, dungeon. The declaration created a royal scandal of the century. Many assumed this was his way of taking her as a mistress; indeed, his servants saw him go down to the dungeons many times, always looking fevered and riled. This was when the rumor of his madness began, even before the madness had thought to look for him.

It wasn't until the young woman vanished from her cage in the deep underground that the real gossip began. Many people were certain that he had released her, some even claimed that they had seen her lounging around the King's summer home, luxuriating in the sunshine and awaiting the doting favor of the king she had enslaved. But it was also said that the King, realizing the cunning and power of the sorceress, had her slain and burned deep in the forest. These rumors flowed until they became a vile torrent King Had could no longer ignore.

One morning at the onset of winter, King Had stormed from his chambers, his heavy winter robes in a fit about him. He burst into the breakfast hall of the servant's quarters, a small room beside the kitchens where the king had never set foot before, much less in his bedclothes. He had charged in and set about his staff accusing and threatening, informing them that if their whispers continued to disrupt his sleeping hours, in fact if their gossiping continued at all he would run them out of his kingdom altogether; or better yet, he would personally run them through with a sword.

Wild threats rarely quiet young mouths as well as one would like, but in this instance it did precisely that. The servants were so frightened by their master that not a single word was ever again spoken in any way ill of the King. Most of the servants realized how perilously close they had been to losing their homes and maybe even their lives.

As a group, the experience solidified their loyalty, but King Had knew nothing of this and knew nothing of their change of heart. What the servants could not know, is that it wasn't their gossiped whispers that kept him awake at night. The whispers that kept him from sleeping were not theirs.

Though the talking behind his back was ended, still the King complained of his restless nights. He refused the tonics of his physicians, for he knew it was not his anxious mind that kept him awake, it was the whispers he heard through his walls. One night, in a fit of rage, the king gave rise to his garrison, and his soldiers swept through the castle to wake his staff from their beds and rid the royal home of all service men and women, sending them from his employ and into the winter cold. The soldiers were then ordered to guard the outside, to assure not a living soul would walk his halls in the night and disrupt him in his bedchamber.

King Had knew he had, at irrelevant cost, finally won himself a night of unbroken rest. He settled into his welcoming bed watching the glow of a solitary candle and for the first time in months, began to feel himself relax. But the poor King had mistaken silence for assurance, for it was then, alone in his castle with no one to cast blame upon, that the whispers again rose up and surrounded him. In a livid fury he rose to rout the incessant gossiping from his house, when he then remembered that no one but himself there remained. The King, turned furious tempest, wrecked his room, destroyed his possessions and bellowed foul oaths, terrible things that could be heard by his freezing garrison at the gate so many floors below him. He screamed throughout the night, throughout the rooms of his house and its echoing stone halls.

By the time morning came, he had fallen listless, communicating only by what his eyes could say. In the following days, news spread. His benefactors came to speak to him, offering comfort; even offering their homes as refuge from the mysterious 'whatever' that ailed him. But the King only stared, his bloodshot eyes and black under-circles telling these friends that none of their proffered comforts would bring him peace.

He refused all help, and instead summoned a carpenter. The carpenter, later interrogated by those same benefactors, gave the confused reply, "I'm simply to remove the wall cover and refinish it with fresh paper." When asked why, the carpenter wrung his hands and become the picture of angst. "He only says that the stain on the wall needs to be taken away. But I don't know to what he refers!" And the people were left to wonder what this riddle meant.

For King Had, this was no riddle. His nights had become much a repetition of the nights before, where he would sit on the end of his bed staring intently at the wall. The wall was re-covered with what the carpenter explained to be a 'tranquil' shade of pale yellow, and still the King remained intense, his maniacal eyes gazing deeply into the wall.

If you looked closely, at least as closely as a mad King would, you too would see it, the darkening of the wallpaper, the faintest shadow the size of a very tall person, though thin like a spirit. With each passing night the stain grew, red-hued and dark according to King Had. He spoke at the wall and the shadow that stood there ever watching him, ever whispering throughout the night, though it never spoke as plainly to Had as he had begun to speak to himself. The King's soliloquies initially were just confused; however, within mere days, fell into nonsensical whispers that conveyed him towards his final descent into madness.

He would not leave his bedroom; he refused all food. Friends and relatives came to see him, but he only sat, wasting away, always sitting at the edge of his bed, bloodshot eyes locked on the stain that only he could see — the stain that spoke in whispers that only he could hear. They looked for the stain on the wall, they humored him and even some lied and agreed to be able to see it, but it was none of it true.

The physicians were at a loss, blaming a variety of maladies but never matching one another's diagnosis. In the daytime, the gossip about the king resumed, but because his subjects could remember him as a good king, they fretted, wondering what was to become of him.

At night, alone in his bedchamber, Had even refused sleep, mesmerized by the form emerging in the wall before him. The shadow of the woman had developed in the days he had waited for it, staring at the wall, waiting for the whispering entity to emerge and meet him. Slower than watching water boil, but as certain as the laws that ensure its eventuality, the woman's appearance became *clear to him, and only to him. So much so, that one night, after weeks of such little movement, King Had suddenly rose. Wrenching his mirror off his wall, he threw it with all the brawn of his madness out of the window, breaking the glass, and then followed by putting himself out through the same window, where he met his death many stories below at the feet of his guardsmen.*

The legacy of a family was ended in that night, and the castle of King Had's inheritance has remained unoccupied in the decades thereafter, by all but a sole proprietor; a nameless deaf custodian who has no fear of whispers.

The legend remains though, and as legends will, has been embellished and honed. It tells of a shadow-etched wallpaper, the shadow of a young witch, so they say, and if you dare to walk the castle's many rooms, she may appear as she once did to the King Haddard, and bewitch you into throwing yourself from the tower, to find your ending on the ground below, where the grass grows freely untended; where a mad king once fell from grace.

Ali let out a shuddering giggle as they finished. "Do you think it was the witch?" she asked with horrified delight. "Do you think he kept her as a mistress?"

Hollo didn't fully understand what a mistress was, but was sure that the story was alluding to something more complicated between the king and the witch than mere 'mistressness'. "Was it her ghost in the walls?" Hollo asked, turning the page to the image of King Had staring at a shadow on his bedroom wall. "Why did she want him dead?"

Ali shrugged, looking around the house with curiosity. "You think your dad had a mistress? Maybe one who's haunting here?"

"Don't think so." Hollo answered. "I would've noticed, wouldn't I?"

The house gave a settling creak that caused both girls to jump.

"Maybe," Ali whispered. "Unless the ghost was here a'fore you were born."

Hollo shuddered, and then so did the house. The girls both stared into the vacant space of the house for several long moments, until Ali cleared her throat.

"Anyone like a ghost in there?" she called out. Her fist balled, and with a little grin at Hollo, she rapped her knuckles on the wall behind them. "Anybody that was a person once? Maybe a ghost now? We appreciate you cleaning for us, just wanted to say 'hello'. Anything to say?"

Silence.

The the wall gave a cheerful creak, and in the very next instant the girls were tumbling themselves out the back door in a panic. The girls huddled together in the garden, huffing to catch their breath. Flynn hooted and squawked, stomping around them with his head jerking in all directions, searching for whatever the source of his girls' distress was, barking loudly and ruffling his feathers in demonstration of his readily prepared ferocity.

Hollo tugged Ali onward, away from the house.

"Let's read another!" Ali said with a bravery that her quaking shoulders belied.

Hollo shuddered at the though of going back into the house, but as their initial fright began to fade, shudders turned to giggles and soon they were laughing together. "C'mon," Hollo nudged. "Let's play outside for a while, in Kit's yard. She realized that she hadn't yet shown Ali her bronze neighbors, and brightened at the thought. Ali needed little more convincing beyond the words 'Kit's yard'.

Hollo led the way, checking on the whereabouts of Chester and the skinny apprentice, not to mention Kit, who she was not yet ready to see again. Just as she saw that the workroom doors were closed, a drop of water fell on her cheek. She hadn't noticed how the day had darkened and grown overcast. Rain was inbound, and Chester, as was his habit, had probably closed shop for the day because of the rain. All the better, Hollo thought, since this way they could have free range of the garden.

The first statue they approached was she who stood nearest them. The Countess was a haughtily poised replica of an aristocratic young widow. Hollo had woken her long ago, and since then not repeated the encounter, choosing instead the company of those statues who did a little better to be pleasant. There was an expression Hollo had come to apply to the woman, which was 'don't judge a book by its cover'. Her expectations of the widow's charm and elegance had been eluded, and instead she had found the Countess to have a personality quite her own. The lace and robes she was cast in gave a strong impression of someone in mourning, though Hollo had never managed to get in the question as to who she was mourning.

In Hollo's right hand, her string wound through her fingers into a star, and she sang a song into the string before laying it against the long gown that covered the woman's feet. Gold light sank into the funeral gown of the woman as she made her rhyme. "Black as night with pain and strife, the Countess breathes and comes to life. I don't know who you've lost today, but you might like company anyway."

The woman's face, so poised and lazily affectionate suddenly fell into a peculiar frown of distaste. Her body, though brought to life, remained so still it appeared she was unaware anything had changed. All that moved was her face, her jaw clenching into a livid irritation, her dark eyes showcased by the harsh furrowing of her frown.

Ali tugged on Hollo's sleeve, wary at the sight. Hollo held a finger to her lips, nodding upward at the woman, who had begun to breath heavily out her nose in little smoky huffs, like a slender, agitated dragon. Slowly, ever so slowly, the Countess turned her knotted little eyebrows and dark eyes onto Hollo. Her lips pursed into a frown, out of which she somehow managed to speak. "What did I tell you about doing that!?" the woman asked Hollo.

Hollo smiled, and gave a little curtsy. "Hiya, sorry, I know you dislike being bothered, but I have someone today-"

"And what's worse," the Countess continued, looking around herself. "I haven't even moved from this tiny jungle into a real estate. You've left me here to *age*," she let her tongue hang from her mouth at the last words, apparently disgusted by the taste it had left in her mouth.

"You haven't-"

"It's been an age since I've had a smoke," she drawled, cutting Hollo off again. She then brightened, and knelt down to Hollo's height, the better to flutter her dark round eyes. "You wouldn't be able to find me some, would you, *darling*," she purred.

"No," Hollo answered. The Countess let a fiery little breath out through her nose. "I'll see you in hell then, won't I," she hissed, rising to stand. "I've had enough of your games, little girl, you and your silly divination."

"It's not divination." Ali corrected her. "You mean enchanting. Hollo's enchanted you. Divination is like reading the future."

The Countess ignored her, though still glanced sideways, as if she had heard a tiny noise from far away. A double take brought her attention around onto Ali, who she immediately lunged towards, her fingers curling into her hair.

"My god!" the Countess barked. "You're so…*cute*."

Ali lit up as the thin, bronze fingers ran through her hair. "Thanks," she mumbled sheepishly.

"You could make a *killing* as a chambermaid," she went on. "The girls would simply murder each other for such a cute girl like you," she winked at Ali. "Tag along with me, I'll take you places. We'll start by parading you around the Officer's Ball, that's where all the pretty young girls go to make a splash. They'll just fall to pieces over you," she cooed, petting Ali like a kitten, and messing her hair around to her liking.

"You're a statue though," Ali said. "How are you going to a dance, and aren't you dressed wrong?"

"I'm never dressed wrong," the Countess answered simply, still smiling, and apparently deaf to the implication that she was not a fetching, young, human woman. "We'll have to change *your* clothes though. Come, follow me, I've had enough of this jungle." She lifted her gown above her ankles, fumbling with the heavy, fluid bronze. "My god," she muttered. "Maybe I'll change as well, something a little less encumbered."

"Cumbersome," Ali corrected. "Where are you going?"

"To my estate," the woman answered. "Hurry now, let's have a ride from whoever lives in that little shack." She marched towards the Casters' workshop and started banging on the door. Hollo leapt into action, first running after her, then changing course as a better solution occurred to her. She knew she couldn't stop the woman who only heard what she wanted to hear, and refused to acknowledge that she was a statue. It would take another statue to reason with her.

Hollo laid her hand on the bronze Knight, the words spilling out of her mouth at high speed, hoping against hope that no one was inside the workshop to hear the woman.

"Fearsome Knight of copper and tin, hurry to life for me again, and help me stop the woman there, who's bronze and loud and unaware."

Armor creaked and the man coughed a little, his nose wrinkling for a moment, distracted by odor, then smiled as he saw Hollo. "The little wooden girl," he said curiously. "Well a happy birthday to you!"

"Not today," Hollo said quickly, looking fearfully over her shoulder as the Countess rapped on the window of the shop with her metal knuckles, causing the glass to shatter.

"I need your help!" Hollo implored. "That woman over there, can you talk to her, make her stop? I'll be in trouble."

If the Knight was confused by this, he disregarded it instantly as he caught sight of The Countess. He puffed his chest out and gave a dashing wink to Hollo before marching forward, stumbling a little as he learned how to walk with such heavy legs. Hollo scurried along behind him, while attempting to waylay The Countess as best she could. "Before you go!" she called, trying to think of a way to catch the young aristocrat's attention. "Please, umm, I have a gentleman who, um, wishes to make your acquaintance."

"Don't be stupid," the Countess called back. "No men of any respectability would be all the way out…" she caught sight of the Knight then, and closed her mouth.

"My lady," The Knight bowed low. "Prithee pardon, madam, but I assure you there are no men in this garden who could stand up to your standard of respectability, though perhaps you would allow me the generosity of a moment?"

He righted himself, all dignity and poise as The Countess looked him up and down. Her fist fell away from the window, and a little malevolent smile curled into the corner of her mouth.

"My my…how vintage," she muttered. Lifting her nose in the air, she flounced past him, away from the house and towards a wrought iron bench back near the fence. She sat herself in it, then folded her legs and leaned away over the armrest with casual poise and closed her eyes. She flourished a kerchief and let it slip from her fingers onto the bench beside her, where the bronze tissue clanged like a bell upon landing.

The Knight grumbled some unintelligible purr of self-satisfaction as he smiled his be-mustached smile and marched over to pick the kerchief off the bench and present it back to her. The Countess accepted it from him with a coy smile that held all the believability of a coyly smiling barracuda.

Hollo sighed, and let herself fall backwards into the grass with her arms outstretched. She stared up at the cloudy sky, catching bits and pieces of their conversation as it turned into a flirtatious singsong that rose in volume, as well as absurdity. Hollo snorted, sitting upright to roll her eyes knowingly at Ali. Ali knew nothing of her knowing eye roll, and sat beside her with glazed eyes, watched the two bronze figures chatting in the humid summer overcast. She hummed a little as she stared at them, a smile spread foolishly on her face, lost in her own version of the scene, which involved a certain young renegade bronze-smith.

Having had quite enough, Hollo pulled herself and her friend to their feet. "I'll show you another," she said to Ali, who remained lost in thought even as Hollo guided her towards a clearing where her favorite statue awaited. "Those two aren't going anywhere so you can come meet Timtree."

Ali stopped them short, tugging Hollo back towards the metal worker's shop and pointed excitedly at a statue new to Hollo. It was nestled in the far corner almost out of sight. It was the likeness of a young man cast upon a tall square of granite, whose face was open in extravagant laughter; his finger pointing toward the distance while his other held the mirth at the top of his stomach.

A tiny grey bird sat on his pointing finger, grooming itself. The stone pedestal was lichen covered, begging the question – how long he had stood there forgotten? No one had bothered to etch words into the stone pedestal. Apparently nothing had ever come of this nameless person.

"What about him?" Ali asked. "The Laughing Man, here? He looks less trouble than a moody rich-girl."

Hollo stared up at his joyous face, agreeing that the young man did indeed seem in good spirits, and would certainly make for some good company, so long as he could keep his laughter to a reasonable volume. She made her threaded seal for the third time, reaching up on tiptoes to place her hand on his shoe.

"Stranger here, who laughs and cheers, take pause from all your glee. Tell me what you love so much, come down and talk to me."

He indeed let out a short bellow of laughter, his eyes tearing up with mirth; but he quickly hushed, his laughter losing momentum. His face slackened, and his expression fell from joy.

"Hi," said Ali. "What's your name?"

Huge, swollen tears of bronze welled in his crinkled eyes.

"Oh no!" Ali whispered. "He's so sad, what did I say? I'm sorry, I didn't mean-"

His head fell back and he set into a slow, rhythmic sob. His mouth open, his sobs became a soft whine as his body fell into a cross-legged sitting position. His fingers clawed half-heartedly at his face as he doubled over, his torso collapsing onto his lap. His shoulders rocked up and down as he quietly whimpered onto his shins.

Hollo stared at him, not knowing what to say, not having the slightest idea what would have set him off, if not simply that for the first time in a very long time had he been able to stop laughing.

"Is he hurt?" Ali asked tentatively.

"I don't think so," Hollo whispered. "I think, maybe he's just worn out. Imagine having to laugh your head off for years and years, and then finally stop. I might cry too. Maybe let's just leave him alone." She ushered Ali away, deeper into the overgrowth, towards the fountain. One last look over her shoulder found the Laughing Man immersed in his silent wailing. He needed time, she knew, then maybe she would know what ailed him so.

Once out of sight, the two girls found themselves in the presence of a smaller statue, Hollo's favorite. He sat with his head resting on his palms, staring at the fountain before him. His body was that of a young schoolboy, though his head and lipless smile was that of a frog, a young frog wearing a newsboy hat on his enormous, amphibious head.

Hollo went to work with the first rhyme she had ever made, the rhyme that had brought Timtree to life years ago. "Tiny toad, stand and play. Hop to your feet on this fine summer day."

The frog-boy yawned wide, sticking out his tongue and blushing as a tiny ribbit escaped him. "S'cuse me," he smiled up at them. "Hiya Hollo."

"Hi Timtree," she said. "Meet my friend Ali."

"Hiya Ali," he said. "You're friends with Hollo, too?"

Ali nodded.

"Why are you so pale," he asked, eyeing her up and down. "What are you made of?"

Ali was without words for this. Her light bronze skin had never been called 'pale' before.

"She's a human girl," Hollo explained. "Like the men that made you, and the one who made me. She's made of flesh."

"Oh," Timtree said in wonderment. "Wow, you're much darker than Chester, how different."

"Different?" Ali chuckled nervously. "I guess so."

"Don't worry," Timtree said with a wink. "There's people made of all sorts of things in my garden."

"This is Timtree's garden," Hollo explained.

"Sure is," Timtree said with a proud smile. "I've been here longer than anyone. Chester calls me his little froggy son. Chester is the boss, you see, the one who made me. He says I look just like his wife, and that's why he won't sell me," he grinned happily, and Ali quickly turned her laughter into a nervous cough.

Timtree straightened, turning his head as a sob caught his attention. "Oh, you woke up the Prince, huh? Well he'll be going on like that for some time, don't pay him any attention."

"How do you know?" Hollo asked. "I've never brought him out before, how've you seen him like that?"

Timtree nodded mysteriously. "We see more than you'd think, statues, if we've been around long enough. C'mon," He said, beckoning them. "There's loads of stuff to tell you since you came over last."

"Oh?" Hollo said. "Like what?"

Timtree's eyelids fluttered as he noticed the darkened workshop that he led them towards. "Oh," he seemed downcast. "They're not here, that means Falermeyer must still be gone."

"Kit?" Ali asked.

Timtree nodded absently, having caught sight of the bronze Knight and the Countess.

"The statues are restless," he observed. "Usually they'd have gone back to sleep by now."

"Sorry," Hollo said. "I didn't think I made it so strong. How do I undo it?"

"No, it's not your fault," Timtree said. "There's more magic in us than just yours. Kit helped make us. He's not actually very good at his job, so he cheats. Uses magic when Chester isn't looking. We feel it, his magic, and we can't sleep when he's running wild. I'll put us all away, you don't need to worry, and I've done it a lot. The Prince used to wake up all the time when Falermeyer started riding his horse. That was before either of them," he pointed at the flirting pair on the bench. "Used to just be the two of us, now we've a whole garden of us who Falermeyer wakes up when he's upset."

"He wakes you up?" Hollo asked.

Timtree nodded energetically. "Yup, when he's upset, but I don't think he means to. The statues start to stir and get restless whenever he's hunting that man."

Hollo's sense of danger tickled her throat. "Why is he upset, what is he doing?"

Timtree hung his head, losing his excitement. "I'll tell you, but only if you promise not to try and stop him… he has a temper. Chester doesn't know what to do without him. He closed the shop up, dunno if he's looking for someone else to hire or what. Without a goodbye, nothing."

"What do you mean?" Hollo persisted. "Where is he?"

"Gone," Timtree muttered sadly. "He quit working here, and then he disappeared."

Chapter Twelve
Hunting the Hunter

A large portion of flesh slammed onto the table in front of him, and a blade, a horrible cross between a knife and an axe, raised up over his head. Bile rose in his throat as he followed the bloody thing through the air and into the overlarge lump of meat.

"Cleanly through the bone, else we don't sell it," the man said. "Shattered bones mean a harder haggle, and folks are keen on talking the price down."

The blade flicked up towards Kit's chest as he nodded his understanding, afraid to open his mouth for fear of losing his breakfast. Eating the Pig'n'Bowl had been a mistake that morning. The meat of pigs was quickly losing its appeal to him.

"You do it now, strong boy. Blacksmith arms like yours should prove useful," the man said.

"Not a blacksmith," Kit corrected under his breath. "Doesn't matter, yeah, I can do it."

The mustached man nodded fervently while scratching his cheek and leaving smudges of bloody fingers through the hairs. Kit shivered a little, positioned the rack of ribs, and swung the heavy blade down into the table. The man, having no fear for his fingers grabbed the cut meat in the blink of an eye as Kit finished his swing. He examined it from all angles before throwing it back to the table, causing another fleck of blood to fly into his moustache.

"Good money," the man winked at Kit. "If you can stomach the work. Man's work. You'll get the hang of it."

Kit nodded, and watched the man chew thoughtfully on the hairs below his bottom lip. Mesmerized, Kit thought to point out the blood in the hairs, but before he could, the man's tongue probed up thoughtfully into his oversized moustache. If the butcher tasted it, he did not have any reaction, only looked confused as the sound of retching drew his attention back to Kit, who had dropped the knife on the table and thrown himself down to the metal grate in the stone street nearby, losing his breakfast into the sticky red drain.

Nearby vendors in the pig merchant's alley shared a laugh as they pointed at him. Kit wiped his face on his sleeve, keeping his eyes down to the ground and reddening as the titters of laughter mocked him.

"Time for a break," his employer said irritably. Kit was lifted forcefully up to his feet and pushed towards the cart behind the butchering table. The man shoved him into the seat of the cart and without words left him there and returned to his table to call back the customers who had been scattered away by Kit's display. In order to court their business again, the man held up a dripping hunk of flank, and at high volume, related the quality of it to those who now sought their meat elsewhere.

Kit rested his head against the wood cart and stared upward in frustration. A butcher's life was not for him, though necessary for the time being. Not much longer, he hoped. Another whole morning wasted in this foul place, and still there was no sign of the Practitioners. He was losing hope that anyone was coming for the statue after all. He thought his plan foolproof, that of course the Practitioners would come to collect the statue of the man named Carr, but his initial excitement had since deflated. It was only just occurring to him the consequence of leaving his job in order to post himself in the pig-merchant's alley. If the Practitioners didn't come to collect the statue, Kit would be forced to beg Chester to take him back, or else remain a butcher's assistant. The thought nauseated him.

How, he wondered, could they not have heard by now? The story was everywhere. The man named Carr chased two girls through the market, and in a display of the strangest magic anyone had ever heard of, the stones, right in front of everyone, and in broad daylight, swallowed up the man.

So why had no one come? Kit grated his teeth as he gazed down the alleyway, where from this distance he could make out the grey stone man beyond the tents. Soon he might have to abandon this plan, and resume his attempts to bait the Practitioners into revealing themselves. But after two years of trying to provoke them into emerging from the shadows, he still had nothing to show for his efforts. Not even his display as the Black Rider had seemed to merit a response.

He had just decided it was probably time for him to get back to work, when he heard the clomping hooves. At that moment, he felt movement in his leg pocket; it felt like something alive. He opened his trouser pocket, not finding a mouse as his imagination had expected, but instead a little, round ball of metal. It had mysteriously appeared in his pocket the night before he met Hollo. He wasn't sure, but he suspected it had come from Fredric. When dealing with Fredric, he had learned not to be terribly surprised by things, so returned his attention to the street and saw a pair of small horses pulling a low wagon through the alley. The commotion had gathered a crowd.

"Think it's them, Smally Ball?" he asked. The ball bounced as if in response. "That why you're bouncing around isn't it? Be useful if you could spot magic, maybe Fred did give me a going away present before he smoke-poofed.

Keeping his eye on the wagon, he saw the occupants were just ordinary men. "They sure don't look like Magickers…"

Several men rode in the back of the wagon, appearing unofficial, not at all like what Kit thought The Practitioners of King Haddard might look like. The one at the front of the cart guiding the beasts forward, though, maybe he could be one…

Chapter Twelve

the way he pushed his way through the crowd with such an air of overblown self-importance seemed pretty Practitioner-ish to Kit.

As the men neared the statue the round metal pushed itself harder against Kit's leg. He was on his feet in the cart now, staring eagerly at the men along with everyone else. The cart halted right in front of the statue. Kit had to resist the temptation to jump in the air and whoop with joy. The butcher, meanwhile, was busy arguing about the mastery of his meat cutting with some buyer, so Kit used the moment to slip out of sight. All the years of waiting for the Practitioners to give him a lead had finally, finally paid off.

. . .

Timtree and Ali scooted themselves closer together as Hollo ran back outside with her father's book held against her chest.

"You're sure they don't need looking after?" Hollo asked, craning her neck to check on the adult statues in the neighboring garden. Timtree nodded energetically, waiting expectantly for her to open the book.

"What about the Laughing Man?"

Timtree glanced unconcernedly behind him, spying the sobbing statue wandering in circles and rubbing his cheeks in anguish. "Meh, he's fine. He doesn't go very far, just paces around. C'mon, I wanna hear the story."

Ali seized the book from Hollo, and her and Timtree brushed their way through the pages at high speed.

"Be careful with it," Hollo cautioned as they flipped faster and faster through the pages.

"Here it is!" Ali squealed. "Listen to this. 'The Black Rider', I told you Kit would be in here, too."

Hollo twisted her head in an effort to read upside down as Ali and Timtree buried their heads together.

"You really think the story will help us bring him back?"

"Dunno," Ali said. "Worth finding out. Okay, I'll read it to you, so listen."

Timtree rested his chin on his hands again.

"The Black Rider," she read.

"This feels wrong," Hollo said softly, before they started. "I don't think we should."

"Why not?" Timtree and Ali said as one.

Hollo looked across the page, running a hand over the drawing of a young boy, tears streaming down his face, and riding a shining metal horse through a field of barley grass. She thought Kit-Falermeyer might be angry if they read his story without permission. Hollo reasoned further that if it was true that most people's magic came about with difficulty, then she the tears on his face were none of their business.

"It's private," Hollo answered. "Kit wouldn't like us prying into his past, right? This is sneaky. We should ask him first."

Timtree and Ali looked miserable, their eyes crinkling into a pleading sort of preparation to cry.

"Don't look at me like that," Hollo grumbled, pulling the book out of Ali's hands. "Imagine it was Kit sitting here, and he got to read all about you and all the sad things that have happened to you."

Ali's cheeks flushed and her expression changed. Hollo looked again at the picture. "I'll bet this story tells what happened to his parents."

Ali let out a sigh. "Well then how else do we look for him?"

"I dunno, but not like this," Hollo said. "If we want to find Kit, we'd have to find Amit. That's who Kit's chasing. Knowing his secrets won't help us get him back, it would only push him farther away."

.   .   .

Kit was farther from home than he'd been in a very long time. Crowds of people his own age milled about at the edge of a park in the north of the city, close to the municipal center of the Artisan District. Children of wealthy families were determinedly enjoying the summer, despite the clouds and light rain. As usual, the younger children tagged along after their older siblings, making their presence known by splashing puddles and screaming their off-key delight into the faces of the older children, who did what they could to ignore them and enjoy their own friends.

Even the young children, muddy as they were, appeared better dressed than Kit-Falermeyer, whose own style of messy laborer's garments was sorely out of place here on the wealthy side of town. At first he had kept out of sight, trailing the wagon that carried the statue of the man Carr, but he finally realized that to the wealthy a poorly dressed artisan such as himself was utterly invisible. Creeping around served no purpose and was exhausting. He had almost laughed as he realized this, though the insult of their attitude kept his delight in check. He walked among them openly, even brushing himself 'accidentally' into a pretty girl every now and again, just for the reaction it drew.

"Pardon miss," he said good-naturedly to a particularly young girl who turned deeply red as she spun around to confront him. "Didn't mean to tap your bottom like that, very rude of me, daresay I'm happy I did though. What's your name, eh?"

The silently blushing girl's friends took an immediate liking to the rogue, asking him questions without pause and chatting about him amongst themselves. While they did this Kit became distracted as a well-dressed man wielding a gentleman's cane sauntered briskly past him. The older man surprised him not so much because he was out of place amidst the throngs of youth, but because of the girl on his arm. Though her face was caked with a powdery makeup, Kit could tell that she had a swollen lip and black eye. No one else seemed to notice this at all, but Kit followed the odd couple with his eyes. The girl's hair was an intriguing collaboration of faded red and straw blond and it stood out against the black of her coat.

"Ouch!" he yelped, reaching into his pocket to feel Smally Ball inside. It was suddenly very hot. "What the-" he mumbled, sucking on his finger and elbowing his way past the group of girls, forgetting they were still speaking to him. He had, without thinking, started to followed the pair, and before he realized what he was doing, crossed the street and nearly caught up to the white-haired gentleman and his young battered escort.

He checked himself, remembering his purpose just in time to see the statue disappear through a gate at the bottom of the lane. To his astonishment, Kit observed the white-haired man guide the girl on his arm through the same gate. He caught up and, peeking carefully, found it remained open and unguarded. Beyond it, twenty yards removed from the street stood the front door of a very large and very old stone structure. One wall was dilapidated beyond repair, while another bulged outward, the dust of crumbling mortar everywhere. If this was a hideout, it was a good one, and guards would have merely made it obvious.

Kit moved casually forward, stuffing his hands into his pockets, and sauntering around like a curious, lost young scamp. If he was seen, this was always his alibi - "Jus' lookin' 'round," he rehearsed in his mind. "Cool old building, bye now!"

"Ouch!" he yelped as the object in his pocket burned him once again. "Look, little bally, if you can't stop doing that I'm leaving you behind." He took another step forward, and instead of cooling back down the ball changed color, the gold metal glowing so brightly he could see the light through the cloth of his pocket. Then, with uncanny swiftness, it cooled down and snuggled in as if having gone to sleep.

"What was that?" he asked of it. "A tantrum?" He began to laugh but then smelled smoke, and, reaching up to his head, found tiny bits of his hair had burned off, and a little dust darkened his hand. He realized what had just happened, he had just moved through a magic barrier and it was Smally Ball's magic that had helped Kit pass through it.

"So it's just like Hollo's house. There's a big invisible wall here, too, eh? You clever little bally you!" he removed it from his trouser pocket and grinned at it. "You get to ride up here in the front with me now," he praised, and tucked it into his breast pocket. "Give us a heads up if anything else wants to kill me, yeah?

Cautiously, he poked his head up to a window and saw only dark rooms covered in dust and long since uninhabited. There were no guards or sentries that he could see, no lights, nor any movement at all. He wasn't brave enough to simply let himself in the front door but there was a stone staircase on the side of the building and that seemed the wiser option.

"Hey," he said to Smally Ball, keeping his voice to a whisper and remaining hunched as he ran. "You were in my pocket at Hollo's place and the house barrier blasted me through the air. Why didn't you help me then?"

The ball, by nature, said nothing.

"I'll assume you had a good reason not to bust through that one," Kit muttered. "Cause if it's just your sense of humor, little bally, we shan't be friends for long."

Around the side of the building there was a small, stained-glass window. It was impossible to see through, and its ancient, rusted hinges refused to obey him. He ducked quickly as the wagon rounded the corner beneath him, past the bottom of the stairs. He saw the wagon was empty and a tingle of excitement gripped him. The Practitioners were definitely here somewhere; they had to be. Now he just had to find them. Hopefully before they noticed him.

He found a window with a large clear piece of glass in its center that was clean enough to see through. Inside was a large high-ceilinged main hall, and standing in the center of it, his mouth curled in a smile, was the very same cane-wielding man and the girl who hung on his arm. Kit moved up to his tiptoes and saw the heads of people at desks staring at the white-haired man. Kit's effort hadn't been wasted. He wanted to cheer, but checked his excitement by reminding himself just how close to danger he stood, just barely out of their reach.

The white haired man was speaking, addressing the rest of them and pointing to the girl at his side who remained listless. Kit left his window in search of another, better vantage point. One window after another was worse than the last, but by the time he reached the far end of the wall, the last stained window had been cracked open some many decades ago and since rusted into place. Sliding his fingers into the gap, he pried ever so gently, biting his tongue at every rusty whine of the hinges until he had enough space to peek one eye and an ear inside.

"We didn't ask you to," came a voice inside, echoing around the hard walls. "Don't bring them here, we don't want to know what you do with the ones you catch."

Kit gulped as he saw that the Practitioner was pointing at the red-haired girl. "Caught?" he whispered, slowly putting the pieces together. "Hey, little ball," he whispered. "Change of plans." This girl wasn't the man's granddaughter or ward, as Kit had assumed. It looked like she was a prisoner, and if that was true, then the man beside her could only be one person.

"Bander-Clou," Kit hissed through his teeth, banging his knuckles against the stone in irritation. He couldn't properly hear what they were saying from where he was, but he doubted he could get any closer, not without a fight anyway. He knew he could find metal if he needed to defend himself, and he knew that he could hold his own against the Practitioners within city streets or even small corridors, but this large room was different. He was at a terrible disadvantage in a big space full of dangerous men and women such as these. If he ended up in a fight, he'd have to first lure them into smaller groups, and somehow get the girl out of harm's way.

While he was trying to decide how to go about this, an argument broke out in the hall, but the echoes twisted the words. Bander-Clou had a stern finger raised accusingly at the nearest Practitioner. In what appeared to be a huff of outrage, he then stormed out the door towards the courtyard, pointing at them and insisting they remain in their seats and leave him be. The Practitioners shook their heads as they turned back amongst themselves to speak quieter. They were apparently perplexed by whatever Bander-Clou had said in his fury, and hadn't noticed what Kit had noticed. The girl remained standing silently where he'd left her, and swayed in place very slightly, as if in some kind of stupor. More importantly, there was the tiniest glint of light that beaded out of her, following the man as he stormed out the door. It was a blue thread so faint that in the light of their desk lanterns none of the Practitioners appeared able to see it. But Kit saw it, and he saw it disappear as the sound of a heavy door thudded behind Bander-Clou. The Practitioner's heads turned suddenly and, in unison, towards the door. A noise on the other side had drawn their attention. The nearest Practitioner approached it, and once he realized that it was locked, began throwing his body against the wood. Another Practitioner rolled his sleeves up and gestured for him to move away. A spark of fire rose in his hands, small at first, but it grew from a flicker into a flame. Kit remained staring at the redheaded girl. A sense of dread rose in him as he watched her regain whatever clarity Bander-Clou's thread had taken from her on their way here. He knew that the Practitioners would notice this in a moment, and once they did, they would have to deal with their prisoner. As far as Kit knew, there was only one way that Practitioners dealt with captured Hermetics.

"Damn," Kit whispered, seeing how she, by the look on her face, was quickly realizing where she was. "Damn!" Kit snarled as he slammed his fist into the wall before sprinting along the rampart. If the girl came to, she'd be in deep trouble, and for some reason, Kit couldn't stand the thought. He rounded around a corner into the back of the building, all secrecy forgotten, and sped down the stairs. Halfway to the ground floor, he froze in his tracks. Below him was the door, and holding the door shut was something Kit had not seen since he was but a boy. The hard, inhumanly powerful arms of a faceless, clockwork man held the door closed. Kit was lost for a moment, torn between his desperation to help the girl, and this sudden unexpected obstacle. As shocked as he was, what he noticed next surprised him even more. There was water coming from under the door, running over the puppet's feet., and to his astonishment, he suddenly felt water run over his own feet. It was cascading down from the top of the stairs. He looked up and saw water pouring out of the cracked window above him, at the top of the stairs water was pouring out of the cracked window and flooding the walkway, the stairs, and running down into the marble courtyard.

It was there in the center of the marble courtyard the grey, stone statue of the man Carr stood. At its base, not forty paces from Kit, was Bander-Clou, and the man's eyes were fixed on Kit, who suddenly didn't dare to move. His face became the portrait of a child caught in the midst of wrongdoing while Bander-Clou leveled silent accusation at him. Their eyes remained locked for a long moment, until Bander-Clou's eyes broke their hold on him and shifted to whatever was over Kit's shoulder. At that moment the sound of faint tapping caught his attention. The beautiful stained-glass window behind Kit displayed a vast panorama of colors, but it was in one of the clear, unstained pieces that Kit saw what the sound of tapping was. A man's face was there, ten feet from the floor, bubbles spraying from his mouth. The drowning man was shouting and banging on the window, scratching and clawing at the glass and looking, it seemed, at Kit, who stood level with him.

The cracking of the glass drew Kit back to his body just as the last bubbles of life left the man. A deep crack split the reds and greens of the stained glass, and as Kit turned to run, it exploded from its frame and a wave of cold sea-water engulfed him. He tumbled, half noticing his body collide with the wooden puppet below. The door was freed to burst outward and another cascade of salt water pushed him away from the building and carried him into the courtyard, to the feet of the man Kit had come to kill. The dark puppet-master Bander-Clou stood waiting, irritated now by the wetness of his socks.

Chapter Thirteen
Reflections of the Mirror Man

A boom of thunder startled them, though none as much as Ali who jerked the open book shut as she flinched, looking up at the sky in fear. "Let's go inside," she said quietly.

Timtree looked sad, but nodded. "I have to go home, anyway. I'll put us all to bed, come visit me soon, okay? If you find Kit make him come home, too, will ya?"

Hollo and Ali nodded, and hurried inside as light rain darkened the bare soil. They set themselves in an armchair in the kitchen room, opening the book across their laps.

"Do you think Amit is in here, too?" Ali asked.

"Probably," Hollo replied.

"And maybe your dad?"

"Might be," she agreed.

They searched the book for some time, reading titles aloud to each other before settling on the Forward. The beginning of which read as such:

Magic.

I can't explain it in reliable accuracy, because the fact remains that we understand it very little.

I will, unlike those before me, neither define the mechanisms of our power, nor argue the reasons it may or may not be. Instead I will, in this collection of stories, attempt to uncover a greater truth about magic simply by examining the nature of its components.

The following essay is titled "A History of Zygotic Pneuma", as we who study the phenomenonology of human beings, or 'Pnuema', call the magically predisposed. Alternatively, you may understand the title as "A History of Magic."

Hollo drew the book closer, a ripple of curiosity shaking her hands. "What is that word, 'Pneuma'…Amit called me a 'Zygotic Pneuma' that night I went in Dad's door."

"What's a Zygotic Pneuma?" Ali asked, but Hollo was already reading to herself, and didn't reply. Ali remained politely silent while Hollo read and reread the Forward, which was less of a story and more of a historic essay.

"This part," Hollo said. "It says that Dinna-Nayla was a wolf man. That his Zygotic Pneuma was what made him a wolf, listen," she read:

Dinna-Nayla is commonly regarded as the first Hermetic man. Though he was not the first person capable of magic, he is known as the first Hermetic man due to the fact that he was the most famous

Zygotic to choose a life in hiding. The famous story of Dinna-Nayla, or as he was more widely known, 'The Wolf Man', explains why this was, but one must first understand the nature of how his unusual gift came about.

"I though you were born with it," Ali said. "You either could do magic or you couldn't. When did you find out yours?"

Hollo frowned. "I was always just like dad. But, I guess most people it happens later."

"What about The Lightning Man?"

Hollo shrugged. "Don't know if he's real or not."

"But he was born with his thunderstorms, wasn't he?" Ali scooted closer and read the text from over her shoulder:

Sometimes, and usually as a result of some trauma in a person's life, a soul fragments into two: The original spirit, known as a Pneuma, and the fractured piece of it called a Pneumatic Compartment.

Ali frowned at Hollo. "Is that what happened to you?"

Hollo shrugged, and Ali continued to read:

What we think we know about this extraordinary phenomenon is that when a Zygotic Pneuma is broken into two, the new shard embodies a new purpose (separate from generating a human being). In situations of great trauma, that purpose usually means the difference between that person's life and death.

Hollo shook her head. "That wasn't how I was born," she said. "I was born in the attic. Nothing bad happened."

Ali ignored her and moved to the next page:

A perfect example is found in the story of Dinna-Nayla. As a young child, he became lost in the woods. Here he was happened upon by a pack of wolves that saw him as a meal. The fearful Pneuma inside of the young Dinna-Nayla, amidst the horror of being devoured, separated, and he became, himself, a wolf.

"So anyone can be magic?" Ali asked, her eyes lighting up. "You never know?"

Hollo continued where Ali had stopped.

At the time of Dinna-Nayla's story, there were already other people with known magical power. There were even people who had attained extraordinary celebrity because of their gift, such as Kaben-Kon, 'The Speaker', also known as 'The Huntress', who was the gamekeeper for the royal family's estate. Her ability to speak with animals garnered her a well-respected place in society, and favor with the royal family. It was this lady-huntress who was elected to uncover the truth behind the stories of the wolf man in the forests. Kaben-Kon found the adult Dinna-Nayla living in a cave deep in the woods, and after speaking to him, ended up killing him.

Another point worth explaining is that the body she returned with was that of a wolf, as Dinna-Nayla had long since been overcome by his magic and his humanity was squandered. Such is the nature of a Zygotic Pneuma. Had his gift been with stone he might have been petrified, had it been with sight, he might have gone blind. When too much of a person's soul is consumed by their new Pneumatic identity, the result is their entrapment.

This incident between The Huntress and The Wolf Man sparked the beginning of what would later escalate into the extermination of radical Zygotics. Those who had already suffered the bereavement of a soul split in two soon faced *decades forced into hiding. However, those whose magic served the monarchy suffered no consequence. These individuals later became an official organization titled 'The Practitioners of King Haddard', whose job was to monitor and tax unlawful magic, and to imprison criminal Zygotics. Historically however, those who practiced magic outside of the law were executed by flame.*

"Isn't that what Kit said happened to his parents?" Ali whispered. "He said they burned."

"He said it was Amit who burned them though, remember" Hollo said. "This was a long time before Amit."

"Doesn't seem like much has changed," Ali said. "if people are still being punished."

"That's why they hide," Hollo said. "That's why my dad and I hid; and why Mr. Packerd did, too. He didn't do magic at all. And Dad only did when he was safe at home."

"What about the man Amit, who attacked you and your dad? Isn't he old? Isn't he using so much magic?"

"It says something about that," Hollo skipped a page and pointed at the last paragraph. Ali took it upon herself to read it, and shifted the book onto her own lap.

Tremendous effort had been exhausted in the study of mending the broken Pneuma to its original whole. Of all the work done, the efforts of the Puppet Master Bander-Clou are regarded as the most successful, and most vile. His work attempted to cage the Zygotic Pneuma in what he labeled a 'Zygotic Stone'.

The Zygotic Stone is a device created to control, and thus belay, or even altogether halt the eventual squandering of the person's life. This work he did was carried out on countless individuals who he incarcerated under the guise of a servant of The Practitioners.

Bander-Clou's work was ended when the Practitioners he served sought entrance to the prison Bander-Clou solely operated, and found instead a graveyard. This prison and its prisoners were used by Bander-Clou in his fabrication of mindless, mechanical servants. Though his work was not allowed to finish, this practice of caging souls was his first step towards mending a Zygotic Pnuema, by moving it into an impervious type of body. In theory, this would allow one to escape the inevitable price of the magic drawing the life out of you, and perhaps even avoiding human mortality altogether. The theory remains unproven, and among Practitioners and Hermetics it is widely believed that, like many before him,

Bander-Clou met his own end by his own hands,

and was consumed by the magic he crafted.

The girls sat in silence for a long while, and Ali chewed on her fingernail as they pondered the information. "So, using magic hurts you," she whispered, sounding deeply perplexed. "Right? They couldn't do magic anymore because they were getting old. So what about Kit? He does so much, will he turn into metal one day?"

"And what about Amit?" Hollo added. "My dad wrote it that he was dead, but he isn't. He's already old, why hasn't he turned to wood like…" she trailed off into silence. She was recalling her father's face, how his skin turned hard, how his fingers dried up into hands made of wood. And then a horrible thought occurred to her. Her father didn't use his magic, not more than he had to. But what about that white door he had made for her to slip through, that enormous, hot power that had saved her? Had it killed him? And hadn't he originally created her with magic just as enormous? Was it because of her that Fredric's body had at last been overcome by the cost of his own use of magic?

Hollo grabbed the book, whipping through the pages.

"Hollo," Ali asked gently. She ignored her, and continued to scan titles over and over again. When she reached the end of the stories she started again from the beginning, reading the titles aloud, frustration growing in her voice.

"Hands of the Sea, The Black Rider, The Lightning Man, where is it, why isn't it in here!?" she shrieked. "Why isn't my dad in here!? Where's his story!"

"Hollo," Ali probed again, concerned.

"I have to know," Hollo raced, still flipping pages. "His story would tell me, I have to know why he did it, why he made me. Why would he do that, if it meant being eaten by his magic!?" Hollo threw the book to the floor and her head fell onto the armrest where she lay, numb. "My dad," Hollo whispered, more to herself than to Ali. "My dad is dead."

She only half heard Ali beside her reasoning against it, saying that it wasn't true. But Hollo knew it was true. She understood how she was made, how she came to be alive. Her father had given her a soul, a piece of himself, half his heart; and still, she could not figure out why. What she did know, was that in the end, he had been left without enough to live.

"I'm a puppet," she whispered. "I'm a broken bit of heart. I'm half of my dad, and he's dead now, and gone forever."

"I'm half of my dad, too," Ali said reasonably. "And he's dead and gone, too."

"But what am I?" Hollo said so softly, not wanting the words to come out of her mouth for fear of hearing an answer.

"My friend," Ali said with fierce conviction. "You're my friend. You're Hollo, and nothing else makes any difference." Hollo buried her face in her hands, sinking into their blanket and Ali's enfolding arms. With her friend beside her, Hollo was able to hold on.

. . .

Coughing and gagging, his limbs were on fire where the torrent of shattered glass had swept around him. His clothing was soaked, and the sting of salt was on his lips and in his cuts, and he had almost reached his feet when hard wooden arms crushed around him. He let out a moan of pain as the puppet squeezed him into submission and held him still. A splash of feet made him twist around in the grasp of his captor, and there he saw Eferee staggering out of the building. Her teeth were bared in a mad snarl at Bander-Clou, who remained facing away from her, while casually running his fingers over the smooth statue.

"You'll need a wagon," Bander-Clou said loudly to the girl without turning. "You've a great many heads to load on to your boat."

She said nothing, but Kit saw her falter in her advance as her legs grew weak. She knelt, struggling to remain conscious.

"I'll bet you're exhausted," Bander-Clou continued. "So much strength you have, but alas, such a frail little girl you are."

The man turned his head to Kit, and he smiled at the boy. "You know, all she wanted was to collect the bounty on those

Practitioners, and now that I've given that to her she's still angry at me. Selfish and greedy, don't you think?"

Kit's face darkened at the man, who only shrugged and began to pace around the statue.

"I'm not your weapon," Eferee growled, nearly too quiet to hear. Her breathing was labored, and her eyelids fluttered. Kit struggled uselessly with the arms that held him, trying to reach her, to help the girl.

"Not *my* weapon," Amit admitted. "But you are *a* weapon, certainly. Everyone is a weapon, honed to kill and conquer anything weaker. Take this statue, for instance." He continued to stroke the statue, Carr, as he spoke. "I think he'll be quite pleased with being allowed to be a weapon once more."

Eferee forced herself up again, and raised a hand forward that immediately dripped with a briny moisture. Amit turned quickly away from the statue as he sensed this, and flicked his cane hard into the girl's wrist. He planted his boot against her chest and kicked her off her feet.

"Don't touch her!" Kit screamed at Bander-Clou's back.

"Oh?" The man seemed amused. "Do you know her?"

Kit did not, but that wasn't the point. "Get you're murdering hands off her," he hissed and clenched his fist, drawing on the metal behind him. The wooden man that held him was torn apart as Kit wrestled the iron out of its body and into his own hand. The pieces twisted into a blade as the wooden remains of the puppet fell about him.

"Hmm," Bander-Clou mumbled, turning away from Eferee, and tapping his cane against the marble in a thoughtful way as he stared at the boy. "I feel like I must know you from somewhere. Or at least, you know me, do you?"

Kit's anger coursed throughout his body, running into his hand and the twisted blade he held.

"You seem to know my hands rather well, to accuse them of murder," Amit said with a smile, spreading his fingers towards Kit and taking a small step forward.

"You don't remember me," Kit said with his jaw fastened by hatred. "You've lost your knack for hunting, if you can't even spot a Hermetic who's slipped through your fingers."

"Enlighten me," Bander-Clou said, his tone reasonable, his cane tucked under his arm, and his hands the portrait of surrender. "Tell me who you are, or would you rather I guess?"

Kit opened his mouth to speak of his parents, to yell the words of execution to this man. But Bander-Clou cut him short as he nonchalantly turned away from him and said, "I seem to recall an angry, little boy who lost his way once upon a time." Bander-Clou spoke loudly, swinging his foot out and planting a firm kick into the stomach of Eferee, whose small body curled around the foot and gasped silently. Kit launched forward, his speech forgotten, only wanting to bury his metal into the back of the man. The cane swung a full circle and Kit's blade was struck clean out of his hand. A half-second later the cane reversed direction and bent across Kit's face and jaw. He didn't feel the impact of the ground, but opened his eyes to find himself staring at the sky.

"He got lost, and a kind old man bought him a cup of tea," Amit continued conversationally. "And the man helped the boy find his way home, and when they got there, the old man killed the boy's parents."

Kit's eyes filled with water as he stared into the dark clouds overhead. The tears pooled and became pink with blood.

"And even though the old man had rescued the little boy from criminals, the little boy couldn't stand the sight of my wooden puppet handling his mother's body as it was, and the little boy screamed out," Amit dug his heel into Kit's fingers and he gasped. "And the little boy said 'get your hands off her!' and then tore all the metal out of the wooden man. The boy raged and screamed and tore the metal from the fireplace, and lit the whole house on fire." Bander-Clou let his foot off, and Kit rolled to his side, holding his fingers and blinking the tears from his eyes.

"I needed their Pneuma, you idiot, but I'll have yours now. You know, I thought you were dead until I heard tell of a boy riding a noisy horse around the streets looking for me." He bent down to look Kit in the face. "Really, though. That was a bit heavy handed, don't you think? Like you're playing chess. Sending out the Knight to bait the Rook." He strode over to the statue, caressing it again. "People always liken warfare to games," he muttered, more to himself than to Kit. "As if clever tricks and games are what wins a war." Amit gave a cruel laugh. "I realized how foolish I had been, to leave you there and walk away. I knew Hor-Gauer was watching me through his mirrors. I should have known he would come to save you, but I didn't think of it. Do you have any idea!" He was suddenly shouting. "How frustrating it is to just barely miss your chance? Had I waited there, Hor-Gauer would have come running to pull you out of the fire, but instead I left. I disappoint myself sometimes…" He trailed off, losing himself in rumination. "I was hesitant to kill a child. But now I have you again," he whispered so that Kit couldn't hear him. "And you know where Hor-Gauer's house is, don't you… where his young little Zygote is hiding from me?" Bander-Clou gave a wicked smile. "She hiding from me behind a protection that weakens every day."

Kit reached a shaking hand to his face to dry his eyes so he could see once more. He faced Eferee, where she lay, trying to rise. Kit reached a hand out towards her, waving at her to stop, to lie back down and die if she could, or else Bander-Clou would rip out her soul as he undoubtedly planned to do to both of them. She ignored his and instead crawled silently, belly sliding along the ground until her hand reached Kit's sword. With laborious effort she threw it to him.

Kit nearly rolled his eyes at her, wanting to ask what she thought he was going to do with it, but her glaring eyes took a hold of his own, seeming to challenge him, to threaten him.

"Stand up or I'll kill you myself," the girl sneered.

Bander-Clou, who had already turned when he heard the sword clatter along the ground, now looked quite happy.

"Eferee, how lovely you're back. I almost expected you to be nothing more than a puddle by now."

Eferee gave a deep grunt of hatred as she came to her feet. Bander-Clou strode briskly towards her, and had almost reached her when she ran backwards, with water at her fingertips. Both her hands raised over her head before she brought them down, crashing into the ground. The impact was immediate and enormous, and where her palms slapped the stone a great detonation of water burst up and outwards. The overcast darkness grew darker in the square, as the high-flying water returned to the earth as a torrent of blinding rain.

The chill of icy water roused Kit, and the sting of salt in his cuts shocked his adrenals enough to get him up to his feet. His sword was in his hands and Amit was distracted, struggling to cough out the water that hit him in the face. His cane had been swept away, he was unarmed, blinded, and dazed. Kit ran as best he could with the blade beside him. Bander-Clou's blue threads shot out of his hands, whipping blindly through the air. Kit dodged them, staggering sideways out of reach as the thread flew past him.

"Bander-Clou," he grunted, a smile curling into his mouth as the man turned around in the haze of falling water, coughing and sputtering. Kit wanted to see his face, wanted to watch as the color went out of it. He raised his weapon up over his head as Bander-Clou was struck by the realization of what was about to happen.

"Dead men are always drawn to the ones who killed them!" Amit shouted, a small smile mirroring Kit's. "Did you know that?"

"You've haunted me long enough," Kit shouted back, swinging his blade downward.

Bander-Clou shook his head, appearing disappointed as he stared calmly back at Kit. Kit's arm had stopped, been completely arrested so suddenly that Kit hadn't immediately noticed that Bander-Clou wasn't dying as he had pictured him doing so. Rather, the man seemed in good spirits.

"I didn't mean *me*," Bander-Clou chided.

The blue threads Kit had evaded, found their true target in Carr and connected into every piece of the stone man, whose hand had halted Kit's swing and now squeezed his wrist until the blade dropped to the ground. The stone man curled his other hand into a fist and swung as Kit cringed, anticipating the blow that would kill him, but no blow came. After a beat, Kit looked up into the face of the stone giant, whose narrow eyes had opened in wild excitement. The powerful hands lifted Kit off the ground, up towards his face. The golem pressed his nose into the front of Kit's shirt, as if smelling him. Kit had only a moment to wonder what was going on, before Bander-Clou explained. "He's caught the scent," he said, his blue eyes sparkling with equal excitement.

Kit struggled to speak and feign ignorance even though he knew exactly what had just become the consequence of his capture. The giant held him aloft, turning him this way and that in the air, smelling his clothes with fervor, becoming increasingly more excited as he did so. Kit fought the hands, though the weight and strength of the stone outmatched his own. Bander-Clou's threads faded from the man, but Carr's excitement stayed the same. He dropped Kit to the ground, where the boy crumbled, unable to stand.

"Death has a way of changing people," Bander-Clou said as he watched the man go. Blue threads came out of his hands and buried into the broken remnants of his clockwork puppet. The body lifted off the ground, the broken pieces of wood and metal reforming, including the sword beside Kit that leapt up to rejoin the construct. The remade puppet pulled Eferee's body off the ground and laid her over his shoulder.

"We'll save her for later," Bander-Clou smiled disarmingly at Kit. "But you, you we will enjoy right now."

Kit was helpless, and barely managed a flinch as a blue thread struck him again in the middle of his forehead. A fountain of blue threads followed in a great cascade that looked like glowing water. These threads sank themselves into Kit's body and slowly, Kit was made to rise. He breathed softly, his chest moved so subtly that one might confuse him with a corpse.

Amit tilted his head slightly upward as a drop of rain fell on his nose. By the time he had raised his head up fully towards the sky, a great fall of rain came upon him, accompanied by a teasing, chill wind. The storm had reached them finally, and unleashed its power in full upon the city. His free hand reached upwards and he paused there for a long while. Turning towards the great stone building, his blue eyes glittered brighter, and his raised hand tensed. Threads poured out of his fingers, a cascade of them swam through the water at his feet and up the steps into the darkened hall, where the bodies of drowned men and women lay. There in the darkness, the broken furniture shook and danced, drawn from the wreckage of the room into the air, melding with the inner light of these people as it was drawn out of them. Cold blue light flickered out of the high shattered windowpanes.

Amit's hand relaxed and fell back to his side as he turned to Kit and said, "You see why the rules of chess are folly in warfare? Because there are never subtleties; there are weapons. Come now, my weapons, and show me your subtlety," he laughed.

Mechanical footsteps and grating joints echoed out of the stone building, and out of the dark doorway came the first clockwork soldier, halting footsteps approaching its master and the wooden man at his side who had Eferee over his shoulder. Dozens more followed out of the building, each one of them arriving before Amit as he stood in the downpour.

"The Practitioners shall be remembered," Amit said to himself. "But not as bureaucrats. They shall be remembered in the same way that monsters are recalled: by the light of campfires, and in the words of parents warning their children to behave."

He brushed the water off his face. "Tonight marks the end of the days when we hide away in fear of common people. We will march through the streets and the people will be made to know who the masters of this world are."

His right hand poised over Kit, he tugged the threads, forcing the boy into action. "Now march, my weapons, onward. And let the whole world see just how powerful you are."

Obediently Kit-Falermeyer marched deeper into the storm, south towards Casting Street, with dozens of wooden constructs at his back.

Chapter Fourteen
The Storm

The rain came hard, just as darkness fell over the Artisan District. Hollo and Ali settled themselves in the attic to weather the storm and to sleep, or at least to try and sleep. Coils of tea-steam rose around Ali's face, and a tiny rattle shook the cup in her hand with every boom of thunder. Seated in her window, Hollo searched the darkness overhead while counting the seconds between the flaring bolts of lightning and the thunder that followed it, but there were few. Never had she seen a storm like this so close to home, so directly above them. Counting the seconds had been fun in storms past, had lulled her to sleep when she would otherwise have been kept awake by the booming thunderclap. Tonight, however, there was no lull, no counting. The storm was upon them, above them, and it would not pass them by.

Wind whipped against the windowpane, shaking it without rhythm, and the freezing wind whistling through the cracks of it stung her limbs. Restless and awake, she leapt off her ledge, thinking perhaps that she would join Ali, and would curl into her bed as she never did in summertime.

Upon rolling off her ledge and down to the floor, Hollo found her bed empty. Hollo had been so intent on watching the sky that she hadn't seen her friend take refuge under the bed. The only hint of this was the edge of the blanket that poked out from under it.

"Ali?" Hollo asked softly, crouching down. A flash of light shone through the little window, and she spotted the girl, wrapped in the blanket with her eyes closed and her hands pressed hard over her ears. "Ali, what are you doing?" Hollo scooted herself along on her belly, slithering her way under the bed to join her, though did not understand fully what she was joining. The girl gave a start and opened her eyes as Hollo wrapped herself up in the blanket beside her.

"What's wrong?" Hollo asked.

Another flash of lightning and boom of thunder drew a terrified squeak from the girl, and Hollo put her arm around her.

"Remember the Lightning Man?" she asked, squeezing Ali firmly. "Tell me the story again."

Ali sniffed, and Hollo realized that her trembling wasn't due solely to fright, but that she was crying as well.

"I always think," Ali said. "After it stops raining, that was the last time I'd be afraid of lightning."

Hollo said nothing, but listened as Ali whimpered and choked on her words. "But every time, it's the same," she continued. "When it rained was when mumma died."

She trembled harder. Silently, Hollo held on with compassion.

"I was in bed," she whispered. "And I thought I heard them fighting, my mumma...and *him*. But the storm was loud and I wasn't sure. I was scared, I didn't know if the thunder was from the sky, or was him yelling. There was crashing, and breaking, and the lightning was bright. I kept saying to myself that it was the storm, and it'll pass, but it didn't. I was scared so I got out of bed and I walked out of my room, and...I saw him standing over her..." she shook and rocked back and forth, rocking Hollo with her. "I thought it was just the storm, but it wasn't the storm, it was him hurting her again, and she fell...and...storms always remind me of him."

The girls sat, hunched over in the small crawlspace as the thunder rolled mercilessly over their heads. Hollo hated the storm then, hated it for how it tormented Ali, and hated the man Carr for what he had done. Hollo thought to remind Ali that, at least, the man was dead, but the thought drew out emotions in herself that she decided would be unhelpful for Ali.

"Do you want more tea?" she asked quietly, having no idea what other comfort to offer her friend. Ali sniffed again, and nodded. Hollo took the cup from the bedside table, and hurried down the stairs towards the kitchen. The darkness of the house was easy to navigate, but it made her hesitant on the stairs all the same. Despite the thunder, the house gave her a chill feeling she was sure she'd never felt at home before. Halfway to the bottom of the last flight, she crouched down on the step. Her eyes couldn't see fully through the dark of the kitchen, but her sense of foreboding prompted her to listen. There was an ebb in the thunder, and the wind blew weaker now, and though it was certainly her imagination, Hollo had heard something that didn't belong to the storm. It was banging, like that of fists against wood. She sat there on the step, thinking of what Ali had said, thinking that her sad story had put fear into her mind that wasn't real.

Yet the sounds persisted.

Still seated, Hollo slid down the steps one by one, hearing the wind and the rain and the thunder, and still the furious knocking. She expected a voice to come with it, to announce the furious labor of someone at work outside, banging on the wooden wheel of a broken carriage, someone shouting for help to revive their carriage to be on their way out of the storm, but no voice or shouting came. The incessant drum of fists could be a tree, she told herself, but what a tree it would have to be to be heard over the wind. There was a chill in the air downstairs, a chill she never felt in this house before. The house never grew too very cold. There was her father's magic to help with that, the magic of her home. But this cold biting air was unusual, as if the magic of her home had gone away and left the air vacant.

There was no soothing warmth to her house now. There was only Hollo sitting in the darkness on her stairs, the beating of fists on her door and the chill air.

The chill intensified as a horribly loud rending of wood split through the night, followed by a whipping wind that blew up the sand all around her. A trail of light spread past the corner at the bottom of the stairs. She realized all in one confusing moment that the door, the impenetrable, shielded door to her house had been broken open. There was a pool of darkness in the midst of the light, where the wind had come in accompanied by a shadow, a shadow with shoulders and a head that stretched into the lighted space on the floor at the bottom of the stairs.

She didn't move, nor even breathe as the air around her dropped in temperature so rapidly that she knew a breath would freeze, and the cloud of it would flow past the wall that kept her hidden and it would float into the hall, and whoever stood there in the doorway would know she was there.

They can't come in, she told herself firmly. They can't walk through the barrier, not unless the house let's them. They can't come in without permission, and she was right. She could see an arm rise in the stage of shadows on the floor, an arm that appeared to reach forward, and a sparking sound like the fizzling of coals doused by water shot through the air. The arm had touched the barrier, and had been repelled. Slowly, carefully, Hollo rose to her feet, and with delicate steps, retraced her way backwards. With all the noise of the storm, she knew she couldn't be heard, but still she crept quietly. She could still see the shadow of the person in the doorway. She saw the person move quickly in a blur of shadows, and then a flash of light danced across the dining room floor that might have been lightning, or maybe the protective barrier that guarded her door. The house itself trembled.

Hollo turned and sprinted up the stairs as fast as her feet would carry her. She heard another impact; this one greater than before. The further sound of wood splintering announced that something else had broken, maybe the doorframe being blown inwards. Falling wood could be heard, pieces of the doorway and the door were being torn away, and whomever it was that wanted to come in was tearing their way past the barrier and into the house. Hollo shut her bedroom door, fumbling with the rusty old lock at the base of it that had never been used in her lifetime, though she didn't know why she was bothering with it, as if there was any use it would have in keeping them barricaded.

In the middle of the room, blanket forgotten, Ali knelt, her fear of thunder cast aside in light of the new sounds from the floors below. "Hollo," she hissed. "What's happening?"

"Someone's trying to get inside," she choked out.

"What? Who? They can't get through the door, right?"

"I don't know, I don't think so," she said, failing to keep the desperation from her voice.

"Someone's after us?" Ali asked helplessly. "And we're trapped up here!?"

Hollo thought to barricade the door, but looking around the room, she knew there was nothing that would stop that door opening, should the person find their way up to it. Silencing Ali's whimpering with her hand on her shoulder, she and Ali sat very still and listened hard. The thunder boomed overhead, but the sounds of the person at the door had faded.

"Please, please be gone," Hollo whispered, without meaning to. Her free hand, she realized, had wrapped itself up in her pocket where her string was kept. She held it for comfort, repeating her plea. "Please, please go away. No one can get through the door. Please."

Minutes passed, and Hollo began to hear the pulse of heartbeat, and realized that she was holding Ali too tight. Her hand relaxed and fell away, and the girls stared at the floorboards.

"How do we get out?" Ali asked, a tiny tremble ill-concealed.

Hard pounding came again before Hollo spoke, though this time from farther away downstairs, without the volume there was before. Hollo's eyes went wide as she heard a far away shout from a tiny voice she recognized from outside her attic window. She ran and leapt up to the ledge while Ali followed her, and a scream escaped the girl as Hollo flung the window open, blasting them both with wind and rain.

"Someone's at the backdoor!" Hollo screamed to Ali over the roar of thunder. A second later lightning illuminated not one, but four people, and not people, but dark statues.

"Hollo!" came the scream from below them. Timtree flailed his arms around, calling to her. "You have to come down! Kit is in trouble!" he shouted.

"Kit?" she said. She hadn't thought of Kit. He might be hurt, she realized; hurt and broken and pounding in vain for help. Hollo nearly fell off the window ledge in her scrambling to get to the door, shouting instructions to Ali over her shoulder. "Climb the rope down to them, I want to check something," she said hurriedly. "If someone is inside I'll follow you down the rope, but if it's Kit, I'll come unlock the back door for you."

Ali looked desperately at her, her eyes pleading with Hollo, but she gulped, nodded, and reached for the rope, trying to steady herself on the wet surface of the window ledge.

Hollo reached the metal hook at the bottom of her bedroom door, and spent another few seconds listening hard for noises of movement below her. She laid her ear against the wood, though the din from the open window made it useless. The only thing left to do was open the door and run, and so she reached for the handle and took a deep breath.

Her hand froze and she leapt away from it just an instant before the door was broken inward, knocking her to the side of the room. Ali froze in the window as she heard Hollo shriek. Wood rained inward around the ramming shoulder of the stone man. Ali's back arched in a feline way as her father's grey stone eyes faced her, froze her movements halfway out the window. He saw her escaping, and ran at her, while Ali remained stunned and cowering at the sight of her vengeful father.

"Ali!" Hollo bellowed, struggling under a piece of the broken door. Hearing Hollo's call brought Ali out of her freeze, allowing her to tumble out of the attic window a scant inch beyond the clutches of the stone fingers that followed her out into the open air. The windowsill splintered as Carr's stone body crushed down upon it. The wall caught him, though only just. Splinters rained again around the room as he ripped his arm out of the wooden hole of the broken window frame, and turned on Hollo.

She remembered then all the reasons the man had for blaming her for his daughter getting away, and Hollo knew that even though stone limited the man's expressions, he hated her with every mineral in his indestructible body.

She was nearer the door than he was, and more agile, and so she turned and ran with all the light and will of her body working to be faster than she ever had before. Out through the attic door and to the stairs, she catapulted herself over the rail and dropped down a flight lower. The bangs and impacts behind her told her that he was unable to take corners as well as she. Even though she fit easier down the tiny staircase, the thuds his stone weight made were just a few strides behind her. She knew that missing her footing would be lethal and could give him the opportunity to break her into a million, tiny pieces as painfully as he chose. She knew this and still she stumbled on the last step, landing on her back at the base of the stairs.

Carr leapt from the top of the landing, his purpose to crush her where she had fallen. Her mouth opened in surprise, not at him, but rather at the odd sensation that someone was tickling her foot. Could this be her spirit bursting out through her soles in the final instant before she met her death? For that last moment, while she watched his massive, stone feet aim at her chest, inexplicably, as if her mind had floated away, she thought of Mad King Had. Perhaps that was because the tiniest morsel of her awareness had seen the shadows on the walls come to life and felt the enlivening glow in the cracks of the floorboards.

Without thought or intent, Hollo's feet and hands found spaces between floorboards, which gave her purchase to propel herself to the side. Wooden shards flew past her as Carr's weight broke holes in the floor, imprisoning him long enough for Hollo to right herself and run for the back door. Before she reached for the handle, the door opened out into the rain.

She came tumbling out, and crashed hard into Timtree, who hurriedly dragged her away from the door.

"Wasn't that a stupendous catch!?" the Countess exclaimed, congratulating herself on having caught the terrified Ali as she had fallen from the attic. She was cradling Ali and awkwardly petting the poor girl's now sopping wet hair. "I should take up acrobatics! At least I would if those circus people weren't so illiterable and smelly!"

Hollo twisted around in Timtree's embrace to locate Carr and found him in the back doorway waylaid by the bronze Knight and the sobbing Laughing Man. They grappled with him, forcing him backwards into the house. Before he disappeared through the doorway, Hollo saw Carr's eyes searching the backyard through the blur of rain, hunting for his prey. When he saw Hollo, his arms flailed out at her before the two bronze men wrestled him inside. Paintings, walls, anything in their way was shattered as they forced him through the house and to the front door where they threw him down the stone steps and into the street.

As frightened as she was, Hollo felt compelled to follow along. She struggled out of Timtree's arms and ran tentatively in through the back door. With equal trepidation, the rest of the gang followed behind her.

When Hollo stepped out onto the front steps, she half expected a crowd of neighbors to have gathered having heard the commotion. But with the intense noise of the storm overhead, no one taking shelter indoors had any idea of what was happening on the street outside.

It was by the flare of lightning that Hollo and the others saw the stone man rising slowly out of the rainwater while the bronze Knight stood aver him, arms crossed and face set in military sternness. And only by the flash of lightning did Hollo then catch sight of a bystander. Where he had come from she did not know, but there he stood not forty feet from the animated men by her doorstep. A white haired man stood in the middle of the road, beneath the lightning, watching them intently.

Eventually they all saw him and one by one became still, wondering what this stranger planned to contribute to the conflict, if anything. Hollo could see now, after a terrified instant, that it was not Amit. He was tall, alarmingly so. A man well over six feet, who by any other circumstance should never walk out into a thunderstorm for fear of his life. There he stood in the road, illuminated by the rhythmic tolling of thunderous lightning overhead, and supporting himself on the copper staff he held with both hands. His weight leaned onto it as if he was an old person, someone whose legs weakened over time, though he was not old, despite his white hair. He was not young either, but rather looked of the age where roads grew a little longer, and strides grew a little slower, and when the weathering of your lifetime starts to appear on your face. His face, with its odd blue coloration, had all the weathering of a salt-crusted sailor, and simultaneously all the perplexed, uncertain recalcitrance of a teenager. By the law of averages, that put his age at an estimation of about forty-five, with a margin of error in the range of several decades.

A single step forward drew a purposeful uprightness into his shoulders, and he accentuated his presence by speaking. His words held all the same curiosity as his appearance. "Are you of the Mirror Man's construct?"

Carr looked wary of him, and confused by the question.

"Are you the guardian of this place?" the man spoke again, impatiently, angering quickly. "Speak you idiot, or is your jaw stone? Or is there no soft brain inside that thick head of yours?"

A terrible grating sound screeched through the night as Carr's stone teeth scraped together.

"No words then?" the man said. "How about you, metal soldiers? Do you guard the Mirror Man?"

The Knight brandished his sword. "We defend the young master. Whom you seek, I don't know. I'm not acquainted with such a man as one of Mirrors."

The man huffed out of his nose, a snort of irritation that sprayed water from his face. He took another stride forward, as lightning flashed overhead, immediately followed by deafening thunderclap.

"The master of this house, this house of mirrors that pretends to be empty, the man who wrote my story in his book of records. He knows of my coming. For you see, he invited me here."

It might have been the stress of the evening that had Hollo immediately believing the impossible, or it might have been her secret hope that her father would appear in the night to protect her, but either way Hollo hurried down the steps, past the bronze Knight and into the downpour. She caught the stranger's attention immediately, his dark countenance changing into surprise for a moment as she rushed out from the cover of the bronze statues.

Carr was quick to his feet, and faster than was possible for his weight, but he had seen his opportunity and intercepted her, bowling into the Knight and knocking him onto the ground while his large stone fingers fastened around Hollo's arm. Lifting her into the air, Hollo shrieked and struggled uselessly to free herself and reach this stranger with the white hair, this man who had appeared out of her father's book just when she needed him.

"Help me!" she pleaded at him, though he did not move, nor react. Ali now ran forward to rescue her friend, but stopped short as the stranger's discolored hand rose up, and lightning then struck into a nearby tree, setting it briefly to flame before it fell. The Laughing Man shooed Ali behind him, hiccupping and silently howling his agitation as he shielded her with his body.

Hollo redoubled her effort to free herself from Carr while calling out again, "You are the Lightning Man! I know you, I've read your story! My father wrote it, he wrote your story and I believe you!"

"The Mirror Man has a child?" the man said, aloud, but to himself in such a way that no one heard him say this. He raised his voice. "Then you are the master of this house?" he asked in his thunderous voice.

"Yes!" Hollo implored. "Please, help me!"

The Lightning Man's expression was unreadable while his eyes roved over the band of bronze statues, over Ali, and then onto Hollo, who fought ineffectually with the stone arms of her captor.

He started forward, slowly, keeping his eyes on Carr. "What are you here for?"

Carr pointed a hand out at Ali, who shrunk behind the Countess.

"Come here, girl," the Lightning Man said to her. "Come here if you want to help your friend."

"No!" Hollo shouted. "No don't!" Carr twisted her arm hard and she fell silent.

Ali went to him, timidly forcing her way past the Countess and over to stand beside the stranger. The man picked her up by the back of her shirt without effort. Ali shrieked and flailed, but the man took no notice. "Trade?" he smiled at Carr. "I need that one to get what I want, and you need this girl. Trade me. Let her run."

Carr's mouth curled into the closest thing to a smile as he was able, and he dropped Hollo to the ground. She was up in a moment, sprinting to Ali as the stranger released her. She threw her arms around Ali, tackling her out of the Lightning Man's grip and to the ground. She would not, no matter what, let go, though she knew she wouldn't be able to resist for long. Strong hands fastened around them both. The stranger lifted them up, and the girls hugged tighter, refusing to be pried apart. The Lightning Man didn't pry, to Hollo's confusion, and instead, he lifted them to their feet and pushed them back towards the house and the statues, who again barricaded themselves around the pair of them.

From where Hollo and Ali sheltered behind their metal legs, they saw Carr's face morph into a delayed realization of betrayal just before he launched himself towards the stranger who deceived him. A stone hand opened, reaching for the white-haired head, the hand large enough to cover it. Hollo tried to shut her eyes, to shut out the vision of his head crushed under the grasp of the stone. She tried to close her eyes but she couldn't.

Fingers tightened over the soaked hair of the man just as the lightning struck, whitewashing the world in front of her, while the cracking of thunder split her ears. The strikes came again, the lightning blasting in rabid succession. Between the strobes, Hollo saw the first bolt run through the two men, leaping from the stranger's body into the stone of Carr's chest. It now burst out of his left stone arm, as his forearm shattered into pieces that rained into the bronze bodies shielding her. Another identical bolt entered him at the chest an instant later, and Carr's leg blew out from under him. Systematically his body was blown apart by the super charge of electricity conducted by the white-haired man.

Hollo's eyes burned, and she squinted them shut until the lightning quieted, and then when it was all darkness once again, she reopened them. The Lightning Man still stood, breathing heavily, his clothes smoldering at the edges. The already singed threads of his ratty, molding clothes steamed in the rain and sizzled faintly as the lingering fire on his body was doused. Around him in the road were the bits and pieces of stone; the sand and solid remnants of the man Carr, who would never again lay his raging hands on anyone.

Chapter Fifteen
When Light Becomes Fire

The lightning flashed, the thunder tolled, and the group of them stood there in the storming rain. The steaming, singed form of the Lightning Man was unmoving, though very much alive, despite all reason to the contrary. Hollo stood Ali to her feet, sputtering, and wiping water from her face.

"I knew you were real!" Ali shouted over the downpour. The Lightning Man looked rather affronted by this, though Ali did not waver. She turned to Hollo. "See!? I told you!"

The Lightning Man appeared to have something to say about this, but something beyond Hollo caught his eye and changed his expression. Hollo turned.

"Kit?" she muttered, squinting her eyes into the distant darkness and stepping forward, though stopped short as a large hand took firm hold of her shoulder.

"This is not a friend of yours," the Lightning Man said. "There is another's imprint inside the boy. Someone else has a hand on him."

Hollo would have argued, but she saw how Kit looked different than normal, how his head hung listlessly towards the ground. "Kit?" she offered loudly.

The head raised slowly and with some strain, so did one arm reaching towards her. Tiny webs of faint blue began to glow faintly out of the darkness around him, a vast number of them, all piercing his body. She knew those blue threads, and knew exactly who stood behind him controlling his body. Hollo had her thread wound through her fingers in an instant; ready, though she did not have a plan. Looking to her statues, she opened her mouth to ask for help, but then fell silent when she saw that they were entirely lifeless and frozen with shock on their faces. It appeared that they had only just registered their creator raising his hand against them when that raised hand had turned them back into the lifeless statues that they were. Kit's hand now fell back down to his side, where it hung limp and doll-like.

"What will you do?" the Lightning Man asked her. "The boy is your friend?"

Hollo nodded.

The Lightning Man continued, "There is no help I can give that won't kill him. If he is still alive, that is, I do not know this magic. He is being swung at you like a sword, is he?"

A sword, Hollo thought. Yes, that was what Amit had done with Kit, turned him into his toy, his weapon. She nodded feebly, her thoughts racing for a solution. She had to stop Amit. She had to make him let Kit go, somehow, and then get the boy inside the house and out of reach. She couldn't see the man, perhaps his wariness of the Lightning Man was keeping him at a distance.

"You have a tremendous source inside you," the Lightning Man said to Hollo. "One unlike most of us. I think you can stop the boy, but I don't think you can save him."

"If that's what you think then I don't need your help," she said. What she really needed was scissors, or something to cut. She thought of how useful Kit would have been right now to fashion some kind of giant blade, presuming the wires controlling him could even be severed. Somehow she doubted it, since Amit's blue threads were obviously similar to her father's, the same threads which ran throughout her own body. No, she decided, scissors wouldn't cut these threads.

Kit's body jerked forward, taking his uncoordinated steps one at a time. Hollo kept looking beyond him, searching the darkness for Bander-Clou. After a moment, a form darkened in the downpour, a large block of something that took her a moment to recognize as a metal carriage, rolling down the street towards her, being drawn forward without horses guiding it.

"Go inside!" she shouted over the downpour.

Ali shook her head. "Kit's in danger! I'm not leaving you to save him alone!"

The Lightning Man stepped between the girls and scooped Ali up into one arm and moved to the side of the road. She was struggling at first, but Hollo saw the man saying something into her ear, and after a few moments Ali stopped, though her face remained wrinkled with strain and fear. Quickly, the Lightning Man deposited Ali into the house for safe keeping before he came back to Hollo's side.

Hollo apologized to Ali in silence as she turned back towards the jerking puppet that was Kit's body. His arms raised, and the carriage fell apart, clattering to the ground in a mess of metal parts. Thrusting his arms forward, the parts rose up, twisting into a tornado. The writhing metal squealed and scraped amongst themselves until the shape changed, and became humanoid. Tiny legs supported a large torso and even larger arms. Huge fists pounded into the stone road as the man-animal shook its overlarge, eyeless head against the rain.

Hollo fell back a step, her chest shaken by the impact of metal fists on stone. The monster moved forward, favoring the use of its massive knuckles for mobility rather than its dwarfed hind legs. Its body swung forward, closing the distance to her at great speed with every gallop. She wondered if she could run, perhaps make Bander-Clou follow her away from the house, but her chances of getting away were slim, even if she could outrun Kit's metal construct. Making her choice quickly, both her hands hit the stone street with her thread already alight. "Stones of earth from deep below, from stone comes sand and a secret hole, filled with rain to ripple and flow," she whispered into the stones.

The monster bounded forward off its legs, and where its front arms would have touched to earth, the stones gave way into quicksand. Though it had no mouth, Hollo heard its surprised whine pierce the night like the misfiring of under-tended mechanics. Splashes of the liquid earth covered her face, and she shook herself hard while restringing her thread. Jumping back a few steps from the struggling monstrosity, she again hit the ground with both hands, spitting moist sand as she uttered her new phrase. "As if the rain had long since passed, earth like water hardens fast."

Without its arms to leverage itself, it was trapped there with the stone street solidified around half its body. As she trembled, Hollo heard a cold cackle from the distance beyond Kit. Amit was there, she was certain now, just out of sight. Somehow he could see her. Perhaps his threads allowed him to use Kit's eyes as well as his magic, and if that was the case she had no hope of luring the man any closer.

Her new plan wasn't allowed to finish forming before the monster stopped it's writhing and the metal components of its body became airborne. The swarm of shards headed towards Kit, whose arms were again aloft. His hands tensed and squeezed at the air; his body shook visibly; his dripping hair began to lose some of its color, fading from chestnut brown into ash. He shook more violently as the metal shards neared him. The dark iron tempest gathered around him, edges of the metal cutting into his shirt as it all whipped clumsily over his body.

"Stop it!" she screamed at Bander-Clou. "You're killing him!"

Kit's eyes remained empty, even as the plates were made to fasten around his body, less seamlessly than if he had made it himself, and he bled in many places where the iron aligned. Even as his hair faded, and the magic within him was wrung from him, poured into the crafting of his armor, he did not react until the armor encased him, at which point he began to move towards her. It wasn't some beast Bander-Clou planned to send at her again. It was Kit, and the longer Hollo fought him off, the more of Kit's life would be exhausted.

Noise in the distance drew her attention away from Kit. A great commotion was growing in the darkness surrounding Casting Street. Voices were raised shouting over the storm in all the streets nearby. It sounded as if the whole of the Artisan district had come bellowing towards her.

"What's happening!?" Hollo yelled at the Lightning Man, whose eyes, so used to the darkness, appeared strained while searching the night. Hollo saw his hand tighten around his copper staff, and the faintest of glows alight his eyes. Overhead came a surge, a white web of lightning, vast and illuminating. The lightning did not strike down, instead it coiled and jumped between the clouds in enormous arcs of light. The street shone like daylight amidst the blurring downpour. She could see past Kit now, into what she had thought was an empty street. Dozens of human forms appeared illuminated by the lightning, and the slow footsteps and halting march of the bodies gave away what they were. An army of clockwork men approached, every jerking step of their inhuman forms drawing them closer.

"We are outnumbered," the voice of the Lightning Man boomed through the night. "We must run."

Hollo felt her knees grow weak, from fear or exhaustion, she didn't know. The explosions returned, this time from a shorter distance. The light from the surging lightning faded and came again, and this time Hollo saw where the sound came from. Beyond the wooden men there was a wall of dark figures moving in unison, approaching quickly. Horses, she registered, carrying people dressed in uniform. Military sabers flashed in the light from overhead, and a faint roar of shouting as well as stampeding hooves reached her. The wooden men turned as the cavalry broke into them. Hollo saw horses go down, their hooves sliding in the rainwater, colliding with the heavy, mechanical bodies in their path.

"There they are!" came an enraged scream from behind Hollo. She turned, finding a sea of people at her back. The

Artisan District had come, not is small numbers, but in an angry mob. Yelling and shouting, the sea of armed men and women closed in on her, though they were fixated, not on her, but on the wooden men beyond. Gunshots rang out, the few soldier who were scattered throughout the mob of common folk fired into the distance, dangerously close to the cavalry in their midst.

"After them!" a frontrunner commanded to the civilian army at his back. He held what appeared to be the oar of a rowboat over his head as the people yelled their agreement over the storm. "No more Magickers in our streets!"

Hollo was knocked back and forth as the angry uprising flooded around her, rushing into the fray. She fell to the ground, crying out as the Lightning Man used his height and strength to fight his way through to reach her. Hollo curled up in a ball, holding the cloak as tight as she was able, knowing that if it fell off her and she was seen, these people would splinter her apart.

She was forced up to her feet, and choked on her breath as The Lightning Man shouted into her face, "Are you hurt!" She shook her head, following the back of the mob with her eyes, and seeing Kit's metal body beating away those who had stopped to fight him; none of them standing against him for long. Soon there was no one left in his way, and Kit marched once more towards Hollo.

Two men, large and bound in the leather apparel of blacksmiths came up behind Kit, each throwing their weight onto him from behind and forcing him to the ground. One of the men had a sledgehammer, and the other held Kit down while the hammer raised up in the air.

Hollo screamed, shrill and terrified as she watched the hammer slam down into his metal helmet. The armor on his head shattered into several pieces, and Kit's head could be seen, exposed and pinned down as the hammer came up into the air again. Hollo struggled out of the Lightning Man's arms and sprinted forward, waving her hands and shouting at them to stop, but the men ignored her.

She didn't see what it was at first, but something hit the hammer-wielding man like a cannonball. It was a person, a small person, who then turned on the other man and slammed a fist into his face, sending a spray of water off his head. At first Hollo thought it was rain, but realized quickly that the briny green glow of that water hadn't come from the sky. She then recognized the fluid fists and dull, red hair of the girl she had seen on the night her father died.

Kit was on his feet throwing wild haymakers around himself. Eferee evaded his swinging arms, though just barely. Hollo didn't know why, but the girl was trying to pacify him, and trying to calm him with words. It became obvious that she had come to help, though Hollo didn't understand why. She caught Eferee's attention, pointing to her front door. "Inside!" she shouted, and neither the Lightning Man or Eferee paused at the invitation. A wild plan struck Hollo at that moment, as Eferee sped past her. Hollo turned and hurried after the girl, while Kit's metal boots could be heard ringing against the stones a short distance behind her. Kit was forced into a run, though his magic was growing weak. Small pieces of his armor fell away, making their noises against the stones as they rained off him. Hollo's thread glowed in her hand before she even strung it through her fingers. She knocked Eferee down as she burst through the door and ran straight past the Lightning Man, who jumped out of her way. A second later metal boots stomping on her wooden floor announced that Kit was only feet behind her.

She stopped, turned and shouted, "Close!" and her glowing hands hit the wall.

The door shook the frame of the house as it slammed into place. The blue illumination of the wires strung from Kit's back went black immediately, cut by the door as if it were a knife. The remaining metal armor fell off him. Mid-sprint, Kit's body went limp and he fell on his face at Hollo's feet.

She remained with her hand pressed hard into the wall, her eyes locked on the mangled, broken door, and her chest heaving. In her mind's eye she could see the raging battle on the other side of it, saw Amit's fury at losing his human weapon, and could imagine Amit breaking in on them at any moment. Eyes never moving, all of her willing it to remain closed, she expected the man to burst in on them with a sinister smile on his face. "A cup of tea?" she heard him ask in her mind. "I'm rather parched, you see."

She stood frozen, her hand pressing harder and harder into the wall the more she thought about it. She didn't notice the Lightning Man until he stood directly in front of her. His large, bluish hand covered her own against the wall. The warmth of it surprised her. Something about his complexion had her thinking his body was as cold as the rain outside, but instead he was warm, and smiling, though kindness was difficult for his weathered features to accommodate.

Eferee had collapsed beside the door, and was having trouble keeping her eyes uncrossed, appearing visibly dazed by whatever effort it had taken her to come this far and help them. Shouts outside could still be heard, and the clash of humans against the mechanical soldiers still raged. Eferee stumbled up to her feet and found the window.

"They're winning," she managed to choke out. "Or Bander-Clou is retreating, either way."

The Lightning Man nodded. "He may be driven away for some time; the man came after you with everything he had. His recovery will be slow now that the people have seen what he's doing. It was foolish to do what he did in chasing you here, and now he has a mob on his hands."

"No better time then," Eferee said, returning to the door and trying to open it.

"You don't mean to pursue him…" the Lightning Man said with a frown. Fear gripped Hollo as she saw the girl yanking on the broken door that was now wedged firmly in place.

Eferee turned a withering glare on the man. "If it's the last thing I do, yes," she spat, then pointed at Kit's motionless figure. "He'd understand, he'd help me. If you all are gonna hide in here, the least you can do is open this damned door!"

"My dad asked you for help," Hollo said, interrupting their argument and instantly hushing them both.

Eferee stopped yanking the handle, and her shoulders slumped forward.

"The night we were attacked, he was talking to you, before he died," Hollo's voice was even, but she struggled to keep it so. "And you didn't help."

Eferee didn't respond, though her subdued posture remained.

Hollo stared at the back of her head, a little afraid of the red-haired girl, not knowing what she would do, whether she was an ally or an enemy.

"Open the door," Eferee said softly. "Just let me out."

"Why'd you come back?" Hollo persisted. "Do you feel bad? Are you ashamed?"

"Open the door!" Eferee shouted, her away-facing body trembling as she struggled again to open the jammed door. "Don't lock me up in here, I can't stand it, let me outside!"

Hollo threaded her fingers, a white-hot anger rising in her. She couldn't have explained why she was so angry; she'd never felt this way before. Her thread blazed into life, glowing through the darkness, and slowly, Eferee looked over her shoulder. Her anger had been replaced with fear, and Hollo was the object of her fear.

"He's dead now, you know," Hollo whispered through a clenched jaw. "He's gone."

Eferee blinked and nodded softly, but her eyes wouldn't raise to meet Hollo's. Eferee kept darting her eyes toward the golden web in Hollo's hands, her shaking growing more intense with every passing second that the girls remained there.

"You're worn out, aren't you," Hollo asked. "You're exhausted. You can't defend yourself."

Eferee winced as Hollo's thread grew brighter. Ali called Hollo's name, but Hollo didn't reply, she was too busy searching Eferee's face for remorse. All she wanted to know was if the girl was sorry, but Eferee wouldn't speak. The

Lightning Man took a gentle step towards Hollo, reaching a hand out and laying it on her shoulder.

"Stop," he told her. "I know you're upset, but stop."

"You could have helped," Hollo said. Eferee was so powerful, so strong, she could have saved them from all this; she could have saved her father from dying so horribly. It was all her fault. Hollo shut her eyes tight, shaking her head and pleading with herself not to burst into tears, but still they came and she cried. The tears felt hot and full of anger. She hated them. Blinking through the angry tears, she saw Eferee bathed in a different light than before. Hollo's thread, her golden light had dulled, the warmth of daylight that always rose from her thread had changed to a shade of darkness. Forgetting her anger, Hollo stared, stunned by the change in her hands. The light was hot, painfully so, and blue, almost like Amit's.

She screamed out in surprise, letting go of her thread when it burned her hands. She screamed, new tears rising in her eyes as she looked at her fingers, where furious flames of blue fire lingered for a second, searing her as the thread fell to the floor. Ali was upon her in an instant, a damp rag quickly wrapping around Hollo's hands as the two girls fell to the floor. Hollo cradled her burning fingers, doubled over as Ali tended her, trembling, wiping her hands of flame with the cool cloth. Hollo barely registered the sound of the door. She didn't know how it had opened, or who had opened it, but she knew Eferee was gone.

Holding her hands limp in her lap, Hollo righted herself and looked down at them. The pale wood of her hands had burnt, and ugly black char covered the insides. The pain was staggering, and no coolness from Ali's cloth helped. Hollo hiccupped through her tears, but the pain was too great and she succumbed to it. She fell against Ali's chest and the world went dark.

Chapter Sixteen
Crafting Glass

Hollo hadn't the faintest recollection of falling asleep, but the burning ache of her hands and soft throbbing of her head roused her. It was morning now, and the faint light of dawn illuminated the house, which remained alarmingly quiet as she listened for her companions. She lay on the couch alone. The exhaustion of the night hadn't yet left her. There remained a deep fatigue in her body that she hadn't ever felt.

Holding her hands out above her she discovered them to be bandaged in white cloth. Ali must have wrapped them while she slept. She was unsure if there was any point to it since she didn't bleed or suffer from infection. The bandage was comforting, at least, and hid the sight of the damage. The tips of her fingers poked over the edge of the white cloth, where she could see the extent of the charred wood. Tiny cracks had etched themselves amidst the black, cracks that would probably disappear over time. Still the sight of it made her dizzy, and she didn't dare look closer.

She rose up, searching the house for sounds of others, curious where everyone had gone, a sudden worry in her mind as she wondered if she had missed something, and if anyone had followed Eferee out into the night. Just then, then sound of a deep voice outside made her jump to her feet. The back door was ajar slightly, and through the window she saw the tall shoulders and white hair of the Lightning Man.

The rain was light outside, more mist than rain. Kit lay with his back against the wall of the house, appearing too fatigued to greet her as she came out the door; even too fatigued to notice Flynn creeping slowly towards him.

"Morning!" Timtree cheered when he saw her. Hollo returned a wave of her cloth covered hand, growing more curious as she saw all four of the statues in conversation with the Lightning Man, who was directing their labor around an object that lay between them.

"Hi, Hollo," Ali greeted her excitedly as she scooped Flynn up into her arms a moment before he launched his surprise attack on the winded Kit-Falermeyer. "Kit made us a copper plate, look how pretty it is!"

"What are you doing?" Hollo muttered.

"It was his idea," Ali said, pointing at the Lightning Man. "We're making you a mirror."

"A mirror?" Hollo repeated to the Lightning Man.

"A mirror," he affirmed, walking over to the two girls. "Your father used mirrors to find people, and so we will make one for you."

"Why," she asked. "What for?"

Ali beamed. "We don't know what happened to your dad yet, so with this, we can find him."

Hollo stared at her feet, opening her mouth to argue, but Ali interrupted. "We can't be sure otherwise."

Hollo shut her mouth, staring around at everyone who was gathered here. "You all did this for me?" she asked softly. Kit waved a lackluster hand through the air and slouched forward, a tiny drool appearing at his lips. Ali went to rouse him, but the Lightning Man beckoned her away.

"Let him sleep, his part is done."

Hollo didn't know what to say. A pang of guilt hit her in the stomach as she saw how excited and industrious her friends worked on her behalf. It was a wasted effort. She couldn't use mirrors as well as her father, but they seemed happy to hope for the best and she couldn't tell them that it was in vain. Even after her behavior last night, and as embarrassed as she was about what she said to Eferee, they seemed not to mind. Full of guilt and apprehension, she approached the copper plate in the grass, and knelt to lay her hands on the smooth metal, but the Lightning Man interjected. "It is very thin, do not touch it yet, not until the glass in laid."

"Glass?" Hollo answered blankly. "You're gonna make glass?"

He nodded.

"Then what do I do?" she asked. "Why didn't you wake me up?"

"We wanted to let you sleep," Ali answered for him. "He says you need to be rested, else it's dangerous, what we're gonna do."

"Yes," the Lightning Man elaborated. "You and I will be contributing equally to the crafting of the glass. You see," he pointed to the Laughing Man who sobbed pitifully while he began pouring fine sand over the surface of the copper. "That mute one there spreads the sand I purchased so that we may pour our magic into it. My storms will provide the heat, and your magic will pour into the mirror. Your father must have made himself a mirror like this somehow, and poured his soul inside it. I don't think there's any other way to make something quite so powerful as to see long distance without it being attuned to your soul."

"How?" Hollo asked, watching as the Countess and the Knight leveled the sand by drawing a plank of wood slowly across the surface, making it smooth.

"Your weave, you will make one over the sand, and it will be held there. Go on, the other girl will help you hold it."

Hollo obeyed, stretching the magical thread until it lengthened enough to span the distance across to Ali, who looked altogether beside herself about being included. The two of them created a weave, though Ali took charge of the shape of it, looping and knotting the rapidly elongating thread until it was complicated to her liking. The four statues took up their places around them, then at Ali's direction, took hold of their own sides of the string and pulled the threads until it spread into a six pointed star between them all. Ali looked intensely proud of herself as she grinned expectantly around the circle of six.

The Lightning Man gazed into the sky overhead. Hollo followed his eyes, wondering what they would do if the lightning missed its mark on the ground between them.

"What now?" she asked warily, just as the wind began to pick up and blow her dress around her.

"Now," the Lightning Man stood straighter. "We call the lightning, and we ask it to strike our four conduits."

"Four?" Hollo mumbled, looking around at the statues who stood stoically staring upward. "You mean you four?"

Timtree winked at her. "We're the best ones for the job."

"Someone has to," The Knight said proudly. "And we've the strongest bodies. Never fear, little wooden girl."

The wind blew harder still, gathering incredible strength. The girls pulled the wires taught between them, Hollo's breath turning quicker as the storm clouds darkened overhead. She turned her head upwards again, suddenly doubting that this would work. The statues were doubtlessly strong, she still did not understand to what extent Kit's magic ran through them, but still she feared the lightning. Even if the statues could withstand the charge, Ali and herself most certainly could not.

"What if it hits us!?" she shouted at the Lightning Man over the roar of the wind. She thought of Carr, and how his stone body was pulverized by the power of the lightning.

"You're not big enough," he answered. "But to be safe, don't move."

Her heart skipped a beat as he said this, imagining her limbs catching fire if the slightest error occurred. How reliable was lightning, anyway? How did he know what the lightning would find most alluring in this circle of statue, human and wood?

"Hurry and light up your wire," he said urgently.

Hollo nodded, attempting to take a breath, but then the wind roared, and her breath was robbed from her. She then imagined what the sensation of flying must feel like, and wondered how it was that birds could breathe in the whipping winds of the high skies. She huffed and panted, and finally managed to draw in enough air to shout her weave.

"Come to life and guide the light," she shouted, bringing an instant glow to the weave.

"And please don't come undone!" Ali shouted back at her, eyes wide and round, eagerly encouraging the wire between them.

"Take the power from the sky," Hollo stumbled, smiling nervously at Ali.

"Between our hands it runs!" Ali finished as the wire darkened into a deep red of cool inferno.

"Bravo!" The Knight nodded. "Well said young ladies, well said, indeed!"

Ali's cackling caught Hollo off guard. The girl's hair whipped around her face and she howled with delight, her mouth wide with excitement.

"This is amazing!" she screamed over the rising tempest. Her small body was jostled around by the wind, and Hollo feared that if it strengthened, Ali would be carried away into the air.

"Hold on!" she yelled back, as Ali squealed with delight, dodging a bit of wood that tumbled through the air and past her face.

"It's like flying, isn't it!"

Hollo hoped it wouldn't be.

The thunderclouds blackened above them, stealing the light from the world, and shutting them in darkness not unlike the dead of night. Flashes of white lit the black clouds above them, illuminating their monstrous depth, and showcasing the enormity of their electric payload. Ali cackled with joy again, the sound of which was lost in the tumbling thunderclap. Hollo squinted her eyes, fighting the impulse to drop her glowing cradle and run away.

"Don't move!" the rolling thunder of the man's voice seemed to read her thoughts, and Hollo tensed her body. Blinding white struck their weave before the sound even announced it. Sightless, Hollo gripped her wire, pulling harder, fearing that one of the ends would go slack, and that she would then find one of her friends laid low by the bolt.

It felt as if they were struck a hundred times. The blinding flashes of light hit over and over again, drawn, as the man had said, into the metal bodies of the four statues on either side of them. The charge hit them, heating their dark bronze bodies into a dull glow of subterranean orange. They were all hit, all of them equally, except for herself and Ali, who she saw for brief moments opposite her.

The amazement that had taken hold of her before now had changed, and Ali's face now betrayed a wrinkle of fear, and Hollo's last anchor of bravery melted as Ali gave in to alarm. Hollo, too, saw what had changed: the bronze statues burned deep inside, the dull orange of their heat had spread and become brighter. Now the lightning ceased, the wind calmed in an instant, and the light came back to the world.

In the return of the overcast gloom, the dull smoldering of the bronze bodies was still visible. The four of them gave out, their hands releasing their hold on the wires, and some of them fell to the ground. The Knight was the first to fall, having had attempted to take a step and found his boot melted to the earth beneath him. His leg came apart at the shin, and drops of hot liquid metal dripped from his overheated, molten core. Hollo only just resisted the impulse to run and give support to the struggling Knight. The fear of pain halted her only a step before taking hold of his red-hot arm. Ali, nearby, had rushed to the same aid of the Laughing Man, who coughed molten orange from his mouth. The two girls exchanged a helpless look between them.

"Ah, well…" the Knight said to Hollo. "So it is that I think we've come to the end of it."

"I hope we were helpful," Timtree chimed.

"Are you hurting?" Hollo sobbed.

"Don't think so," the frog boy said, puzzled by the question. Upon his large amphibious head, his charming, newsboy hat gave way, sliding apart in a thick slow wave over half of his face. "Not painful, no."

"Are you dying?" Hollo whispered, kneeling, fighting tears. "Can't we fix you back?"

"I don't think so," the Countess answered haughtily. "I don't believe it works like that." Her elegant arm fell away at the shoulder, and a long spindly leg started to collapse in on itself. "I told you all this would happen," she sighed.

Hollo turned back to the Knight, wondering what expression of guilt she could possibly utter to convey not only her gratitude, but also her self-hatred for being the cause of their destruction. "I'm so sorry," she whispered. "I'm sorry."

"Children," The Countess said with distaste. "I'm so glad I have none. It's very simple, Hollo, that you helped give us this life, and so of course we'd give it back. Don't grovel, it's unattractive."

"She isn't groveling," the frog-boy corrected. "You mean grieving."

"Certainly," the Knight said, with a frown at The Countess. "Though I think I can say it better," he smiled his knightly smile at Hollo, causing half his moustache to break off. "Oh blast," he muttered, touching at his face, then shrugged gingerly. "What's a body that cannot age?" he asked her kindly. "What use am I if I remain unchanged by my usefulness? Fear not, little wooden girl, the scars of battle are to be endeavored towards."

And those were the last words from any of them, though the girls waited patiently seated, staring around into the faces of the statues that had since cooled, and the life gone away from them.

The Lightning Man, having sat without interrupting, now rose. He lifted the great round plate of metal and glass from the ground and held it out for the girls.

"You see?" he asked them softly, as the light rain returned, chiming against the metal remnants of their bronze guardians.

"The mirror is crafted." He cast his iron eyes around the circle of broken statues. "But magic has its price."

Chapter Seventeen
The Opening of Doors

Kit growled as he was made to rise, and led indoors. Hollo held the mirror in her hands, staring into it without the faintest knowledge of how to operate it, or even what she wanted to see in it.

Ali and Kit settled themselves at the kitchen table, then stared expectantly at Hollo, who abandoned them, and instead placed the mirror on her father's desk and again stared into it.

"Now what?" she whispered.

The Lightning Man came up beside her. He reached a hand out, and very slowly, pulled the loop of string out from her pocket. She watched his hand do this, and was entranced by it. In deciding the age of this man, she had not taken into account his hands; hands that might have dated back to the very construction of the world; hands that might have held the world aloft during its inception. The blue coloration of his face was present in his hands as well, where it mixed with the red inflammation and peeling, pruned skin that had changed from looking human over so many years spent in the elements and constant rainfall. His fingernails, or the thick yellow-white mess of fungal claws that were there instead, gave his hands such an alien quality that Hollo was surprised in herself for not balking at the sight of them nearing her.

The hand now held the thread before her eyes, swinging it lightly back and forth in front of her like a pendulum.

"Remember who your father is," the Lightning Man instructed. "Remember that you share a bond with the man. The gift of sight is ingrained within you. All he could accomplish, he passed on to you. Hold your mirror, and find him."

Hollo gripped the cool metal disk, wanting to argue her case, wanting to explain how it was impossible to see her father because the man was certainly gone forever. They watched her closely, waiting to see if the mirror came to life, if it glowed, or what. Hollo stared deep into it for a long while, her eyes darting around while her company remained silent.

"Nothing," she said.

The Lightning Man let out a slow breath.

"Maybe it's not working?" Ali offered. "Maybe try someone else?"

"That is possible," the Lightning Man said thoughtfully. "Perhaps try another person. There's a story that isn't in this book. Perhaps it's a story your father preferred to keep private. There is a woman, whose name was Luca, and she was called the Woman in the Walls."

"The Witch," Ali said. "From Mad Had."

"Yes," the Lightning Man agreed. "You should learn who she was. Look into your mirror and see if you can see."

Hollo obeyed, tightening her hold on it, half expecting the glass to remain inert as it had in her search for her father. A small part of herself preferred the mirror to remain lifeless, so that she would not have the proof that her father was gone.

Despite her resistance, the glass did indeed illuminated. A woman appeared before her, very tall, as tall as the Lightning Man himself. After a moment Hollo saw the woman change, growing smaller, father away. The tall woman appeared to darken until her features were indistinguishable. She became a shadow, a dark stain against the wall behind her.

"It's just like in the story," Hollo related to them. "Just like in the King's bedroom, a shadow in the walls. Does that mean she's still alive? Trapped?"

Ali shivered, looking around the room. "A ghost?"

"I suppose," the Lightning Man said, his words sounding careful. "Do you see where she is? What wall she is trapped inside?"

Hollo shook her head, staring into the mirror harder. She did not have control over what she saw, couldn't make the image turn to the right or the left. All she saw was the shadow in the wall grow farther away.

"Wait," Hollo whispered. "There's a floor now."

The wall moved away slowly, but eventually the rest of the room was revealed. The ceiling came into view, and then a staircase beside the shadow, a staircase that looked all too familiar. Hollo twisted around in her chair and saw the mirror on the wall behind her. The mirror appeared ordinary, though as she stood up from her chair to examine it, she saw there to be more than the normal reflection within it. She looked back into the mirror in her hands, and gasped when she saw Kit. He was seated attentively with his back to the wall where the woman's shadow lingered.

Hollo nearly dropped the mirror as she pointed and ran forwards. Kit appeared startled as Hollo hurried past him, and Ali squealed with delight as she realized what Hollo had seen.

"I told you!" Ali said. "I said it that it was haunted in here!"

Hollo stood in the hallway near the door, looking up into what would have been the face of the woman, had she been more than a shadow.

"The mirror works," the Lightning Man affirmed.

Hollo reached a hand out to the dark wood of the wall, laying her palm across it, deaf to the conversation in the room. She vaguely noticed Ali and Kit talking animatedly, badgering the Lightning Man with questions about the woman. Who she was, where she came from, and why she wasn't still trapped in the old castle of kings. Hollo had her own questions, though at the moment all she cared to do was gaze in wonderment up at shadow of the woman in the walls.

"Have you always been here?" Hollo whispered. "Have you always protected me and my dad?" She didn't need an answer, nor expected one. Her magical house had more than just her father in it after all. She had known that, some part of her had always known that.

"My dad saved you, didn't he," Hollo whispered again. "After your spells that trapped you in the King's walls, it was my dad who rescued you, it must have been."

The Lightning Man appeared beside her while Kit and Ali remained in the kitchen simultaneously astonished and terrified.

"I suspected this," he told her, holding his own hand out to lay on the wall beside Hollo's. "Though the Mirror Man never did tell me this secret, I had guessed. I wondered what happened to Luca."

"You knew her?" Hollo said. "You and dad knew her?"

He smiled sadly at the shadow, meeting the eyes levelly at his own height. "I have many sisters and brothers," he said. "But Luca was the oldest, and maybe the only who remembered me."

The shadow had started to fade, as Hollo pressed her hand harder into the wall, trying to draw her back. She was unwilling to part with Luca just yet. It felt like she was meeting an old friend, or even a long missed relative. If the woman in the walls had shared her home with Hollo for all these years, that certainly made them something. After another moment the shadow had faded entirely, and Hollo's hand fell away. The Lightning Man's hand, however, lingered.

"She was your sister?" Hollo asked. "You left home when you were small, didn't you?"

"Younger than you are now," he said. "And I had hoped my family forgot me, and yet not all of them did. It was the Mirror Man who told me about her. It was the Mirror Man who told me that others in my family held odd power like I do. My sister moved through walls, into rooms where secrets were told; where kings and lesser people schemed to undo people like us. King Had is known as the Mad King, but would be better named the Witch-Hunter. That is a story that few living people know besides myself and Luca. Your father knew."

Hollo let the Lightning Man escort her back to sit with Kit and Ali, who both had quieted to listen as the Lightning Man spoke.

"Luca was accused of being a harlot, when what she really was is actually much more sinister. She was a dangerous woman, my sister. Her eavesdropping got her in a lot of trouble with the Practitioners. The Practitioners had their own bounty hunter, who arrested Luca and presented her to the king. What they did not know was that she herself was a Hermetic. She tried to argue her case with them, tried to blackmail the king and others, but in the end they locked her away to die."

"Bander-Clou," Kit said. "He caught her, it must have been him."

"The man who attacked you," the Lightning Man said under his breath. "Yes, I recognize him now, at least I recognize his craft."

"Then what happened?" Ali asked.

"She did the only thing she could, she escaped," he said. "But she refused to lose, and instead of running away, she remained in the walls. Weeks she stayed there, tormenting the king into madness until he finally threw himself out the window."

"She's a hero," Kit said solemnly from the table. Hollo had forgotten him. "Luca..." he trailed off, frowning at the space where the shadow had vanished. "She tried to drive the king to madness so that the Practitioners would lose their power. If the man who created them proved to be insane, then it seemed only natural for the common people to refute them."

The Lightning Man shrugged. "I don't pretend to know her well, but the Mirror Man may have agreed with you."

"May have," Hollo whispered, realizing again what else the mirror had told her.

She looked into it again, pressing her father's name and image into it with her mind. Now that she was sure the mirror worked, this was her chance to find him, to see his face hovering over the pages of a book, his glasses shining in candlelight. She searched for him, but the glass remained dark. The Lightning Man and Kit were in conversation, and Ali was busy paying attention to Flynn. Hollo hunched over the mirror, alone, staring at her own reflection.

"Hollo can use the mirror," Kit said, drawing Hollo out of her own thought and back to the conversation.

"For what?" she asked.

"I'm against it," the Lightning Man said firmly.

"Against what?" Hollo persisted, drawing silence from the others. The three of them all shifted uncomfortably, seeming wary of her.

"Last night," Ali said delicately, "after you collapsed, when that red-haired girl went outside after you yelled at her, there was still fighting going on in the streets. The people were fighting the wooden men, and we assume that she went chasing after Amit. We thought the fighting was done, so we went out to see. We heard a girl scream, we saw her get taken by the wooden ones."

Hollo gulped, anger welling up inside her. She didn't dare say the girl deserved it, but ashamedly, she felt that way.

Kit grumbled, seeming pained. "Bander-Clou rips out souls, Hollo. If you think that's a fitting punishment for her, then-"

"No," Hollo interrupted, her eyes burning. "I don't want that."

"He might have captured her," Kit whispered. Ali shivered beside Hollo as Kit's face darkened with that familiar inconsolable anger. He stood suddenly, the hurt in his body forgotten, and his fists balled. "I have to go help her, she's one of us above all else," he said. "I know what it feels like to have him inside your head, it's unbearable, the worst kind of torment. I can't let that happen to her."

Hollo knew as well what that felt like. The man invaded her own mind before Kit's. In the days past, she had almost forgotten who her real enemy was. Eferee wasn't to blame, even though Hollo absolutely did blame her. Amit was the one deserving of hate.

"You're defeated," the Lightning Man said passively to Kit. "You lost, don't do anything stupid."

Kit ignored him and turned to Hollo. All sign of anger was gone as he implored, "Hollo, Bander-Clou has her. Please find them for me."

Hollo shook her head, hugging the mirror to her chest.

Kit appeared on the verge of tears now. "Please, I can't bear it, I owe her, and I owe Fred, and I owe my parents. I have to stop him, do you understand?"

"What if he kills you?" Hollo asked. "Why do you always leave, why won't you stay with us?"

"Because I can't," he answered. "This is my whole life. It's like your dad, he was your whole world. Bander-Clou is mine. I have to have this, so please. Tell me where they are."

Hollo rocked in her chair for a long moment, while Kit stared at the floor, shame on his face.

"Don't make me live like this anymore," he whispered. "Don't make me live in his shadow. It's my fault he found you, and it's my fault that girl is suffering. It's my fault my parents were found, my fault they died."

The Lightning Man appeared thoughtful, and Hollo looked to him for guidance, but received none. She let out a breath, and leveled at Kit. "Promise me."

His eyes came up from the floor, a nervous hope in them.

"You have to promise me that you won't go to kill him. I'll find Eferee, and you can go and save her, but you can't fight Amit."

They stared at each other for a long time, while Kit chewed his tongue in the side of his mouth.

"If we're making deals, then I have one for you," he said. "Go somewhere I can't find you, if Bander-Clou captures me again."

The Lightning Man nodded his agreement. "The city isn't safe, after what the man did last night, there is a witch-hunt in the works. The people have risen up in fear and hunt the streets. The Mirror Man's shields have faded away, and the door is broken." He turned to Kit now. "I will keep them safe."

Hollo looked back and forth between the men for a moment, before tightening her grip on her mirror. "Okay," she whispered into the glass.

. . .

Kit's legs felt like lead, his joints had stiffened. He was depleted, not just in the body, his soul itself felt heavy, weighted down as if it too had begun to harden into metal. He forced the thought from his mind, quelling the fear that Bander-Clou had forced so much of his own magic out of him that it was claiming its price on his body. He was worn out. Any more magic might be the end of him, like Fredric.

Struggling with his stiff limbs as he walked on, he couldn't help but turn his thoughts to what Hollo said had happened to the man. Fredric had pulled Kit from the fire as a boy, rescuing him from the house that fell to ashes around him and the bodies of his parents. The kindness of the man was how Kit always remembered him, his loving face, and his calm countenance. His imagination pieced together a terrible picture of the man turned to wood as his magic drained the life from his body. A fate that Kit knew rested in a delicate balance for his own flesh at this moment.

The streets were littered with straggling uniforms and beaten civilians. It appeared that the fighting had persisted long into the night as Bander-Clou and his mechanical soldiers were forced to retreat through the streets. Kit had only to follow the trail of broken, wooden bodies and the people who examined them to know where he was going. Hollo had showed him where to go to find Eferee, though it appeared that he was not alone in trailing Bander-Clou.

As he neared the former headquarters of the Practitioners, he found that a siege had been laid on the building. Much of the stone wall had been wrecked, and in its place, a wooden barricade had been thrown together outside the old stone building. The people of the city had gathered here, though they were being pushed away half-heartedly by the soldiers who had staked out a perimeter on the road. Kit forced his way through the throngs of the poorly armed artisans and made his way to a young soldier, his left eye closed tight over what Kit guessed to be an injury. The one-eyed soldier's hands were raised up in the air to placate the looming mob that pressed the rear of the wooden barricade.

"Let us do our jobs!" the young soldier said, a note of panic in his voice.

"What's going on here?" Kit asked him forcefully. The young man raised an eyebrow at him.

"The Practitioners have gone mad, there was an incident last night, and we've cornered them in here."

"Isn't it dangerous for all of us to be here?" Kit said, feigning distress.

"There's sense left in some of you!" the young man said with obvious frustration. "Listen to this guy here, he's figured it out!" The soldier returned his attention to Kit, relieved to have a friend in the crowd with a sympathetic ear. "They've got some crazy magical guard, wood men who've laid low every advance we've made on them. What's worse," the young man choked. "They're making soldiers out of a few of our dead. They suck the life out of them and turn'd 'em into one of those ratchety devils." The soldier sobered for a moment, staring into the sky. "Some of my best mates got themselves sucked dry, now they're up there," he gestured to the windows of the building, where wooden guards could be seen. "Guns don't hurt them much, we're stuck until reinforcements come."

"You got reinforcements right here!" shouted a burly man beside Kit as he raised a pair of baler's hooks over his head. "Storm the foul place and let's be done with it, no more taxes from these damn deviled Magickers!" The crowd rallied and surged in on the young man, who all but fell down as his face went white, shouting placating words that fell on deaf ears. Kit moved away, forcing himself backward through the crowd until he was free of it. The frenzy intensified, and odd weapons sprouted up above them. Kit knew there weren't enough soldiers to keep people from storming the building. Bander-Clou was a merciless man, which Kit knew better than most. He'd have no problem killing bystanders if made to defend himself. There wasn't any way to sneak inside like this; the barricaded soldiers had made sure of that. If left to their own devices, they would only get themselves hurt trying to rout the clockwork guard while trying to fight off the mob as well. Kit couldn't reach Eferee any way besides the front door. He tested his joints, finding them much as stiff as they had been. The risk of using magic was too great, but he had no choice.

"C'mon lads," the burly man incited the crowd. "Magic ain't no match for the lot of us, lets break 'em to pieces!"

A roar followed his words, as the militia's weaponry waved through the air. The burly man held his baler's hook on high as he pushed forward. In a moment of confusion, the man stopped, staring up at his tools in surprise.

"Go on!" one of his mates yelled. "What are you waiting for?"

The man growled as he wrestled with the hooks above him, seeming perplexed and nearly lost for words.

"Go on!" another shouted.

"I can't!" he sputtered. "They're stuck!"

A moment later they flew out of his grasp as he fell onto his backside. Other instruments followed the hooks, flying backwards over the heads of the crowd. Weapons were wrested from their owner's hands as heads all turned to the lone man standing behind them. The metal weapons flattened and twisted around Kit's legs, up around his body, while a misshapen mass grew under his legs. The metal covered him, and the lump beneath him grew into a horse.

The young soldier's remaining eye stared dumbly into Kit's face just before the head of a shovel molded itself into a mask. It took the young soldier a moment to register how the crowd that he had barely been able to keep in check a moment ago suddenly parted in front of him. As he was wondering why, a great, metal horse bore down on him. In shock, he threw himself out of the way and scrambled up to watch the horseman charging past him, all the way up to the front door of the besieged building. The young soldier's comrades gave chase, following after the rider towards the building where the rider broke down the heavy doors. A moment later a dozen wooden men poured out of the doors and engaged the trailing soldiers. The young one-eyed man fumbled for his rifle, his hands shaking despite his training. He checked his weapon, gulping as sweat beaded at his forehead. His rifle was in satisfactory condition, much to the young man's dismay, and without cause to retreat, he rose to his feet. He then realized how he stood alone, how the mob had dissolved now that it was weaponless. The man whose baler's hooks had been taken from him sat on his backside, alone in the road, staring at the fighting.

"Left you your rifle I see," the burly man said to the soldier without looking at him. "My hooks," he added blankly, "he's using them for stirrups…'magine that…"

The soldier breathed deeply, clutching his rifle to his chest. Standing rigid, he focused focusing his quaking shoulders towards the front door. "Right lads!" he shouted to no one. "Charge!"

Meanwhile, Kit charged through the front hallway, seeing wooden men chasing behind him. His neck tightened as he strained to look back at them, and it took a painful effort to turn forward again. He could barely move his body with the rolling gallop of his mount, and he knew that at any moment he might be thrown off.

The scream of metallic friction announced the failing of his magic, and the collapse of metal began in the feet of his horse. The legs began to crumple, and all at once the metal gave way entirely. Kit fell to the floor in a wave of scraps and slid to a halt some feet beyond. The wooden men followed close, and quickly bore down on him. One last effort on Kit's behalf picked the metal off the floor around him, melding into a solid sheet that filled the stone hallway. A heavy impact sounded, and a moment later the beating of wooden fists could be heard hammering against the other side of the barricade.

Kit let his arms fall back to the stone floor, his eyelids fluttered, and sleep threatened to take him. He tried to rise, but his limbs entirely resisted his command. Even bending his arm could not be accomplished. He closed his eyes, knowing he had pushed it too much, knowing that he may never move again. There was no telling whether or not he would ever stand by his own will again, no matter how much will he had left. The effort was claiming him.

. . .

Hollo stared at the mirror on the table, a tightening in her chest as she battled with herself. She wanted to find Kit in the glass, wanted to make sure he was alright, but knew there was nothing she could do for him. She had already watched her father die; she couldn't bring herself to follow Kit into danger.

"Don't," the Lightning Man said to her, reading her thoughts. "You've done all you can do."

"There's always more I could do," she whispered. "More I could have done."

"You're talking about your father," the Lightning Man said.

Hollo didn't reply, knowing it was obvious where her thoughts were turning.

"Let me tell you about your father," he said, settling himself down in front of her. "I've known the Mirror Man since I first began walking the road. I could not have lived if it weren't for his guidance."

"How old are you?" Ali asked.

"Much younger than he," the Lightning Man replied. "The Mirror Man remained ageless as I grew up. He has remained that age for a very long time. He would never tell me precisely, though he once gave me a hint by accident. He made a reference to a character of history that he lived with as a boy in the country. This man you call father lived before the King Haddard himself was born. In excess of a hundred years."

"Dad was a hundred?" Hollo whispered.

The Lightning Man nodded. "When I was a boy, I left home, but didn't yet know how to sleep on the road, so I spent money on a room at an inn on my first night after leaving my home. He appeared to me in that room, by means of a mirror. He calmed me down, stopped me crying, and told me stories. I traveled to his home, this home, many years ago. And he gave me this," he drew the locket from beneath his shirt, and opened it to reveal the tiny mirror inside. "Not often, but every once in a while I would have the fortune of traveling with the man. It is a lonely life on the road; never staying for long in one place. Though it can be dangerous at times, it has its safety. The Mirror Man could not be persuaded to come with me often. He preferred to see the world through his mirrors."

"You traveled? You and my father?"

The Mirror Man nodded, smiling. "We did. It was less lonely, on those occasions. I got to know him well. Your father changed my mind about things more than once. This curse that haunts our kind, the 'strangeness' that we are…we all feel the weight of it bearing down on us. Your father saw it differently. He saw it as a wonderful thing, even though it kills us. He told me that we all die, every last one of us, and each one of us dies too soon. There is never enough time to live, no matter how many years you have in the world." The Lightning Man laughed out loud, a booming mimicry of thunder. "And I was young, and I disagreed with him so adamantly. The thing about your father, is that he knew that when I walked from place to place, I had nothing but my thoughts. He would say things to me, and I'm sure he said those things knowing that I would have nothing to do but argue with myself about them. He told me I was not a cursed man. He told me a story, called The Lightning Man, one he had written. The fairy tale he wrote in his book speaks of my becoming, but not of my purpose, he told me. The man who was born to water the land, he called me. I was born to walk from shore to shore, to see the world, to water the land."

"So what about me?" Hollo asked him. "I have magic, what was I born for?"

The Lightning Man stared hard at her for a long while. "Would you like to find out?"

Hollo didn't reply.

"You know we cannot stay here," the Lightning Man said, finally addressing the source of Hollo's anguish. "You want to find out what your magic is for, but you will never answer that question while hiding in this house. I'll ask you again, would you like to find out what you were born to do?"

Hollo nodded slowly, her eyes wide, unsure of him.

"And you?" he asked Ali. "What about you?"

Ali looked once at Hollo before nodding her agreement. "I want to be a merchant," she whispered.

"That is an odd thing to say," the Lightning Man said, though not unkindly. "You needn't decide your fate right now, you are young." The Lightning Man stood up suddenly and raised a pointed finger at the girls. "You each are allowed one thing, whatever one thing you care about most in this house, bring it here, both of you."

Ali leapt out of her chair and scurried out of the room. Hollo thought for several moments, before she realized what she held most valuable; her father's book of stories. She retrieved it from the desk, as Ali came dashing back into the kitchen holding Flynn in her arms. The Lightning Man frowned at the bird, but then upon a second of consideration, seemed to decide to allow it. He turned about and wrestled the damaged wooden door out of the way. He stood to the side, gesturing with a hand for the two girls, beckoning them onward.

Hollo hugged the book tight to her chest, shaking her head. "I want to stay, here, where I lived with dad."

"Do you want to stay and remember your father?" he barked. "A moment ago you wanted to find your purpose. Here it is," he pointed out into the storm. "An open door."

Hollo could feel Ali's eyes on her. The decision was hers, for the both of them. She hugged the book tighter, then pulled it inside her cloak and walked outside.

Chapter Eighteen
On One's Own Two Feet

Kit's body twitched violently, shocking him awake again. He forced his torso to bend himself upright, and a calming breath escaped him as he found his barricade remained intact. He didn't know how long he had passed out for, but the moments of unconsciousness seemed to have released some of the stiffness from his body. Though he struggled, he could stand. His steps were slow, but he managed to keep himself upright and moving forward. The wooden men had obviously given up trying to get through to him and were undoubtedly looking for a passage around. He knew they might head him off, and knew that there was little else he could do to stop them now. He played with his magic for an instant, reaching out with his soul for the presence of metal, but what normally happened effortlessly now only left a tingling in his fingers like the blood had left them and the muscles had gone to sleep. Sleep, he thought wistfully. All he wanted to do was go to sleep, and as he neared the final door of the hallway, he knew that sleep might not be too far away for him. Raising an arm to the door wasn't worth the effort so he pushed with his shoulder, causing a great creaking of wood from the large, oak door as it moved slowly inward.

The room was dim, only lit by the light coming in from the vacant window frames, where the seawater had shattered the glass. Bodies of the Practitioners remained here in the great hall that had been their headquarters. He noticed how the moisture seemed to have been sucked out of the drowned corpses, even though the floor remained damp from the flood of the previous day, and the rain that blew inside. They had been harvested of their light, Kit knew, and at that moment, saw the man who had done this sitting among them. Bander-Clou raised his head as Kit staggered inside.

"So it was you who broke the door. Have you come for tea?" he said humorlessly.

"Have you got any?" Kit replied, not entirely meaning this as a joke. Having tea was a fine way to die.

Amit snorted, and Kit wondered why the man hadn't risen yet, why he remained sitting in the shadows. Even if Kit tried, he would not have been able to fake any semblance of a threat towards the man, staggering and limping as he was.

"Stop," Amit barked weakly. "Stay where you are. Yesterday...you broke the shield around this place. How did you do that? That...was something I hadn't expected. Extremely sneaky of you. I should have wondered how you got in. I disappoint myself sometimes..."

Kit ignored him, continuing to approach. A single blue thread slithered across the stones to a small body on the floor between them. At once he recognized it was Eferee. The blue thread hovered over her, poised to strike. Bander-Clou appeared to know that Kit had come for the girl as much as he had come for vengeance.

"She's still alive," Kit grunted.

"Always save at least one weapon," Amit said. "She was going to be my last stand, but the time for that has passed."

Kit examined the shadowy face of the man, whose white hair had become disheveled from its military grooming and fell around his face. He couldn't tell from this distance, but Kit wondered how extensive were the man's injuries. He appeared to be unwilling to face him, and hid his eyes behind his hair.

"So do we stand here?" Kit asked. "Waiting for one of us to attack the other?"

"You can't attack me," Bander-Clou chuckled. "You can barely move."

"Don't need to move to attack you," Kit bluffed, hoping the man would be wary of Kit's gift with metal.

"Don't make my laugh," Bander-Clou said. "Laughing hurts now."

Kit stepped forward again, throwing caution to the wind. "Then let me be on my way."

The blue thread coiled menacingly over Eferee's closed eyes and Kit stopped again.

"Stand up at least," Kit said. "Face me if that's what you want. Last stand?" he chuckled dryly. "I bet you can't even stand."

A terrible grating sound echoed around stone walls as the dark form of Bander-Clou's body straightened up. Mechanical misfiring shot around the room with each pained step the man took forward. Kit stood his ground as the man came forward into the pool of light cast through the windowless hole in the wall.

"I may be many things," Bander-Clou said as his wooden face came into the light. "But I am a man who will die on my feet."

He pointed a finger towards Kit's face, a wooden claw more than a finger. "You've come to kill me, so try."

Kit would have balked and recoiled at the sight of the man, but he was beyond that, beyond the energy for surprise. "I can't," he said simply. "I promised the little girl I wouldn't."

"You promised?" Amit said, his poorly attached wooden jaw opening wide as a chattering of metal and wood mimicked the sound of laughter. "You promised…don't tease me. You couldn't kill me if you wanted to. I, a broken, old man, and you don't even have the strength to do me in," his mechanical laughter echoing through the great hall.

"You gonna kill me then?" Kit asked. "Since I promised not to kill you, either give Eferee to me or kill me."

"And then what!" Amit barked. "You'll escape? Carrying the girl? Through those ordinary cattle out there who want your blood the same as mine? You think you stand a chance without the Practitioner's hovering over you? I was the only one who hunted our kind before, but now there will be scores of those pawns after you. I'm falling to pieces before your eyes, and still it is you who is doomed."

Kit's eyes burned. He knew this was true, and knew that this was, subsequently, the end of the road for him. Amit creaked and shifted and his blue thread left Eferee and came to hover in front of Kit's face.

"If you like," Bander-Clou hissed. "I'll save you all that trouble. Join me for a cup of tea, boy. Join me for tea in the great darkness beyond this blazing hell, where our kind are all fated to end up sooner than they expect, once the hunt begins."

Kit stared numbly at the needle of thread that danced around before him. He grew dizzy watching it, his eyes crossing as it neared the space between them.

A tumultuous blast split the room, just as Kit's eyes had closed to wait for the end. He came back to life in time to see the highflying splinters of Bander-Clou's face fall back to earth. Kit watched as it appeared to happen slower that it should, Bander-Clou's remnants returning to the floor. It had been gunfire, Kit realized. The soldiers had conquered the wooden men outside and finally made it here. Kit readied himself for another gunshot, feeling a tingling between his shoulder blades where he could feel a rifle aimed. He turned, slowly, expecting a firing squad to be training on him, but found instead a lone young man. He was ghostly white, and gulped as Kit faced him.

The young soldier shook visibly where he stood, his left eye squinted tight as the other sighted down the length of his barrel in Kit's direction. Kit waited for the shot, but a coughing sound spun him back around. The noise of the blast had revived Eferee enough to choke the water out of her mouth. Kit flinched at the sound of the rifle hitting the ground, while the young man shivered and shook. "Dunno how I made that shot," the young soldier said while holding a trembling hand out in front of him and inspecting it. "Always been lucky, I guess."

Kit eyed him warily, unsure what would come next. Surely there were more soldiers following closely behind him, they would be here soon.

"But look at that good luck there," he pointed at the rifle. "Out of ammo. Guess the last damn Magicker got away," he said pointedly to Kit. "Couldn't be helped."

Kit stared blankly at him for a moment, before he realized what the young soldier was doing. He hurried to draw Eferee to her feet and slung her arm over his shoulder before the young man changed his mind. It was a good thing Eferee was small. The young soldier held the door for him as Kit struggled past. He stopped just outside it, and turned back to face him.

"You left me my gun," the young soldier said to Kit, before Kit could even open his mouth to ask the question that hung in the room.

"What?" Kit managed to choke out, still keeping his eyes warily on the rifle in the boy's hands.

"You left me my gun," the soldier elaborated as though it were obvious. "You took everyone else's but left mine. Don't care if you are a Magicker…" he trailed off, a great surge of emotion rising inside him as he gazed at Kit with respect. "You stopped the mob, you saved a lot of those people out there." The young soldier continued after a moment of choking back his brimming emotions. "I couldn't have done it if it wasn't for you. You risked it all to help us, even though you're one of them."

The young soldier wiped his eyes on his sleeve and then pointed down a small corridor to the left. "I got lost looking for you. There's a door out that way no one else will see you, go on. Carefully. Go on."

Kit hoisted Eferee higher onto his shoulder, wincing at the pain of it and hurried off as best as he was able.

. . .

The rain drummed against her hood, and wind whipped around her. For a moment she considered running back into the house for shelter, but the sound of the door being slammed into place behind her put an end to the thought. Ali stood beside her, shivering, clutching Flynn, who barked and shook his head against the rain. The Lightning Man walked out into the road while the girls hurried after him. They followed him along Casting Street, seeing no one on their way. After the night before it appeared that even the market square would remain vacant today, perhaps because the storm had been so bad, or perhaps because the fighting in the city still raged somewhere.

Hollo's thoughts turned back to Kit, wondering if he was caught in the fighting, wondering if he'd survived until now. Not knowing his fate was almost unbearable, and yet she knew it was for the best. There was no changing him, just as there was no changing the Lightning Man. She wanted to complain to the old weathered man, wanted to ask what they were doing, where they were going, and how they would avoid fatigue if made to march onward in this heavy rain? Just as she opened her mouth to yell over the storm, the Lightning Man turned out of the street and up the steps to a closed, dark shop. The sign overhead read 'Packerd's Historical Halfway and Pawn Broker'. The Lightning Man tried the doorknob halfheartedly, before using his shoulder to break the lock and force the door inward. He ushered them inside, and they stood in the middle of the dark room shaking and wet. The Lightning Man busied himself amidst the racks of merchandise, until returning to them with a pile of clothing and two backpacks.

"Dress yourselves for the cold," he told them. "You will be cold for a very long time ahead of you, but you will grow used to it. For now, wrap yourselves tight. The road is long."

The Lightning Man left the room. The girls heard him in the kitchen, probably harvesting food from Mr. Packerd's pantry. Hollo and Ali wordlessly changed their clothing as Flynn dried himself. Once dressed, they waited, listening to the Lightning Man as he rummaged. He returned with a canvas bag over his shoulder. His other hand tore the drawers out of the desk, searching heavy-handedly until a smile spread over his face, and a silk purse jingled in his hand.

"I have lived beneath the storms for a very long time, but I understand how that is a poor place for daughters to grow. There is a small town not far beyond the gates. We will buy a wagon."

Ali, who had matched Hollo's dismal expression until now, brightened. "We'll see the world," she whispered to Hollo. "We'll be like merchants."

Their backpacks were heavy, but the Lightning Man allowed them a kind pace as he led them through the city streets. Wordlessly, he walked on, out the open gate at the west edge of the city, and beyond it.

Hours of moonlight and miles of road passed beneath their feet until the girls were beyond tired, but the Lightning Man led them farther and farther from home. An hour ago they had begun to climb a hill, a gentle slope, but nonetheless the pain in their legs began to grow unbearable.

Ali and Hollo collapsed at the same time, their woolen pants darkening with mud. The Lightning Man heard this and returned to them. Wordlessly, he picked them up by their backpacks, and with one girl in each hand, carried them beyond the edge of the road, where he tucked them into the dry space beneath the roots of a fallen tree. The two of them panted and heaved, too tired to speak or move, and barely able to even watch the Lightning Man tearing pieces of dry wood from the underside of the roots. Soon a small fire crackled into life between them. The Lightning Man seated himself down, brushing dirt and splinters of wood from his hands.

"Every day you will grow stronger," he told them kindly. "Do not begrudge the effort it takes to live like this. It is a gift that will aid you for the rest of your lives."

The girls said nothing while the Lightning Man freed Flynn's body from the backpack that had carried him. Flynn ruffled himself furiously, and then bounded around in the dirt searching for bugs.

"We're not far away now, your bird can walk the rest of the way," the Lightning Man said reasonably. "We can rest here as long as you need though."

Hollo stood, brushed herself off and drew Ali off the ground. The girls gathered their belongings and headed back to the road. He watched them walk, a twinkle of approval lighting his face.

Dawn crept through the clouds as they arrived at the summit. Before them, at their vantage point, chimney smoke marked the town in the valley ahead. Behind them, the Artisan district sat illuminated in sunlight. The clouds had moved away, bathing the city in the dawn of late summer. Hollo and Ali took a moment to stay there, where they could see their home, both wondering when they might ever see it again.

"A place worth visiting," the Lightning Man called back at them. "Come now girls, before the road softens too much." He continued to walk until out of sight, while they remained there, staring back at the place they were leaving.

"I don't want to go back," Ali finally said.

Hollo stared at her.

"Not until I'm grown, and a rich merchant, and seen the whole world. I want to stand here again, but not until then."

Hollo grinned slyly. "You mean not until you've grown into a woman?"

Ali blushed and ran after the Lightning Man. Hollo chased, calling mercilessly after her. "You'd better hurry and sprout hips before Kit finds someone else!"

Ali squealed and shook her head as she ran, with Hollo chasing after.

Chapter Nineteen
The Woman in the Walls

The rain had gone, and with it returned the hints of an approaching fall. Soft warm wind swept in from the east and brought with it the scents of wild anise and ripe apples from the farmlands beyond. It was a cleansing kind of air, one that remained ever at your back lightly carrying you along. The wind had led Kit here in the early morning, and the broken door had done nothing to prevent his entry. He took that as a mark of truce, though he knew better, and had begun his work.

Standing to examine his effort, he tested the swing of the door experimentally, grinning a rare grin of self-satisfaction. He then gathered his tools and returned them to the tiny shed beside the back door. It had pleased him to find Flynn gone; he had dreaded the idea of having to find a new home for the poor, abandoned beast. He should have known Hollo wouldn't have left him; that she would never knowingly abandon anyone, even himself, he thought with a guilty frown. She hadn't abandoned him, had even placed herself in danger on his behalf, and this puzzled him a little. In payment, he had taken the morning to offer his last respects, and repairing the door was the last helpful thing he could do. He returned to inspect his work, running his fingers over the wooden doorframe before shutting it and testing the lock, further assuring himself of a job well done. It had been a long time since he had used his hands in his work. Metal crafting came to him without effort, but wood only obeyed him if he put in his honest labor.

In the darkness of the unlit house he stood, marveling at how the world was changing him, that his sense of gratitude towards a wooden girl had made an honest worker out of him, if only for a few hours. In this darkness, the hair on his neck raised. He felt a presence agree with him, and a tickle of humor titter from somewhere behind him. 'Honest?' he could have sworn he'd heard the word spoken, but knew better.

He remembered the sensation of someone looking over his shoulder his first time stepping into this place, and how it had alarmed and confused him, and though the house now remained dark and empty, he now knew it was not entirely vacant. Raising his voice a little, he spoke into the house. "Thought I'd come and say goodbye," he said, and no reply came. He stuffed his hand into his pockets, taking his time to stroll through the house, and then settled himself at the table where he stared out the kitchen window. His mind turned toward the bay, where he imagined the ship waiting for him, and Eferee making ready to sail. He was a little nervous; he had never traveled before, nor had he ever been on a boat. The Docks District of Thedes was not too great a distance away from the Artisan Harbor, and they would come to arrive there soon. There was work for him there, and the money would be good.

"I read his book years ago, I hated the story he wrote about me," Kit spoke aloud into the silence of the dim kitchen. "But I've been thinking about those stories a lot lately, and I think I figured it out. Who you are, who you really are."

When normally there would have been the sound of a floorboard, or perhaps a wrinkle in the air, there was nothing but stillness. Kit smiled, turning himself away from the window and towards the hallway, where there in the wall, where he had expected, slowly appeared a darkening in the wood. Tall, slender, and unmoving, the faint shadow of a woman bled through the boards.

"The curse of the Zygotics," Kit whispered, reciting from the text he knew, the text that Fredric had left behind. The shadow in the wall remained unmoving, much the same as it did when it had appeared to the mad king Haddard.

"Kingslayer," he said, giving a sad little smile. "Luca, isn't it? Luca Tor-Falerum: The Woman in the Walls. I know you. I've finished what you started. Rebellion worked, we won. The Practitioners are gone, mostly." He scratched the table with his fingernail for a moment, pensive, wondering what the woman would say to him if she could. Whether she would be proud, relieved, or unimpressed by his efforts. He certainly felt he deserved praise, but deep down he knew what her answer would be. He could almost hear the words she would have spoken.

"It isn't over is it?" he whispered. "The Practitioners weren't the problem. I guess I didn't understand that before. I thought it would be different for me when they were all gone, but here I am, sitting in a secret house talking with a ghost, and hiding from the world. Magic is still scary, we're still feared, I'm still cursed." He sighed, eyeing the shadow again, a little smile creeping into his face. "You're definitely a mother, listen to me spilling my heart out. Might as well curl up in bed and let you read me a story."

Kit suddenly wondered if that was insensitive to say to a woman who had never so much as touched her own child, who was trapped just out of reach and now more alone than ever before. He hunched over a little in his chair, speaking now at his shoes. "Fred should have told me he had a wife, I'm sorry I didn't puzzle it out until now. I never really wondered what Hollo was, before. I just thought Fred was so clever all on his own. I should have asked how he made her. He couldn't carve anything to save his life. You made her body from the wood of this house, I'd bet. And then Fredric gave her his magic, proper parents, you both. I wish I could have told her for you, before she left. She thinks she's all alone in the world. She thinks it was her dad's heart she stole to be born."

The creaking floorboard beneath him seemed to disagree. He nodded. "But then she might have stayed," he agreed quietly. "It must have been hard to let her go."

On the table before him lay Hollo's mirror. He smiled at it, running his fingers over the glass. At the desk he tore a slip of paper from the scraps and penned his words, 'if you ever need friends, you know how to find us'. He lay the note on the glass, and walked towards the door, but paused briefly. "She'll be back, I'm sure she will. She'll figure it out when she's older I bet. Maybe when she understands a little more about love. And don't worry, I promised I'd look after her. My eyes and ears will be open. You have my word."

He had one last thing to leave: a small round piece of metal that he drew from his pocket and placed on the table beside the mirror. "This," he began, "damn thing hit me in the chest one night. Bright light blew up in front of me and this came shooting out. I figured it was something Fred needed me to have, but I didn't understand what it was. Should have figured it out once I saw Bander-Clou's little stones. I thought I should've given it to Hollo, but I realize that would have been wrong cause she doesn't need it right now. So, I thought you'd like to keep it safe. I always wondered how old Fred was, suppose I was right to think there was more to him than middle age. Dunno what light the thing has left, but I suppose whatever it does belongs to you."

Out in the street he faced the building one last time, standing straight and respectful. "Kingslayer," he said, placing a hand over his heart and bowing low, uninterested in those nearby who stopped to stare at him do so. He then stuffed his hands back into his pockets and the warm wind carried him away to the west, where Eferee and her ship waited on him to embark.

Inside the home, all silent and dark, the shadow had disappeared from the wall, yet something else moved therein. A thread, golden, glowing, and inching through the air made its way from the ceiling to the table, passed over the mirror, and curled around the metal stone that lay cold beside it. Slowly, reverently, as if time slowed down, the thread curled around and around the stone, glowing brighter, until just before it was enveloped, the faint, ancient light inside the stone began to glow back.

Epilogue

There was land between the districts of Thedes. Not expansive, but enough distance to keep travelers cautious of becoming stranded on the road in times of storm. The Artisan District sat very much in the center of the Thedan Empire, protected from the world by farmland and the other districts and cities that surrounded it. Linking the Artisan economy to the rest of the empire were many roads that cut through farms and mountains and carried the wealth on its course. These roads created circulation, with the artisans living at the heart of it, and though the commerce in Thedes thrived, there was still a place in the empire where riches went to die.

The Docks district lay farthest from the heart of the Empire, at the outskirts of the circulation, and was the severed artery of Thedes, where the healthy circulation of an empire had a habit of washing away into the sea. The docks are a place of thievery: in the arts, on the streets, on the seas, and in the halls of powerful merchant families. The docks were where you went to make friends you would otherwise not be able to find: friends in nefarious business, friends who would grant you secret passages by vessel, or even friends you might only have for a single night and by whom you would soon be entirely forgotten. The docks, for all these many types of friendship they offered, had other opportunities if your skill, of whatever variety, was great enough.

The Docks housed the majority of the performing arts within the empire, due to the simple fact that performance thrives best in places where no one is allowed to silence it. This was how the arts came to find a home amidst the many friendships, impoverished persons, secret societies, and virtuosos who mingled along the vast southwestern coastline of Thedes. Traveling there was easy, but leaving was an entirely different thing. Performers who wandered to the docks often got lost through the cracks, and sometimes into the sea. Fortunately for some, getting lost was precisely what inspired them to come here in the first place.

A very tall, dark skinned young woman stood under the overhang out of the heavy rain. A roof without walls had been erected long ago to serve as shelter for those who found themselves too far away between the districts or towns to ride on for shelter, and some roads had dozens of them. This tiny shelter was a dry blessing in times of storm, especially unseasonable storm.

This storm had caught most of them by surprise at a time of year when wheat was being brought in from the farmland. Small trade families could be run bankrupt by a severe storm at the wrong moment, as their covered wagons could only stand against so much weather. Several of these families bound towards and away from the coast took shelter here now, and were delighted to find themselves in the presence of a traveling performer: the tall, dark skinned woman who used wires to move a puppet. Not just any puppet, mind you, but a puppet who told stories, and told them so well from the puppet's mouth that the woman's own mouth couldn't be seen to move at all. It was a very clever act, they thought, one that would surely gain her reputation in the theaters along the coast.

The puppet waved to the children, who gathered before her while their parents took only a moment longer to join them. The puppet introduced herself, telling them of their travels, all the while referring to her operator as if they were different people. The children believed her, and their parents appreciated the performance. She told them of the lands beyond these, where they themselves had just returned.

"Do you know The Lightning Man?" the puppet asked, and many heads nodded excitedly. The puppet continued, "He is a friend of ours, and we're meeting him soon. He's nearby, in fact." The puppet extended a hand towards the sky and the storm overhead, and the giggles of adults were silenced by the excitement of their children. "We are going to the coast, because, you see, we have many stories to tell. Would you like to hear one of our stories?"

The children were delighted, and were more delighted still when the puppet girl smiled at them. They were nearly as impressed as their parents by her smiling, and the parents gasped and laughed, shaking their heads in wonderment at the masterful marionette whose mechanics baffled them all. How could a puppet be made to smile? They whispered this to each other, and the children hushed them.

"What would you like to hear a story about?" she asked the children, whose wide eyes searched her vividly human face. They knew she was wooden, just as they knew the tall woman was making her move. Though as she spoke they forgot these things, and met her luminous golden eyes believing with all the power of their imaginations that this wooden girl was as real as they themselves were.

"A love story," piped up an older girl directly in front.

The puppet nodded slightly, a fidgeting motion that appeared more lifelike even than her haunted golden eyes. "You may have heard the story of Mad Had, have you?" The puppet girl asked them, her mouth moving so seamlessly with her words that the adults were quickly caught believing the impossible. "In the story he had a mistress, do you remember?"

"The witch!" a child said.

"Yes," the puppet nodded. "Now let me ask you, have you ever heard the story of the Mirror Man?"

All before her shook their heads, and the puppet continued, "The Mirror Man once loved a woman, a woman quite as tall as my friend here," the adults giggled as the puppet girl turned to address the same person who certainly spoke these words. "That woman happened to be in a great deal of trouble, and had come to hate the man who had imprisoned her. King Had was his name. You know him from his own story, but this is another story. This is the woman's story, and how she came to be loved by a man who only saw her through mirrors."

While the puppet told them this story, the rain grew a little fainter, and the people listening grew a little quieter, and all those watching were certain, if only for a moment's wild imagination, that they saw a tear fall from her face when the story was done, just before she bowed.

"So," the puppet asked them. "Is that a good story about love?"

Children, whose luminous faces glowed with tears, nodded their heads, while behind them, adults smiled sheepishly and fidgeted with their things. The applause was forgotten as the adults sat in silence amongst themselves, casting nervous smiles towards the remarkable puppet. The storyteller however, was offered praise, and even one family with a wagon offered to give her a ride, but no, they had their own wagon, and thanked them anyway.

The few coins offered were pocketed by the puppet, who, to the deep amusement of the gathered folk accepted the coins offered to the tall woman while stating politely that it wasn't the tall woman who had told the story, though the puppet-girl assured them all that her assistant would be paid for her time accordingly. This was very funny, and earned them a fourth coin.

The rain eased enough that those who gathered here decided it was time to be on their way, and thanked the dark, young woman. When all had gone the little puppet-girl gathered a cloak about herself, and looked up to the sky.

"He's a full day ahead now, we'll have to catch him up soon."

The tall girl busied herself with their cart, removing the feedbag from the face of their small mare and preparing her harness. The puppet crawled into the seat of the carriage, gently pacifying the restless red chicken, who a moment ago had been entirely invisible amidst the crates of bright red apples that filled their wagon.

"That's the last of the oats," the tall girl said, patting the mare.

"Gonna have to start feeding her apples," the puppet replied.

"That cuts into my profit," the girl grumbled. "Oats are cheaper."

The puppet reclined in her seat as the wagon began to trundle down the muddy road. "We'll catch up at the next halfway, I'm sure he'll wait for us there." The puppet inspected the four coins she had earned that day. "We'll buy oats. I'll even buy some for you."

The dark-skinned girl's stomach rumbled violently, and after a moment of the puppet smirking at her, reached into the back of the wagon for an apple.

"Not a word," the girl grumbled as she bit into it.

The puppet grinned, and lay her head back again, watching the storm clouds before them loom ever closer.

We hope you have enjoyed

HOLLO
The Magic of Thedes, Book 1
by Devon Michael

To read more by this author please visit:
www.devonmichael.com

Books and their authors survive on the words of their readers.

If you enjoy a story, remember to share it and leave a review.

This way the stories will continue.

Made in the USA
Middletown, DE
11 May 2019